Calamity Jane

Calamity Jane

BERNARD SCHOPEN

BAOBAB PRESS
RENO, NEVADA

ISBN 978-193-609-7050

Library of Congress Control Number: 2013912319

Baobab Press
121 California Avenue
Reno, Nevada 89509
www.baobabpress.com

Printed in the United States of America

MIX
Paper from
responsible sources
FSC® C011935

To Annie and Barb
Excellent Sisters

and

To the Memory of Another
"Taddy"
Mary Katherine Schopen Krejci

Acknowledgements

This novel was a long time in the making, and many people read and commented on all or parts of various manuscripts. I would like to thank particularly for their efforts Michael Binard, Kathy Boardman, Phil Boardman, Michael Croft, Margaret Dalrymple, Danny Goeschl, Gaye Nickles, and Verne Smith.

I also wish to thank Christine Kelly, the publisher of Baobab Press, and her staff for their painstaking efforts to transform a pile of manuscript into a handsome book.

Finally, I want expressly to thank Anne Harvey and Paul Starrs, who were kind enough to answer my questions about ranching in Nevada.

Innocence and violence are terrible things.

– LOUISE BOGAN

October 23, 2009
Blue Lake, Nevada

J ANE HARMON'S FILM about the death of Brock Walden has made a great success Out There. Since *The Last Roundup* was shown on PBS, reviewers and critics have lined up to present Jane bouquets of encomiums and accolades. All acknowledge the aesthetic sensitivity and dramatic flair with which she shaped her materials into a story. They applaud the vision that saw in the life and death of a Western film actor a fable about the American West. They admire too Jane's technical skill, the way she fit together narration, musical passages, still photos and clips of scenes from Brock Walden films, blending these with her own inspired shots of Walden Ranch and Gull Valley and Blue Lake and the people and the world Out Here. And they all accept – most rise to congratulate – Jane's assessment of that world, of the rural West and the American desert, of what should be done in it and who should do it.

Out Here opinion differs, at least about Jane's opinions of our past and future, about her understanding of the desert and those of us who live in it.

Blue Lake had made up its mind about the film even before watching it. We had already seen the effects that Jane could create with light and shadow, so we expected *The Last Roundup* to have its attractions, yes: it would be pretty and poignant, would please and touch. But to grant Jane the authority to speak about our lives and ways – that was quite a different matter. She had lived Out Here for over a year, searching for a story and creating havoc, and when she departed she left behind ruin and uncertainty – two men who had fought over her now confined, a woman disappeared, the future of Walden Ranch in jeopardy. So when she returned last May with Carlyle Walden to preview the film, Blue Lake filled the high school auditorium with an understandable, if maybe not altogether justifiable, resentment. It was easy to deny Jane Harmon the right to speak about lives whose rhythms and pulse she had never really felt. It was easy to see her as just one more Out There interloper who would use what she found Out Here for her own purposes. It was easy, and satisfying, to ignore her. It was easy – too easy – to blame her.

That evening Carlyle Walden greeted us warmly at the door. If he detected in the crowd a sense of injury, he gave no sign. Taking the stage as if he owned it, he offered a welcome and a joke about world premieres, but he could not quiet the harsh hum of discontent that deepened as the room grew dark. Silence came only as Jane's elegy on the death of Brock Walden made us an audience. When the lights rose once more, what seemed a single sigh acknowledged her achievement: she had moved us, deeply. Watching Brock Walden die, we had felt something of ourselves die with him. We were left, momentarily at least, with a sense of loss, an awareness of inevitable endings.

Then the moment passed.

And Jane was among us, decked out in denim and leather and plaid, smiling on those present and admitting no absences, attuned to compliments and nothing else. She accepted my embrace and commending murmur: "It's very good, Jane."

"Yes, Miz Waner," she said. Her scent hinted at lilac. "I know."

"But I don't think you've swayed Blue Lake to your point of view."

"Some see quickly, some never." She beamed, pleased with herself. "That's what you told me the day we met, remember?"

"You obviously got Carlyle to see – his narration works wonderfully with your images," I said. Then I smiled. "Did you persuade him with your art or your love?"

For a moment her gaze narrowed, as if she suspected my remark might carry a criticism. She glanced across the room at Carlyle Walden, who was listening studiously to Eleanor Broadhurst. Then Jane too smiled.

I had seen that smile before. It was the smile of a woman who would dismiss from the world all that did not conduce to her desire.

"I didn't do anything, Miz Waner," she said, slipping past me. "I just made my film."

Walking home with Eleanor, I recounted this exchange.

"She's done more than that," Eleanor snorted. "Carlyle Walden's sober, and he seems almost a man. Or is it being free of his father that's bucked him up?"

"Both, probably," I said.

"Well, it's about time. He's over forty years old, for crying out loud." Then she snorted again. "That's quite the buckaroo outfit she had on."

After a moment, I replied: "Ione Hardaway."

"Ah."

Eleanor, who always has something to say, said no more. We walked on through the evening, the streets quiet now, the heat of the day softened, the desert wind stilled, and we didn't speak of Ione Hardaway, the woman who was no longer with us.

Eleanor returned to Los Angeles the next week, and my life in Blue Lake went on, and if over the long summer and early autumn I often thought about Jane Harmon and wondered about Ione Hardaway, I gave little concern to Brock Walden or his dying. But since *The Last Roundup* was shown on television, I've found myself brooding over the death that windy day in the Rocking W ranch yard, even as I discover that I seem to remember not what I witnessed but what I saw in Jane's film – violence rendered beautiful, images of shattered bone and torn, bloody flesh composed into a harmony and so made to seem somehow just. At the same time, although I recognize the truth at which Jane's film gestures, I feel it at odds with my sense of things. Something seems missing, so I can't quite fit together what I see and what I feel.

Others saw Brock Walden die, but their accounts don't help me, for they were almost immediately shaped into fanciful yarns that Blue Lake was amused to spin for Out There reporters. Details of the death became more "Ol-Bee-Dub-Ya" lore that, like the anecdotes about his sex life – most ribald if not expressly obscene, most exaggerated if not finally false – both Blue Lake and the media preferred to fact. And when the reporters moved on in search of spicier scandal, Blue Lake was less interested in revisiting the accident than in pondering the future of Walden Ranch and the Rocking W. Then came the realization that the very person who had placed the cattle operation under question would surely influence the decision about whether and how and when things would change. At which Blue Lake dismayed.

Calamity Jane.

Blue Lake had given Jane Harmon the sobriquet soon after her arrival, local wit being pleased with both its echoes out of Western lore and its suggestion of her effect on everyone she encountered. Accidents small and large accompanied Jane as she made her way through our lives. Whither Jane, disaster.

Persuading myself that Brock Walden's death was but one more of these mishaps and catastrophes, I have recently tried, in memory and imagination, to track the spills and bruises and breakages, the dead horses and burned homes, as if I could follow their trail to a final truth. As Jane did when she was with us, I search for a story. But what I come to, again and again, is the on-going confrontation of Jane Harmon and Ione Hardaway, and invariably my tracing of events shifts into a contemplation of character.

Projecting images, I watch Jane search for the story she couldn't find because she was living it, watch a proud and angry Ione lose what she never had because she wouldn't take it.

Jane, with her graceful gestures and earnest innocence, appears before me a woman men mistake, her dance a solitary sway, her attention given over wholly to her art, which is to say, to herself. Ione I see concealing secrets – under leather her beautiful hands, under anger a mind high and solitary and most stern, behind her glare a powerful attachment to the land and her life on it.

One who also makes art and keeps secrets, minor as both may be, I see these two women, each in her fashion dear to me, and I wonder if their contest was inevitable, or if it might have been prevented, or if the outcome might have been changed. I wonder if I might own some responsibility for what happened.

But now Brock Walden is dead, and Jane and Ione are gone, and I am left alone with intuitions and impressions that, as I reflect on them, somehow slip beyond my understanding. So I have determined to fix them in ink on paper, to record them in this journal – that's what I do, after all, what I have done since I was a child: write, fashion life out of language, pen thought and feeling onto a page.

Writing, I would tell the stories that make up the story of the death of Brock Walden, and I would try to find in this story what so far I seem to have missed. I would determine whether this story has any real significance, or if my worrying of past events is but an old woman's refusal to accept the end of things as she knew them. I would discover too why, when Blue Lake accuses Jane Harmon, I rise to her defense.

And, scribbling, I would address another question, one that Eleanor broached as, still under the sway of Jane's art, we made our way along darkening, desert-scented, Blue Lake streets last May: "Could Jane be right?"

I **ONE HARDAWAY**, the only witness to and victim of the first accident, accounted for it with derision. "Gawkin'." Blue Lake understood.

Approaching town from the north, the highway climbs an unimpressive hill to a sudden high desert panorama that can evoke, in those taken unawares, a complex response. The Turquoise Range looms, a massive, tree-dark, overbearing presence that intensifies what is otherwise a vast drab absence: bare foothills and rocky alluvial fans that decline to an expanse of playa, flat and dun and utterly empty, and sage-stubbled rumples of earth that spread to a horizon made vague by distance and desert haze. Confronting such sheer space, many travelers involuntarily turn inward. Some think of the movies of John Ford and his epigones, several of which featured Brock Walden. Some recall the fly-over shot of this very scene, a blankness of earth and sky nicely accentuated by a small band of startled wild horses, that for a decade opened Brock Walden's television program. Some shape the absence into an empty beauty.

All of which Jane Harmon was doing that hot, windy, late-May, midday Friday.

Her small SUV weighted down with film equipment and towing, as if an after-thought, a low, slat-sided, quite overloaded and wind-whipped trailer, Jane was halfway down the long shallow descent from the ridge that Blue Lake calls The Rise, gawking at the billboard on which a grinning Brock Walden welcomes travelers to Blue Lake, Nevada, "Where the West gets Wild." Thus distracted, she allowed the wind to edge a trailer wheel off the pavement. At the jolt, she reflexively jerked, and metal shrieked, rubber squealed and smoked, and trailer and automobile separated. Spun violently, the car dove to a fender-crunching stop in the bar pit. At the same time, the trailer let fly one of its wheels, which bounded down the highway, while the platform flew the ditch, hit, and burst apart. Slats snapped and skittered, boxes somersaulted into the sage, and papers leapt up on the wind like white and gray birds as the trailer sheared off shrubs and the wheelless axel gouged the earth in a long, dust-raising skid.

Thankfully – should I say typically? – Jane was not injured. Ione Hardaway was not injured seriously.

On her way back to Walden Ranch with a pickup load of wire, Ione was starting up The Rise when out of the sudden cloud of dust and smoke ahead hurtled the wheel, which she could avoid only by taking to the ditch. The rough passage bounced her unseat-belted bottom into the air, knocked off her Stetson, and banged her eyebrow into the rearview mirror. For a moment, as the wind raced away with the dust, she sat stunned. Then she clamped her hat back on, took from its concealment in the door panel her small, nickel-plated, .32 caliber pistol, stepped out into the wind, climbed from one bar pit and aimed herself up and across the highway toward the other and the gawker who'd nearly wrecked her.

Jane, also stunned, stared at the figure bearing down on her, wide-shouldered and long-shanked, in worn denim and dusty plaid and a stained cowboy hat that shadowed the features beneath it, leaning into the wind with a thrusting assertion of self, wielding a pistol. The driver of the pickup seemed… well, I don't know, even now, what Jane thought was advancing on her, other than masculine menace.

At the same time, approaching, Ione thinned her anger with concern. She saw that the gawker was a woman whose empty stare and rigid grip on the steering wheel suggested shock and maybe injury. As she would when happening on any creature in distress or pain, Ione thought to help. Descending into the ditch, incidentally dangling her pistol from a gloved finger, she dipped her head and bellowed against the wind into the rolled-up window: "You OK?"

To which Jane mouthed, slowly, unmistakably: "Leave... me...
alone."

Which Ione, being Ione, instantly and angrily did.

Even as Ione's pickup was clawing back up onto the highway and
raging off, other vehicles gathered on the roadside. Jane, in her confusion unable to distinguish between inquiry and assault, remained
in her car. A local ne'er-do-well named Norman Casteel, all beard
and belly and self-satisfaction, came up to contemplate the stove-in
fender and, surreptitiously, Jane, while two other oafs posed for her
blonde benefit in the slouch that some western men have been persuaded by western movies signifies a most virile presence. Out in
the sage Norman's girl friend of the moment, Mina Pasco, and a few
other arrivals – an old ranch couple, a trio of tourists, a BLM crew –
began to help collect Jane's belongings. A sheriff's cruiser raced
up, roiling dust as it slued to a stop, and soon Jane, assured by the
authority of George Burleigh's bulk and badge and neatly ironed
uniform, allowed herself to be helped from her car. Satisfying
George that she was uninjured, she marveled that the accident had
happened just as in films, so fast yet in slow motion, and allowed
that, yes, there had been someone else involved, in a way – a pickup
with a big W on its door, a scowling person with a bruised eye? And
a little pistol? Ione Hardaway, sounded like to George.

"Ione? A woman?"

George nodded, not quite smiling. "You bet."

Then there was paperwork. While Jane talked and George wrote,
in the sage men and women continued to assist and, it would eventually be discovered, acquire. Another deputy arrived and saw to the
security of Jane's belongings – clothes, shoes, tapes and DVDs, kitch-
enware, lotions and linen, photographs and papers – which were
restored to boxes to be trucked to temporary storage. Another truck
would haul off the trailer. A wrecker arrived, dragged the SUV from
the ditch, and trundled it into town, George and Jane following.

As the afternoon swelled and ebbed, Jane learned that the fender
looked bad but wasn't and the car would be drivable by the next
noon; that the cameras and equipment in it had been well packed

and were undamaged; and that her insurance would pay for the destroyed trailer, the storing of her belongings, and the expense of an overnight motel stay. She also learned that Blue Lake, Nevada had much to say about Ione Hardaway.

Jane checked into the Desert Vista Motel and took a shower and a nap, sleeping into evening and the easing of the wind, which, as she stepped out, whispered ominous night sounds in the unfamiliar streets and the shadowy recesses along dark storefronts. Seeking safe haven, she slipped into the Silver Sage, where neon flickered and hummed, the air was greasy with decades-old tobacco smoke, coins clattered into slot machine trays, and in the lounge a guitar trio and a flat female voice ground up country tunes.

Jane was in the dining room, picking at a salad, when up shuffled a buckaroo in clean jeans and a pearl-buttoned shirt. He removed his hat with an old-fashioned, nearly comical sweep.

"Don't mean to interrupt your meal, Ma'am. Miss. But I'd like to apologize."

Jane was puzzled. "Apologize?"

"My sister, this afternoon, on The Rise. Ione can be unmannerly, sometimes."

"No," Jane said, understanding. "I didn't – it wasn't her. She wanted to help. Like the others."

Jane would maintain later that only his mention of his sister, not his aw-shucks charm or boyish good looks, persuaded her to accept Troy Hardaway's advances, such as they were, that evening. Her interest in Ione, sparked by their encounter, had been fanned into fascination by the discovery that a woman was the manager of the local area's largest livestock operation, Walden Ranch. Over the afternoon, Blue Lake had offered evidence of Ione's enviable abilities and odd ways – her knowledge of the land, her skills with tools and animals, her impatience with people. Now Jane invited Troy to take coffee and tell her more about his sister's competence and talents and toughness, her anger, her glares, her pistol.

Troy was pleased to oblige her. Ione, eight years older, had raised him after their mother died, was his sister and mother and boss. She had rough edges and sharp points to her personality, he admitted, mostly because what she cared about was getting work done – branding calves or feeding cows or maintaining engines or building fences or ordering supplies or figuring expenses – and she couldn't countenance in others a lack of attention and devotion to task. She was friendly enough to friends, and usually polite if cool to others, but she didn't suffer fools, lollygaggers, or gawkers. Her glare, Blue Lake had said, promised unpleasantness, and her anger was so easily provoked that it seemed a constant seething. What she was angry about her brother didn't know.

"But why does she carry a gun?"

"Dad give it to her," Troy said. "Uses it for snakes, rats, varmints."

Jane pursed her lips in a comical moue. "Which did she think I was?"

"Car goes into the ditch on a empty highway in the middle of the day, whoever's behind the wheel might be drunk or doped up, who knows?" Troy grinned. "She likes it handy."

As they spoke, the sound of voices and laughter in the lounge had swollen. Now over the music came an alcohol-harsh hooting. Jane, who did not drink, who did not care to be around those who did, thought it was time for her to go.

"Friday night," Troy said. "This's about the only place in town to go to, at least for a lady like yourself. The band ain't great, but maybe you'd like to dance a little?"

Jane declined. "Thank you, but it's been a difficult day."

"I see how that'd be," he said, "But there's this problem of a hundred dollars."

Jane had made to rise. Now she settled again. "What hundred dollars?"

"The hundred I win if you dance with me, or the hundred I lose if you don't."

"Oh, a... wager."

Troy grinned.

She hesitated, taking him in.

I use the phrase deliberately: taking him in. When Jane focused her attention on another, she didn't look or observe or study – she appropriated. She located her subject within an inner understanding, which sometimes involved a radical reshaping, effectively denying him consequence beyond her consideration. She took us in, made us materials to be worked by her art, and didn't really recognize us otherwise. But of course we weren't aware of that.

I don't know what she saw or imagined in Troy Hardaway that evening. I do know that what she had felt earlier in the shadowed street still flickered at her nerve ends and charged her response.

"One dance," she said. "If you'll walk me back to my motel."

I was to hear several versions of what Jane, once she and Troy became a couple, called "the hundred dollar dance": of the displacement of energy in the lounge when they entered; of the space the other dancers gave them to waltz in, as if in a rite of passage or communion; and of the badinage of Troy's friends at the payment of the debt.

I was to hear too of Jane's disquiet under the gaze of three men at the bar, her sense of being, in her dark slacks and silk top and lightly highlighted blonde hair, quarry. Then one of the men, all gristle and bone, pony-tailed and tattooed, spoke to the others, slid off his stool, and approached. As she had that afternoon watching Ione Hardaway cross the highway, Jane stiffened.

Troy, with an easy thin smile, stepped forward. "What's happening, Haas?"

Pete Haas also smiled. "I'm about to ask the lady to dance."

"She's here for one dance. She had it."

Haas still smiled. "I'd like to hear it from her."

"I'm her spokesman for the evening," Troy said evenly.

Hass let his gaze drift over the other buckaroos arranged, quiet, still, around the room. His smile slid into a grin. "Another time."

He was grinning at Jane, who seemed not to breathe. But he was addressing Troy.

Haas and his two companions left. A guitar twanged. Voices rose once more. There followed laughing importunities for Jane to remain, to dance, to drink, which she warded off. She did accept Troy's arm as, at their departure, they passed through a shower of hoopla and innuendo. Out in the dim street, she tightened her grip. Troy thought that he understood.

"Don't worry about Haas. He's likely over at the Adaven, drowning his sorrows."

"I hate that," Jane said then, as in discovery.

Troy, not knowing quite what she referred to, didn't respond.

They walked silently down the street splashed with pale neon colors to the Desert Vista. Neither apparently gave a moment's thought to sex — I remind myself that I write of a man and woman both over thirty. I can account for this only by assuming that Troy was already hopelessly enamored of her, of her blonde comeliness and elegant carriage and graceful movements, and no more inclined to persuade her into bed than to urge a carefully bred filly into harness behind a plow. I suspect that Jane was oblivious to all but her own intent.

They parted with a rather ceremonious handshake, Jane believing that she would never see him again, Troy, without plan, without promise, convinced otherwise.

DRIVING INTO TOWN that first day, still a bit shaken, Jane looked with her artist's eye at what she had come to, and she grew glum. Much later, in her film, she showed us all why what awaited her she had found wanting.

There is no lake in Blue Lake, Nevada, and the spring runoff that briefly shimmers on the playa is often silver, other times gray, but rarely blue. From The Rise, the town appears as a smudge between the playa — The Flat, as Blue Lake has it — and the foothills. Nearer, the prospect is even less appealing. Just below the turnoff to Gull Valley, the desert begins to bloom with weathered single-wide mobile homes stuck up on blocks, warped plywood hay and tack sheds, pipe corrals and sagging wire fences, abandoned stock trailers, junked vehicles of every sort in every stage of rusting desuetude, and signs tattered or mud-smeared or bleached to blankness — all leading to the cluttered sprawl around the Pinenut County Fairgrounds and the Blue Lake Indian Colony.

At the edge of town, newer motels and gas stations rise from the rubble and mold of those older and failed: a Texaco Mini-Mart stands beside a crumble of oily concrete over which soars the red Mobil Pegasus. Main Street is a wideness that seems empty even when it isn't. Along it small, asphalt-shingled homes and littered lots gradually give way to commercial and institutional buildings of diverse style and construction and antiquity. Some of the storefronts are open and active, others blank or boarded-up, but all bear the marks of earlier enterprises now defunct. Squares of plastic or blotches of fresh paint or swirls of neon only deepen the prevailing shabbiness.

Beholding this, and the stir of dust under the wind, and the glare of the huge sun, and the creep of shadows across the afternoon, others beside Jane Harmon have felt forlorn.

By the time Jane and I met the next morning, her opinion was only slightly altered. Arising early, she had run through cool, quiet residential neighborhoods, glided around the high school and down to the Dirt Plant, over to the edge of the foothills, and through the sage to the irrigation ditch, which she followed up the nub of earth Blue Lake calls The Hump. There, under the face of a large granite cliff, she stopped.

I was on my patio, occupied by a line of verse, when I saw her stretching, bending her body with an economy of effort that brought to mind Japanese watercolors. Then she paused, as if transfixed by my mailbox. Noticing me, she came up the graveled path and enquired, as if asking after the highest improbability: "Miz Waner Ma'am?"

She was as splendid as the morning. Flushed and damp from her run, exuding health, soundness, she seemed a woman to encourage large hopes for all of us. I was immediately taken by her.

"I'm Winnefred Waner, yes," I said. "Good morning."

"This is... wonderful! I didn't think − I mean, I didn't know you were still..."

The word she wanted seemed obvious. I offered it: "Alive?"

She laughed, almost as if she had phrased a witticism.

I set aside notebook and pen, urged her to a chair shaded by a broad umbrella, and went into the house, returning with iced tea and orange sections and a plate of cinnamon wafers, which I served as I tried to recall her face, her pleasing if unremarkable features.

Visitors had appeared unannounced before – former students or
their children, usually, but a few times readers.

She introduced herself as the daughter of Constance Lesperance,
who had taken one of my English classes over three decades before.
"Connie. Red hair, slim? Her dad, my grandpa, worked at the Dirt
Plant. It was only one class, but she never forgot you."

"I don't remember her, I'm sorry," I said. "I taught so many young
women."

She took me in.

Then, just as her silent stare neared rudeness, she astonished me.
"I used to pretend you were my mother."

That morning on my patio, Jane sketched the outlines of a story
to which in later tellings she would add emphases, nuances, shades
of emotional color. She was ten, confined to her room until all her
toys and games were put in their proper place, sulking and ignoring
the western movie on her television. Her mother entered, holding
in her red-nailed grip a Manhattan, not the first of the day, intend-
ing, Jane was certain, to chide. Instead, taken by what she saw on
the TV screen, she settled onto the bed, swirled slowly the ice in her
drink, and smoothed the bright red pattern of the pressed cotton
draping her knee.

Then together mother and daughter watched a wide-shouldered,
thick-chested man astride a beautiful Appaloosa ride through a
mountain meadow toward the camera as bass notes of a guitar resonated reassuringly. At the curve of a green knoll, the rider reined
in, and the camera swung to gaze with him out onto the land: a
pretty valley of Technicolor green, rivulets tracing it, cattle stippling
it darkly; smoke rising into the blue sky from a large log house set
amid corrals and out-buildings; snow-capped, pine-dark mountains
enclosing, sheltering, protecting all.

The camera panned back to the rider, angled up so that like the
mountains he towered. Tipping back his hat, he exposed an expanse
of brow. Leaning forward, gloved hands on the saddle horn, he
smiled. The music, shifting from note to chord, swelled.

It was a pivotal moment in Brock Walden's career. *Under the
Mountain* marked the transformation of his screen persona from the

flawed and dangerous but ultimately decent B-movie hero to the restrained patriarch who had overcome his past. Playing this role on his own television series, he would become a representative figure in American popular culture.

It was a pivotal moment as well for Jane Harmon, the beginning of her love of western films.

"He looked so... sure, so steady," Jane said to me, "You knew you could count on him."

Confidence, stability, reliability – old-fashioned virtues to reassure a young girl who lived in fantasies and imaginings – these Jane found in Brock Walden's screen presence. So did others. With his mass of torso, his solid, pistol-bearing hips and shapely thighs, he seemed fixed, secure. Even astride a horse he seemed planted in the earth, a part of the land, constant. All an illusion of art, of course.

Then Jane's mother, a strange softness in her voice, had said: "He kissed my hand."

"What? Who?" Jane had asked, confused. Her mother's red mouth too seemed soft, as if it belonged to someone else.

"Brock Walden." Constance Harmon had nodded at the screen, where the rider and Appaloosa picked their way down the hillside. "He got off his horse – that horse – and he took my hand and he kissed it. Then he got back on his horse and rode off."

That morning on my patio Jane laughed at her childish confusion. "At first I thought she meant she was in the movie. But she was talking about the real Brock Walden, meeting him here in Blue Lake. Well, my mother and a movie star? – naturally, I made her tell me about him. That's when she told me about you."

I took a nibble of cinnamon wafer, listening.

"That year Brock Walden was at his ranch during the local celebration – what do you call it: Wild West Days? He rode in the parade. My mother was standing with you in front of the drugstore when he came along and stopped and asked you to introduce him to her and he kissed her hand and then yours?"

Brock Walden had ridden in several parades. I didn't remember watching one with a student, but that didn't mean I hadn't. I did remember a vile kiss.

"She said he was... nice."

"He could be," I said.

"What is he like, really?"

Jane was to ask me this question on several occasions, but I never gave her a complete or completely honest answer. Before I could reply this time, she added. "My mother said he never put on movie star airs. She said he was just like all the other men, only more so."

"That's an interesting way to put it," I said.

"She thought you were nice, too, even if you were a little reserved, sort of. But that was okay for an English teacher. Everybody called you 'Miz Waner Ma'am,' like a title."

"My first students started that. They were mocking my serious-ness." Only a few months removed from college and Winnefred Anne Westrom, I had been adjusting to a new name that still seemed to designate someone else, a new career that I feared I was hopelessly unprepared for, and a new life. "It stuck."

"She said you told her she could be intelligent, that she didn't have to be just..."

Jane, I noted that morning, sometimes groped after simple, obvi-ous language, but half-heartedly; the word she wanted might come, as "pretty" did in this case, or not: what was important wasn't what she said but that she had something to say.

"Over almost fifty years in the classroom, I made that point to many young women – usually to no effect." I couldn't keep my curi-osity penned up any longer. "How did I come to be your mother?"

"Oh, I was always pretending." Her smile flickered. "My father was a navy pilot, he died in a crash before I was born, and I just felt sometimes – it seemed like he couldn't have been my real father, you know? My stepfather was nice, he adopted me, he loved me, but he wasn't..." She sought a word, which she didn't find.

"Anyway, after we watched that movie, I started to make believe sometimes that I was the daughter of Brock Walden. But my mother was still my mother, which meant that he and she... well, I couldn't deal with that, so I rearranged everything until I was your daughter – you and I were blonde, and you understood me the way you'd understood her, and she had stolen me away, or you'd had to give me up…"

What began as a laugh softened into a rather wistful smile. My own smile seemed to blossom from a bud of affection.

Jane stayed with me over two hours that morning. A filmmaker who had just finished a two-year stint teaching at the University of Wisconsin, she talked intelligently of art and authoritatively of movies. We spoke of westerns especially, and directors from Ford to Eastwood, and stars from Tom Mix to Roy Rogers to John Wayne. We also talked of Nevada and the desert, which she was traveling through for the first time. She'd deliberately routed her trip from Madison back to Los Angeles through Blue Lake: "I wanted to see if it was like I'd imagined."

"And?"

My patio offers a view of town and playa and desert. Jane looked out. "It's…"

Wordless, she raised her hand and let it fall limply, and her wrist brushed the tip of the spoon she'd left in her iced tea, and the glass toppled, sending watery slivers of ice onto and across the table. As if witness to the unaccountable, she stared. "Oh."

"Don't worry about it," I said, quickly retrieving my notebook and pen and, with the edge of my hand, sweeping the wet onto the patio bricks.

She looked out again. "I didn't think it would be so… desolate."

I smiled. "Out Here we see it differently."

"Out Here," she repeated. "I heard that yesterday: Out Here, Out There. I – how long does it take to become a native of this place."

I knew what she meant. "Some see quickly, some never. It helps to have been born to it."

"Were you?"

"On a hardscrabble ranch in Amargosa Valley," I told her. "Then after my mother drifted off and my father died, I lived with my aunt in Pahrump. It wasn't too different then from what Blue Lake is now."

"Your mother abandoned you?"

"She was given to fits of melancholy. When I was nine, she went into herself one day and never returned." Even after sixty-five years, the loss pained.

"I'm sorry," she said, and she seemed to be. What she said then should have been my clue that Jane's sympathy was ever and only for Jane. "So we're both orphans."

"But I'm a daughter of the desert," I said, smiling.

"I'm not the daughter of anything, I guess," Jane said. "Just America."

I nodded down at the small white house near the base of The Hump, where a man and woman were hauling boxes out the door past a lilac bush still in bloom. "When my husband and I lived there, where my tenants are moving out, I often came up here to enjoy this view. We decided to build here because of it."

Jane's conversation could proceed like a smooth rock skipping over a pond. Now she said, "They still read your essay in college, the one about all the women who go crazy out in the desert."

"I'm flattered."

"I wish there was a way to make a film about it."

Jane had been making films since high school in Tom's River, New Jersey, winning prizes there and at UC-Santa Clara and in Los Angeles. Her productions concentrated on women in travail. Her most recent, a study of Chicana agricultural workers, had brought her national recognition sufficient to secure the contract at Wisconsin. But her tenure there had not gone well. She'd done no good work, found nothing to engage her imagination: Madison was all smooth surfaces, her students all smiles, her colleagues all slogans, and her classes a drain that sucked away her creative energy. She gestured at, obscurely, an aborted relationship. Now she was returning to Los Angeles, where she would apply for another grant. She would make another film. She wanted to create something beautiful and powerful. It was in her, she felt, this film, if she could only find a subject.

She gave me too, that first morning, her version of the accident the previous day, of Ione Hardaway's actions and her own misunderstanding. "But the gun — would she actually shoot somebody?"

"She hasn't," I said. "Yet."

"She's so…" Once more the word she wanted didn't come. "The Wild West that Brock Walden welcomes us to — is she part of it?"

"That's an enticement to tourists, a marketing ploy."

"Yes, of course, but… do you suppose she'd talk to me, let me film her?"

I smiled. "As I say, Ione hasn't shot anyone, yet."

It took her a moment to realize that I was joking.

After a few more minutes, she prepared to take her leave. When I rose with her, she gave me a sudden hard hug. "I really do feel like you're — I mean, I feel like… fate brought me up here this morning."

"I've enjoyed our talk," I said. "Have a pleasant, safe trip."

She turned and walked down the path.

Jane, moving, pleased the eye. I watched her until she disappeared below the lip of the hill. Then I returned to my efforts.

Eleanor returned an hour later from the cemetery, where she had been planting at her husband's grave. She sat where Jane Harmon had, covering another chair seat with the broad-brimmed sunhat she took off. While I got her a glass, she lighted her second cigarette of the day. "Henry's grave looks nice."

"Thank you," I said. My husband was buried only a few paces from Reverend Broadhurst.

I told Eleanor about Jane Harmon, her odd fantasy, her encounter with Ione Hardaway, her opinion of my view.

"Desolate is the word," she said. "Sometimes, anyhow."

Eleanor's love-hate relation with Nevada had begun over sixty years earlier, when she arrived in Blue Lake the new bride of the new pastor of St. Basil's Episcopal church. The sun and wind and dry air desiccated her Celtic skin, the brown emptiness offended her green-seeking Massachusetts eye, and what seemed to her Nevadans' willful ignorance and cultural impoverishment assaulted her Sarah Lawrence sensibility. Yet she admired much of the desert world: the indefatigable spirit of some of the people, the hard creatures and the spiny plants that clung to life here, the twisted shapes, the lovely light and subtle hues, and the silence. Now she enjoyed all this, and my company, over her annual Memorial Day visit, but she would not stay long. A drunk driver had killed John Broadhurst a quarter of a century before, and she had made another life in Los Angeles.

"She wanted to know where she could find the Wild West."

"She wants grime and mayhem? Spittin' an' fartin' an' eye-gougin' an' knife-fightin'? Louts and slovens and scofflaws?"

I laughed. "She seemed to think Ione Hardaway could help her find it."

"No grime with Ione, at least once chores are done." Eleanor sucked in smoke. "Mayhem, now, that's another matter."

I smiled. "Have some more iced tea."

Three days later I received Jane's letter, asking if she could rent my little house.

WHAT, JANE HAD ASKED me that first morning, was Brock Walden really like? I don't know that I can say, even now. I do know that we – Jane and Ione and I, Troy Hardaway and Carlyle Walden and Cletus Rose – all of us fluttered and swooped in the disturbed air of his passage through our hours and days. He irked and angered and enlivened us, he dared us to love him, he charmed us even as he rejected our claims on him. He was to us, as to Blue Lake, Nevada, a swirl of wind and wet in our desert.

Jane Harmon was not alone in wondering about Brock Walden. The question of his identity and character had been in the American air for over half a century, from the moment Hollywood first guessed that money might be made by outfitting in cowboy togs another war hero with a Horatio Alger history. I had wondered myself, which was one of the reasons that, a year after Sputnik began to circle the earth and the newly-wed Waners arrived in Blue Lake, Henry to do geology for Consolidated Mining and I to teach Blue Lake youth to read carefully and to write clearly, I found myself one June morning in a twelve-year-old Ford churning up the dust of Gull Valley as Eleanor Broadhurst drove and smoked Herbert Tarytons and talked about the new owner of the Rocking W.

"Walden. Named himself after a mud puddle. The Chamber of Commerce thinks he'll be a tourist attraction. Will they carve his manly visage on Mount Adams? Make up bumper stickers: Blue Lake – the cow town that cow-tows to a B-movie star? It's a tax dodge for him, of course, but at least he's going to run cattle. That'll keep some people busy and money circulating. But my, wouldn't it be nice if Blue Lake did come alive? New people settling in instead of assorted hard-luck types just passing through. Maybe God would make them Episcopalians. Is the smoke bothering you?'

After purchasing the ranch the previous summer, Brock Walden began flying Out Here in his small plane, delighting Blue Lake children when he buzzed the town, frightening adults when he buzzed their automobiles. He came to hunt deer and elk with his pals, to see to his property, and to assure Blue Lake that the Rocking W was for him not just a retreat into reality from the artifice of Tinseltown but even more a business opportunity. He intended to invest goodly sums of his own money on improvements and, when he could make a deal, other pieces of property. Should his special needs be served by special arrangements – on taxes, roads, utilities, water and grazing rights – he would be a permanent economic force in the community. He was eager, he avowed, to be a good neighbor.

All this augured hopefully. After the war Blue Lake had experienced little to encourage optimism. The production of beef was up but the price down, the price of gold fixed but the cost of mining it climbing, and unless other uses for diatomaceous earth were found, the paychecks of those employed at the Dirt Plant were imperiled. The population was declining. Travel was easier and faster, which made it cheaper for Blue Lake to shop for large items Out There. And while more people drove their automobiles Out Here, Blue Lake had nothing with which to entice them to stop and spend, nothing to sell. Except Westness, Wild and otherwise.

By the time Henry Waner and I arrived, Blue Lake had already mythologized and commodified its past. The rodeo, once an occasion for unruly and intoxicated men to sport with animals and fight with each other, was now a family affair complete with parades and carnivals and fairs. Businessmen donned raiment authenticated by movies, pearl buttons and string ties, and dressed their wives and daughters in crinolines and calico. Enterprises sprouted signs featuring horses or shovels. The Chamber of Commerce erected a plinth and plaque before an old cottonwood, a branch of which once bent under the weight of a horse thief. Visitors were offered the opportunity to tour a worked-out silver mine or an erstwhile brothel, to attend the reenactment of a trial of a claim jumper, to pan for flakes of gold in Cottonwood Creek, to ride horses into the mountains or desert, or to wager on ore wagons racing across the playa.

All this Blue Lake chose to believe represented a real tradition, much as Blue Lake chose to believe that Brock Walden, born Walter Waldo Broekenworth in Newark, New Jersey, was a real Westerner.

"Ol Bee-Dub-Ya," Eleanor snorted. "He sits a horse well and hits what he aims a rifle at and buys drinks when it's his turn – which makes him, in Nevada, a paragon of virtue. Speaking of which, we'll have to guard ours. He's notorious."

"You could have brought your husband along instead of me," I said.

She took in a lungful of smoke. "What fun would that be?"

We were on our way to examine a mahogany secretary that had been found in a Rocking W shed, where it had been buried under the dust and detritus of decades. If it proved to be restorable, Evelyn proposed to claim it for her husband's congregation. Brock Walden, it happened, was at the ranch supervising the construction of a landing strip between the road and Molly Creek, and in answer to her telephoned inquiry, he had invited her to come out and inspect the piece.

"I told him I knew he'd want to donate it to the parish. He said he looked forward to 'nee-go-she-a-tin' with me. Even me, broken down wreck that I am."

Just thirty, Eleanor for her own reasons assumed the character of a crone. She had the fair, freckled skin that the desert sun savages, but her blue eyes were lovely, and her figure even after the birth of three sons was trim. Men noticed her. She gave no sign of noticing them. Smoking, which she did not do in public or her home, was her only vice. She once told me it was her way of committing adultery.

"We'll confuse him," she said. "I'll dicker while you distract him."

"How do you propose I do that?"

"Breathing should suffice."

I laughed. I had been looking forward to meeting Brock Walden. I'd seen several of his movies and heard the tales broadcast over Blue Lake and was curious. I would be happy, I thought, simply to breathe and observe.

Eleanor slowed as the dirt road roughened and took the curve of a slope into what seemed a deep calm harbor in a sea of sage: the Rocking W. In the morning sun, meadows and fields of wild hay greened, and small earthen ponds shimmered. Molly Creek was a narrow rill that drained from reedy seeps and soughs adorned with bright-winged birds. Across the valley, Eagle Creek twisted through pastures and neat rows of old apple trees and the deeper green of alfalfa fields. Nearer the road, a man guided a scraping blade over a strip of land recently chained free of sage. Up ahead, a collection of mismatched, poplar-protected buildings and pens and corrals sprawled over a brief elevation commanding a view of road, fields, and desert. Beyond, above, the Turquoise Range curled in a huge and sheltering embrace.

"Buckaroos think they'll come here when they die, if they've been good."

"It's a lovely spot," I said.

Clanking over the cattle guard, we met the disorder of the ranch yard. The old stood with the new, the discarded with the still serviceable: structures and enclosures and vehicles and machines and materials. The ranch house was an original square of logs that had been added onto in several separate constructions. But for all the disarray, the Rocking W pulsed with life, seemed a place where appearance didn't matter, where doing was everything.

A pair of handsome horses watched from a corral beside a large, weathered barn. As we pulled up before the house, a pregnant mixed-breed Collie challenged our arrival, and a small man wearing what appeared to be several layers of clothing stepped from an outbuilding, gave us a glance, and disappeared back into the dark doorway. Another man dozed in a rocking chair on the house porch.

Then Sheila Brenner, a two-year-old on her hip and a six-year-old peeping from behind her leg, came out and called sharply to the dog, handed the younger child to the elder, and crossed the ranch yard to greet us. B. W. had ridden out to check the spring in Icebox Canyon, and her husband, Jim, was picking up irrigation equipment in Reno, but she could show us the secretary, which she and Cletus Rose had cleaned up as best they could. We found it in a rickety shed Sheila had thought she might turn into a chicken coop. The dark finish was spotted and scratched, a brass door-pull was bent and a pigeonhole insert warped, but Eleanor thought the piece worth restoring.

We went back to the house. As we approached, the man on the porch put down a paperback book and rose from his chair. Noting his size and shape, I took him, in a confused moment, for Brock Walden. Then Sheila introduced us to Cletus Rose. He was thirty, of somber expression and soft, intelligent eyes. One of his large, powerful looking hands lifted his Stetson high enough to reveal his baldness. He would see to the furniture.

We women went inside and drank iced tea and talked. Sheila Brenner, pretty in a frizzy-haired and chipmunk-cheeked fashion, wore a faded cotton housedress over a strong ample body and a pleasant smile over a deep anxiety. The only woman on the ranch, she was obviously happy to have other women to talk with about the weather and Blue Lake doings, about her boss, about her husband. Jim Brenner had returned from Korea physically sound but silent, subject to dead-eyed tears that pained and frightened his wife. His oddness made others uncomfortable, but his inattention cost him jobs, so he had drifted from one to another, Sheila and daughters being forced to settle for brief periods in one of her mother's bedrooms. The Rocking W, Sheila said hopefully, was a fresh start. The responsibility B. W. had given Jim seemed to ground him.

When Eleanor and I went to load the secretary, we found that Cletus Rose had wrapped it in a blanket and tarp and lashed it securely into the trunk with a length of new rope.

Eleanor smiled. "There's our excuse to return, if we want. Rope's expensive."

Then Brock Walden rode into the ranch yard. He walked the high-stepping, beautifully groomed bay toward us. When suddenly the horse started, tossing its head and stomping its front feet heavily into the dirt, he reined it into a slow circle, speaking softly: controlling the animal, he seemed to take on its power. Then he stopped, patted the horse's neck, and leaned back in the saddle. He looked at the secretary, at Eleanor, at me, and he smiled.

It was a performance of the sort at which, after a dozen years in Hollywood, he excelled. His delivery of lines on screen was convincing enough, but his appeal as a film actor came largely from the pure if not at all simple masculine force projected by his physical presence. I felt it in the small shiver that danced over my skin.

He stepped down from the horse, greeted Eleanor and, removing his hat, extended his hand. She took it, returned his greeting, and then introduced me.

"The schoolmarm. Been hopin' I'd have the pleasure." The drawl, with its slurs and elisions and lazy rhythms, was an obvious, faintly mocking affectation that seemed nevertheless real. His hand swallowed mine and resisted, for the briefest of moments, its withdrawal.

Then he smiled at Eleanor. "Seems like you negotiated with yourself."

"Junk," she said, moving to the back of the car. "This looks like its been in the bottom of a birdcage. The glue's so dry it's dust."

"Woman's touch'll bring up the shine on it.'

"So it will be shiny junk."

"Fine piece hidin' under there."

They joshed with one another. Eleanor flushed under her wide-brimmed straw hat, delighted by the banter. I stood silently enjoying the fun.

Cletus Rose had returned to the porch and his book, but now at Brock Walden's elbow there arrived the small man I'd noticed earlier. He wore three pairs of pants and at least that many shirts, none of which or the flesh beneath them, the sharp funk of him argued, had been washed for a long time. The dirt on his face didn't obscure the rather unfortunately repaired harelip; a cleft palate revealed itself in the harsh slur of sounds that he addressed to Brock Walden as he took the reins of the horse.

"Thanks, Lonnie," Brock Walden said to his retreating back. To Eleanor he said, as the small man moved out of earshot, "Thinks he's part of the place, like the mustangs hang around Mud Springs."

"It's charitable of you to take him in," Evelyn said.

"Earns his keep. And it's the way we do things Out Here, isn't it."

"Precisely. Which is the very reason that you want to let St. Basil's have this piece of furniture."

He feigned chagrin. "Walked right into that one, didn't I."

Through all this I had been ignored. Then Brock Walden turned to me, squaring his shoulders, seeming, nearly, to grow larger. He smelled of horse. "What do you think I should do?"

"I think you should follow your finer instincts."

"If I did that,' he drawled, grinning, "I'd never do anything exciting, Miz Waner. What do your friends call you?"

"Winnefred," I said, startled.

"Winnefred," he repeated. "Awful stuffy for such a bright young thing. How 'bout your husband – he got a special name for you?"

On its face, nothing in the question approached the unseemly, yet something in his voice made it seem so. Still, I smiled. "No. He's one of my friends."

"More 'n that, I hope." He grinned. "How 'bout Win?"

Suddenly uncomfortable, I retreated into my somewhat starched classroom persona. "I'm not a person others usually address with diminutives."

"Address with diminutives, huh? I guess not," he laughed. "Awful young to be usin' words like 'di-min-u-tives.'"

I felt my face reddening.

"An' nobody calls you Win?" He was still grinning, but a deeper, more forceful current sounded in his drawl. "Maybe I will. That way, you'll always know who's addressin' you."

Sheila Brenner came out on the porch then, calling to him to the telephone.

"Miz Broadhurst," he said to Eleanor, "the parson's married a witch. Turned me into a philanthropist."

"You'll get a star in heaven," she smiled.

"Use all I can get." He tipped his hat. "Ma'am."

Then he turned to me, and his smile changed. "Win."

Eleanor smoked and chattered all the way back to town. Sheila Brenner couldn't take much more moving and uncertainty. Lonnie McClary had been living in a desert hovel he'd built out of used tires when Brock Walden brought him onto the Rocking W. Cletus Rose was not a buckaroo, not any longer; he was an ex-drunk who had, after losing a bar fight of epic proportions with Brock Walden, become the actor's stand-in, stunt double, and bodyguard, and who, when at the ranch, made thrice weekly trips into Blue Lake to meet in the basement of St. Basil's with a group of not very anonymous recovering alcoholics. He hadn't been dozing when we arrived at the ranch. He'd been reading.

"How anybody can slog through more than a page of *Absalom, Absalom* without getting a headache I'll never know."

"Faulkner always seems forced," I said in my schoolmarm voice, "as if he wants to shock us for the shock of it."

"You're too innocent to appreciate him, Winnefred," Eleanor said. "The stories my husband hears from our Blue Lake friends and neighbors make Faulkner seem like a Sunday School teacher."

We were drinking coffee in her tiny dining room when she finally raised the subject of Brock Walden. "So what do you think?"

"I think I made a fool of myself. Diminutives."

"Oh, I don't know," she said. "There's something to be said for being an intelligent and sensible twenty-two-year-old thoroughly in love with her husband. You held your ground. Lots of women would have swooned into his arms."

"I grew up around men like that," I said. "I learned how to keep them at a distance."

"Those men weren't Brock Walden, though, were they?"

I smiled then, shivered. "Actually, he is a little... scary."

Eleanor stopped smiling. "At least you have the good sense to see the danger. You'll want to be careful with him."

This had become too serious. "He flirts with everyone, Eleanor. He was flirting with you, too."

Soberly now she said, "He's a stallion, Winnefred, and he's taken your scent."

I was shocked by her image, so unexpected, so coarse. "What?"

"He'll always be there now, nose up, advancing on you. He'll never push, but he'll always pressure. If he can't charm you, he'll try to wear you down. He won't care how long it takes, and he won't be satisfied until... you present yourself to him." Her manner was so serious that for a moment I thought it might be feigned, a jest.

"Which I will never do," I said. "I'm not interested in his attentions. He must see that."

Eleanor shook her head. "You are only twenty-two, aren't you?"

Something in her tone, a sad maternal concern, kept me silent.

"I'm sorry," she said, "I didn't mean to patronize. But a man like Brock Walden doesn't care what you may or may not be interested in. To him you're a sexually viable female of his species. He'll consider you, Winnefred Westrom Waner, about as much as the stud considers the mare he covers."

I found that difficult to accept. "But finally he's not a horse. He's a human being. And you're not suggesting that he would resort to violence...?"

Eleanor leaned across the table, took my hand and enfolded it within her own, freckled and veined, her gold wedding band loose on her finger. "No. He never needs to. I'm simply telling you to be careful. Don't allow yourself to think that he is other than he is."

"What is he, Eleanor?"

"He's a lout on a fine horse."

I resisted, then and later, Eleanor's assessment of Brock Walden. Certainly I did not pass it on to Jane Harmon when she enquired. It was too simple, he too complex, the evidence of his character conflicting.

Brock Walden was said to be, and would often prove himself, a congenial, generous man, loyal to and undemanding of friends, hospitable to all, charitable to the ill-fated, helpful especially to veterans wounded in flesh or spirit. He was cheerfully civic mind-ed, giving his name and time and money to local projects. As might be expected of a war hero, he sang jingoistic, xenophobic paeans to America, even as, unexpectedly, he placed under the protection of his reputation those few Out Here who looked or spoke or believed differently. He provided for drifters, one of whom he himself had been as a teenager, working his way across the country, when he hayed for a week in Gull Valley. This experience Blue Lake fixed on. He had toughed it out. He had labored with his hands and his head, with muscle and brains and grit made himself the man who would come to own the very Gull Valley place on which he'd built hay-stacks for a dollar a day and found. He was, in Blue Lake, Nevada, what we would have ourselves be.

Of course, Blue Lake heard the stories from Out There, of wrecked Southern California nights, of brawls and binges, insults and gauche-ries. We heard whispers about marijuana. Always we got accounts of Brock Walden and women. And when, the summer after I'd first seen the Rocking W, Jim Brenner rode into the hills, turned loose his horse, and shot his dog and himself, rumors surfaced about his wife and his boss. Over the years, Brock Walden's sexual escapades in the high desert, actual or imagined, became a staple of discussion among locals: "Guess who Ol' Bee-Dub-Ya cut out'a the herd this time." No one – not the cuckolds, not the fathers or brothers, not the wives and daughters and sisters involved – seemed to mind. Quite the opposite: Blue Lake, while not actually pandering for Brock Walden, took his mounting of local mares as a source of bizarre pride.

At the same time, watching Brock Walden, the good neighbor, buy out at a cut rate those small Gull Valley ranchers who had been backed into the final corner by the perversities of nature and eco-nomics and the human heart, Blue Lake said, "Business is business." As he carefully put together the pieces of Walden Ranch, we said: "He's shrewd, Ol' Bee-Dub-Ya." Not his fault that the smaller outfits couldn't compete.

Blue Lake looked at what Brock Walden brought to and took from us and called it a fair exchange.

But I told Jane Harmon none of this. Some of it she heard, in and about Blue Lake, once she had begun her search for a story. Nothing in these accounts, however, could shake her faith in her fantasy.

I **WRITE SLOWLY**, some nights but a few sentences, some nights only a paragraph or two. Since I began this account, winter has hardened the land with cold. Soon we will have snow. Already we have less daylight, more darkness.

I write in a cloth-bound notebook like those stacked a lifetime high in my closet. When I die, someone will find them and, perhaps, wonder.

I write with a lovely tortoiseshell fountain pen, a gift, marking no occasion at all, from my usually parsimonious young husband a few months after our wedding. The slim barrel fits my fingers; the colors and patterns put the desert in my hand. I enjoy watching the ink seep from nib to paper, soaking, bonding.

Jane Harmon, who came Out Here with a head full of ideas and attitudes given to her by her Out There teachers, once, as we sat at my table, suddenly sat upright and pointed at my pen, exclaiming: "Fo!"

I didn't understand. "Pardon me?"

"It's faux tortoiseshell, isn't it! Your pen."

"No," I said, "I'm afraid it's real." I described the sentiment attached to it.

"But tortoises are on the Endangered Species list," Jane said. "Pens like that, and combs, they're illegal, you can't buy or sell them anymore."

"And rightly so," I said.

"But you still... use it."

"It isn't as if I could give the shell back to the tortoise, Jane," I said.

"Yes, of course," she frowned. "But to some people, even the sight of it might be... disturbing. Offensive, even."

"I see," I said. "You want me to sacrifice my pleasure for your ideological comfort."

"Well... yes," she said.

In my will I have left my property to the Blue Lake School District, my personal possessions to the Blue Lake Community Center, and what little money I have to Ione Hardaway. But I'm thinking of adding a codicil bequeathing my tortoiseshell pen to Jane Harmon.

After our first visit, Jane had returned to her motel to find Troy Hardaway waiting with French bread, sharp cheese, and plums, by which she allowed herself to be lured to a bench in Cottonwood Creek Park. She enjoyed the food as much as she did Troy's stories about his sister and his description of the country he could show her if she would return, as he urged. Hours later, driving into the gathering desert darkness, she decided to do precisely that.

"It wasn't Troy," she told me. "I just suddenly knew there was a film here for me to find."

So on the first day of July, her SUV came to be parked in the drive of my rental. The next day, while her belongings were being transported from storage, she had Nan Bailey at the Snip 'n Clip shear off her Out There coiffure ("Defrosted her," Blue Lake waggishly noted), leaving a boyish blonde crop that she stuffed under a flat-crowned Stetson she purchased at Millar's Western Wear and Saddlery. She also bought a pair of Tony Lamas, and with them she was soon wearing denim and plaid and in them walking with a slight forward lean. Blue Lake saw by her outfit what she wished to be taken for. But Blue Lake had already taken her otherwise.

Calamity Jane. The accident outside town suggested the epithet; those following kept it current, justifying Blue Lake's sense that wherever Jane was there would be some sort of upheaval.

Around Jane things fell with uncommon frequency. Displays in Foodmart or Hasweldt's Drugs shuddered, cartons dropped, bottles bounced or broke, cans wobbled down aisles. In offices papers slipped from folders, folders slid off desks. Moving through her day, Jane seemed almost of necessity to bump into things and people, and we in Blue Lake, avoiding her, ran into things or each other, even as she proceeded in a blithe, Buster Keatonesque oblivion that transformed splat and thump into a ballet danced to the rhythms of

High Farce. But objects sometimes fell on toes, painfully; knees and elbows offered or accepted bruising; there was jostling and disconcertion and spilling. And always someone had to clean up the mess.

The few times Jane recognized her part in these occurrences, she apologized, sometimes with an extravagance that inflicted more damage, other times simply smiling, as if ignoring the disorder made everything orderly again.

We were drinking tea and nibbling at pastry one morning when, apropos of nothing, she asked: "Calamity Jane. Do they call me that? Me?"

When I hesitated, she went on: "Calamity Jane was a...masculine kind of woman, wasn't she? Crude? I don't understand the connection."

"They're amusing themselves. You seem to be in the vicinity of an unusual number of mishaps."

"Oh." She frowned uncertainly. "A joke?"

"Not intended unkindly," I said, politely prevaricating.

"I see," she said, suddenly smiling. "They've given me a name. It's like calling you 'Miz Waner Ma'am' – it's a form of acceptance, isn't it."

It wasn't that, but I didn't say so.

Now the notion became, like the denim and plaid, part of her Out Here costume. Henceforth, Jane was pleased to agree that she was something of a klutz. This was one of her typical revisions of reality, however, for she was beautifully coordinated, the gestures that wreaked havoc seeming effortless and inevitable. No, what Jane was was thoughtless. She took in, she mused, she imagined, but she didn't pay attention, she didn't consider consequences, she didn't think. She gawked.

One evening soon after her arrival, Jane appeared at my door with a question about electrical circuit breakers. Tea and small pecan cookies held her at my kitchen table for an hour on that occasion, and she returned with regularity over her first weeks in Blue Lake. I came to look forward to her visits. I was, I discovered, lonely – so many friends had in one way or another departed – and Jane could be a delightful companion. Although most of what she knew of history and literature came from movies (I once joked that she must have never read a book, which she seemed to take as praise), she spoke interestingly of art, and she discussed political and cultural issues as if they were the stuff of oddball comedy. She enjoyed recounting her misadventures among the rich and famous in Los Angeles, when she worked, for a brief period after college, for organizations that advocated for the arts, soliciting and disbursing funds. We laughed together at the imbroglios she created, at her gaffs and deflations; but while her humor was always at her own expense, it was also indulgent. She seemed charmed by her own stories, which she told as a child might, discovering in them something wonderful about herself.

As I listened, I began to get a sense of, and to relate to, what Jane really wanted from Blue Lake. Her career was stalled, she said, because her life was cluttered: she had been distracted by unimportant projects and ideas and people. Now, in the emptiness of the Nevada desert, she would free herself of personal obligations. Now she would give her art her all. It was time she made an important film, a beautiful and powerful film. It was past time. Time was running out.

Hearing this, I smiled. "You're a young woman yet."

"I'm thirty-two," she said. "I have a reputation in some circles, yes, but I haven't done anything really impressive. And competition for grants is fierce. Even knowing a lot of people, I can't be sure how many more chances I'll have."

From Blue Lake Jane also wanted a subject for her beautiful and powerful film. To the organization supporting her she had proposed a study of Nevada's wild horses, which, however, she had no intention of making. "That's so been done." She was after something else, something different. She wanted to find and film what Brock Walden had welcomed her to on the billboard outside Blue Lake: "the Wild West." She wanted to locate the essential spirit that created all those classic Western movies she loved and loved to talk about. It was Out Here, that spirit — she sensed it in the spread of space, felt it in the grit of the desert air. She just needed to find a story that would give it shape and substance.

Conducting the business newcomers must, Jane bumped about town and took in images — the skyline of storefronts on Main Street, the color of the dust on the cottonwood leaves, the glint of sunlight on the water tank. She measured forms and faces: a smear of childish cowlick; the sag of a matronly breast; broken hands, gouged cheeks, rheumy eyes. She asked questions, assayed answers. She perused relics and texts and photographs at the museum, old maps and newspapers at the library; she listened to tales at the BLM and Sheriff's offices, and she talked with elders at the Blue Lake Indian Colony. Soon she was out in the countryside, trying to see like a native and taking photographs that at night she uploaded onto her computer.

Jane did all this, but she didn't find the real Wild West. She didn't find a story. And she didn't see that she was the main character in a story that Blue Lake was telling itself.

As Jane bumped and bumbled about, Blue Lake waited for the real fun to begin, small disasters being but the cartoon, so to speak, before the main feature. Jane was amusing, with her Out There ideas, her cowgirl costume and smooth sashay, her bangs and thumps, but Blue Lake was eager to see how her presence Out Here would affect the interlacing of local lives. Some relations would undergo a readjustment, assuredly, for she was female and single and attractive. She was also, at first, wholly ignorant of Blue Lake's intentions for her.

Jane had come to Blue Lake to simplify her life, to reduce it to essentials. She wanted to shed especially the layers of feeling, the imbricated indulgences and anxieties that American women have come to denote with the term "relationship."

"I'm not good at love," she told me early in our acquaintance. "I care, but apparently not enough. I really just want to be let alone, to do my work, like…"

I looked at her denim and plaid costume, aware that Jane had sensed that Ione Hardaway had removed herself from any consideration of sexual intimacy. "Like Ione."

"I was going to say, like you, Miz Waner."

Jane's belief that she would be left to herself I attribute to her innocence. When she finally concluded that what she wanted was not possible, I could offer no consolation.

"In a small rural community like Blue Lake, a single, sexually viable woman is considered a sexually available woman."

She protested: "But I don't want to be with anybody."

"It doesn't matter," I said. "Alone, you call other relationships into question."

"But I haven't encouraged anyone. I didn't do anything."

"That doesn't matter either. Until you're accounted for, you are trouble, perhaps calamitous."

She didn't smile at my little jest. "It isn't fair, Miz Waner."

Ah, Jane. Who but the innocent expect life to be fair?

Encountering Blue Lake men, Jane could not fail to know that she was the object of their most male intent. They strolled Foodmart aisles with empty carts as if shopping for some delectable tidbit, or fingered magazines in the drug store, or posed with tools in the Ranch and Garden Emporium whenever she was in these establishments. Vehicles of every stripe trailed her as she walked about Blue Lake or, night and day, rolled down the street where she lived, my driveway serving as a turn-around on their circuit. Bold men stopped her on the street to offer invitations, more timid men phoned or sent her notes, these attentions giving rise in Jane only to mild irritation and quiet frustration.

Troy Hardaway, of course, was among her suitors. A half-hour after Jane walked down The Hump with the house key, he was helping her unload. In the hot days and long nights that followed, he regularly found excuses to be in town and at her door. But only once did Jane's conduct suggest that Troy might not be merely one more amorous pest.

From the moment of her return, Jane had asked about Ione Hardaway as often as she had inquired about Brock Walden. I was able to confirm Ione's skills and intelligence and character, and when Jane brought me more of Blue Lake's stories, I could also attest to Ione's eccentricities, if that's what they were. Jane had taken the fact of a female ranch manager into her imagination, making Ione a feminist hero, a woman misshaped by her struggles in a man's world, which she had ultimately conquered. (Jane's imaginings were not wrong, merely incomplete; there was more to Ione that Jane could then know or her ideology could ever account for.) But when, her first week in Blue Lake, Jane thought to drive out to the Rocking W to apologize to Ione for her brusqueness after the accident, I gently proposed that such a visit wouldn't be welcome. Troy, appealed to, made excuses: Ione was real busy, she didn't "visit," she'd forgotten about the incident and wouldn't want an apology anyhow.

Troy put Jane off, yet this, only this, was what she wanted from him. Denied, she denied him any advantage in the contest for her favors. He became, so to speak, just one more blind seeking squiggle.

Then, in early August, Jane appeared with Troy at a Friday dance at the American Legion hall. They arrived early, danced exclusively with one another, and left long before alcohol and sexual energy heated up the crowded room. Troy took her home, spent a polite half-hour in her living room, and then drove back to the ranch house he shared with his father. Blue Lake did not know quite what to make of this until the following Monday.

At mid-morning, Ione Hardaway sat with her brother in a booth in the Wagon Wheel Café. This in itself caused comment, for Ione rarely took a break from the string of tasks she began and ended in darkness. Yet here she was at ten o'clock, among salesmen and retired ranchers and teenage shop girls, drinking coffee with Troy and seeming to enjoy her ease.

Then Jane Harmon came in. Acting out a surprised delight at the sight of brother and sister, her shoulder brushing a coat rack into a perilous teetering, she approached. When Troy got to his feet and introduced the two women, Ione studied Jane's extended hand for some time before meeting it with her own, bare and beautifully shaped. Then at Troy's invitation, Jane sat and began to talk. Ione almost at once tugged on her gloves, eyeing Jane as she would a growling calf-killer: slowly, squint lines deepening into scars, eyelids drooping, her gaze steadied and set and shone.

Ione's glare, which had stopped hard men in mid-sentence, had on Jane Harmon no effect whatsoever.

Then Ione spoke, and Troy gave a small start, but Jane's smile didn't waver. The women exchanged words, Ione, having the last one before she rose and stomped out.

On all this Blue Lake agreed. About what had been said in the encounter, however, the only consensus was that it didn't matter because it didn't seem to have mattered to Jane.

That evening Jane recounted the meeting for me.

"Our little plot, Troy's and mine, didn't fool her at all. But I admire her so much, what she's managed to achieve, the position she's earned. When I said so, though, she got upset. And when I told her about my film, how I was sure she would want to be part of the project, she — isn't that a wonderful Medusa look she has?"

"It doesn't seem to have turned you to stone," I said, smiling.

Jane laughed. "It only worked with men, wasn't it?"

"And what did she say about being interviewed?"

"Oh," Jane replied blithely, "she said no. She was quite unpleasant about it."

Ione had read Jane as an opportunist, one more Out There exploiter Out Here to take and then leave, a patronizing sensibility who would presume, as she furthered her own interests, to explain us to ourselves. (This reading was fundamentally correct.)

"I don't see why she's so... negative," Jane protested to me. "I just want to make a film that gets to the heart of things Out Here. I'm beginning to sense — well, I don't know what I'm going to do, but Ione will be part of it, somehow."

"But she told you she doesn't want to be in your film."

"Oh," Jane replied with magnificent aplomb, "everyone wants to be in a movie."

The last word that Ione had had in the Wagon Wheel was directed, it turned out, not at Jane but at Troy. "She told him to get back to work."

Which he did. But the bargain — a dancing date in exchange for a meeting with Ione — seemed not to have led anywhere that Troy would have their relationship go. He became again just another swain.

Over the next weeks, aspirants to Jane's affections were as unceasing in their attentions to her as Blue Lake was implacable in its resolve that she be bound to someone, anyone. Still, Jane might have resisted longer – for that matter, she planned on staying only a year, she could have put up with what was after all mere nuisance, she could have toughed it out – had it not been for another suitor, this one most unpleasant.

IN THE FINAL MINUTES of the day of Jane's accident on the highway, the Blue Lake police had been called to the Adaven Bar, where a dispute had erupted. Bloody but brief, the altercation ended before officers arrived, Norman Casteel suffering a broken nose and assorted contusions at the hands of Pete Haas. Because both insisted that the row had been, if not friendly, at least one between friends, and because no on-lookers would swear to having witnessed a public disturbance, and because the proprietor estimated that the damages to his place of business were minor, the police, to their great disappointment, could make no arrest that would lead to a filing of charges.

Haas, in town a year or so, already had caught the eye of local law enforcement. He'd done jail but not prison time in Southern California, and he'd fled to the Nevada desert seeking, he proclaimed, his birthright as an American: freedom. He didn't actually assert but neither did he deny that he was Brock Walden's natural son, a rumor that Blue Lake found less preposterous than his purporting to be a geologist. He filed a few claims and disturbed enough dirt to pass as a working prospector, but the money he flashed, George Burleigh was convinced, came from distributing methamphetamines and fencing burgled goods. He had brawled in other bars, establishing dominance among men like himself, enjoying the rush of violence, and the pain. He had taken up with a succession of Blue Lake slatterns. He had hard eyes and a filthy mouth.

Norman Casteel also wished to be free, to roam the wilderness, or so he said. A self-styled frontiersman, he was a homegrown oaf who trapped an occasional pelt and sometimes guided Out There hunters, but he spent most of his time in the Adaven, his drinking financed by whatever woman he was living with – at the moment, Mina Pasco – or, more often, his elderly Aunt Shirley, retired from the county assessor's office, to whom he was oddly devoted.

Haas and Casteel had battled over, absurdly, Jane Harmon. Caught up in a lurid fantasy, Casteel had drunkenly toasted the blonde who drove her car into the ditch that day, insisting that he would soon be off to the Desert Vista to take his pleasure with her, punctuating his point by twirling on his finger as if it were the lady's favor a skimpy satin undergarment. First on the scene of the accident, where he had stolen the panties, he asserted Right of Discovery. Hass, arguing that the woman owed him a dance, registered his own claim. Savagery ensued.

This might all have been of no consequence. But a week after her return, as Jane cooled down from her run, delighting in the quiet of the streets, the shade of the elms and crab apple trees, the smell of dewy grass and desert dust, she suddenly found herself at a street corner confronted by a huge, shining, rumbling pickup, by a leer and an invitation.

She recognized Haas immediately, anxiously, and she ignored him.

As she made to cross the street, he revved the powerful engine and inched the truck forward, back, forward again, blocking her way. He repeated his invitation.

Jane looked directly at him, and she spoke: "Leave… me… alone."

As he grinned, Jane became aware of her damp and clinging T-shirt, her skimpy shorts, her bare limbs glowing with sweat. She felt naked, defenseless, gripped by fear and an inexplicable shame. But all she could do is what she did: she ran.

The pickup pursued, at a distance, its engine roaring as if in angry amusement. Even after she had gained the security of the house, of a door and deadbolt, she didn't feel safe, and wouldn't until the machine ceased to bellow.

What had he said? I asked this question when, sometime later, Jane told me of the encounter. George Burleigh, on my patio in response to my call, asked it as well. In both cases the answer, when Jane brought herself to give it, was the same: "You wanna dance?"

By the time Jane told me about this incident, others had occurred, so that she could offer evidence that she was being stalked. He was, this saturnine figure, in his truck or out of it, in the distance or suddenly near, always there, watching, so much so that she felt his presence even when she couldn't see him. He had phoned and not spoken (it was him, she knew; it had to be him). At ominous hours of the night she heard noises that might be a prowler or was awakened by the snarl of his truck's engine. She altered her running routes, took different streets on her walks downtown, shopped randomly and on no schedule, only to find him, finally, there.

George Burleigh told us who and what he was. George also explained that he could have a talk with Haas but do little else. Stalking was tricky to establish, and Haas was breaking no other laws. He was, George suspected, enjoying Jane's fear.

So he continued to lurk. Until the September Saturday morning when, as Jane stepped out of Mercer's Stationery with the advance Los Angeles Times Sunday edition under her arm, she found her progress blocked by Norman Casteel and Mina Pasco in one direction, and in the other by Pete Haas, who, as if in a ritual of exaction, held up her red undergarment, blotched and mottled and stiffened now with the stains of dried fluids.

He smiled. His companions laughed. Hass spoke. What he said Jane blanked out. She would recall only that the language was obscene, the message depraved. He offered her no specific threat, yet each word was intonated with savage sexual intent.

There were others on the street that morning. Some didn't see, some didn't realize what was happening. Some, confused, gawked. Until Irene Walters, glancing out the Thrift Store window, saw the grouping of figures on the sidewalk and, having for decades carried the tray in Nevada bars, immediately took its meaning. Stepping outside, she shouldered her way past Pete Haas, slid an arm around Jane's waist, advanced on the retreating Mina Pasco, and escorted Jane into the Thrift Store, all without a word.

The next weekend, Jane Harmon took Troy Hardaway into her bed.

In settling on Troy, Jane had made the easy, obvious choice. He was single. He was good looking, charming in his boyish, old fashioned, buckaroo style, steady and healthy and fun loving. Women liked him. More than one had sensed that he might be emotionally soft, malleable material to be worked into a shape suitable to her purposes, only to be disappointed as, after a brief dalliance, with an innocent smile he drifted off beyond enticement.

I had known Troy Hardaway all his life. Hardaways had ranched in Gull Valley for several generations, declining in vigor and fortunes until Troy's father sold his small place along Boulder Creek to Brock Walden and continued to live in the house as a hand for Walden Ranch. Like his son boyishly handsome and friendly, Bill Hardaway was a competent buckaroo, an excellent horseman, and a dandy of the colorful bandanna and carefully groomed mustache sort. Inexplicably, he carried in his hip pocket a dainty .32 caliber pistol identical to the one he gave his daughter on her twelfth birthday.

Troy Hardaway had his father's way with a horse and concern for his appearance, but he had much of his mother too. Mindy Brown had been sweet, unassuming, and calmly, rather strangely unaware. She married Bill Hardaway because he asked her, raised the daughter so unlike herself with an absolute if unengaged devotion, and when, six months after the birth of her son, she was diagnosed with cervical cancer, she accepted her fate with equanimity, suffered for some months without complaint, and died quietly.

In her son all this surfaced as an amiable contentment. Good-natured, easy-going, Troy Hardaway was without, it appeared, ambition. Caring for his horse, working cattle, hanging around the Wagon Wheel Café or the lounge at the Silver Sage, he seemed to be a wholly satisfied young man. As his mother had, he took what life offered him and asked for nothing else. He took as well what women offered him, his elaborate courtesies and willingness to be agreeable actually serving to protect him from their designs upon his future. More and more it seemed to Blue Lake that he was a bachelor – not one of those made by nature or habit single, dedicated to dogs and guns, or to wood carving or fly tying, or to extremist politics and conspiracy theories, no: Troy Hardaway would remain unattached because it was less fuss.

And then along came Calamity Jane Harmon.

"Miz Waner Ma'am – you know where I can find Troy?"

There was in the air that September morning a hint of fall, a crispness beyond cool. Ione Hardaway, in her anger, didn't seem to notice.

As it happened, I did know where her brother was. So did she. Troy's buckskin gelding, Tango, was cropping greenery in the rectangular enclosure, once a vegetable garden, between my patio and the irrigation ditch. That told all.

"Come in, Ione. I've just made coffee."

"Gotta run him down. He's supposed to be up in the mountains collecting cows."

But Ione had come to my door, not to Jane's. She wanted what in her oblique fashion she had off and on through the years sought from me – comfort, confidence. I smiled. "We haven't seen each other for a while."

After a brief hesitation, she removed her hat and stepped inside. "I could use some coffee, I guess."

At my kitchen table she sat quietly as I put out cherry turnovers and poured coffee. Her hands, nicked and lumped by years of labor but still lovely, lay bare and folded on the table. Each of her leather gloves, mottled by old sweat and dirt and grease, curled stiffly beside her Stetson like the discarded carapace of a desert crustacean.

She wrapped shapely fingers around her cup. "I was hopin' it wouldn't be him."

My silence wasn't much consolation.

"What's she got that makes them yahoos all trip over their... selves?"

"Be nice, my dear."

"Why?"

The exchange had precise, practiced timing. It was a joke, and acknowledgment of a secret sharing, one we had discovered when Ione had been my tenth grade student a quarter of a century before.

The intervening years had marked her. A pale band separated her dark auburn hair from her weathered face, made that face a mask, rough-finished, primitive. As a young woman Ione had been handsome, to some sensibilities compellingly so, her dark eyes flashing with intelligence, her skin taut over features high-boned and striking. Now that skin was runneled and those features sharpened; her gaze was wary, sometimes fierce. Nevertheless, had she chosen to get herself up for the dance, so to speak, Ione still could have attracted a discerning male eye. She did not so choose.

"What'd you guess she wants with him?"

"Security." Troy Hardaway was safe, I thought, would offer Jane no threat while protecting her against those who did.

I had had ample time to consider what urges and imaginings might have led to this particular coupling. The previous noon, returning from town, I espied a rider turning off the dirt road along the irrigation ditch and onto the street. Troy Hardaway saluted with a brush of fingers against his hat brim. The hat was gray and stiff, his rose-colored shirt bright in the sunlight, his jeans a new blue, his boots glossy. His grin took a decade off his thirty years.

As I parked, he nudged Tango down the low hill. The horse was well featured, powerfully muscled and sleekly groomed, and Troy was upright and easy astride him; animal and rider made a pleasurable impression, which was to Troy's purpose. Certainly he had trucked the horse into town, and he could just as well have hauled him to Jane's front door, but, aware of the figure he cut on horseback, he had chosen to arrive for all the world as if in his spiffy duds he was searching Blue Lake streets for strays.

Troy tethered the horse to a branch of the lilac bush, which I had planted years before, in Jane's dooryard. An hour later Tango in a pretty prance came sidling up the street, Troy controlling its pace with a tight rein and gripping knees. Behind him Jane Harmon clutched at his hips.

Just after sundown, Troy appeared at my door, hat in hand, asking permission to water and pen the horse in my now-barren garden. Jane had had a minor fall, turning an ankle. He would tend to her needs and ensure her comfort and, within an hour, two at most, he assured me, he would reclaim the horse and ride back to the fair-grounds, where he had left his truck and trailer. Nothing in his voice or bearing intimated that he didn't mean what he said. Yet the darkness deepened and he didn't reappear.

Sometime after midnight I was startled out of near-sleep by the thumping of hooves on the soft earth. Rising, I went to the window and in the faint light saw Troy's shadow beside the horse, heard a soothing murmur and a contented wicker. I returned to my bed. Minutes later I felt water pipes shudder, heard the squeak and then the hum of the garden faucet. After another few minutes all was silent.

Sleepless, I had considered Jane Harmon and Troy Hardaway.

Now Ione scoffed at my conclusion: "What security? He's a twelve-hundred a month ranch hand."

I didn't reply. Instead from my window I watched as Troy and Jane stepped out her front door, clasped hands, and started up the hill. Troy moved with the slow, awkward uncertainty of a man truly comfortable only on horseback; Jane, limping slightly, seemed to imitate his gait.

"Maybe you can ask her," I said.

Ione leaned forward to look, her gaze taking on the shine that Blue Lake knew to portend unpleasantness. I rose and went to stand in the door and await the lovers.

Troy ushered Jane around his sister's pickup with the exaggerated courtesy usually practiced only by old men. When he saw me in the doorway, he placed a hand on Jane's waist as if to confirm her reality, his grin a glow of delight and wonder. Observing him, I came to a new understanding of the term "enchanted."

Jane was more difficult to read. In boots and jeans and plain white blouse, she stood smiling in a stillness that at once issued from and enveloped her. She seemed soothed. I suggest nothing so simple as sexual release, though doubtless that contributed to her mood. No, what Jane was enjoying was resolution. Now, for good or ill, her relation to Blue Lake had been determined. Now, coupled, she would be left alone.

That is what, pressed, I would have said then. Today I would add something more. That morning Jane was prepared, I believe, to love Troy Hardaway. She didn't know, I believe, that she would be unable to.

Troy touched his fingers to his hat brim. "Miz Waner Ma'am."

I invited them in. Troy removed his hat and placed a guiding hand on Jane's elbow, with stiff formality escorting her in and seating her across from his sister. Then he placed himself before Ione and grinned. "Mornin', Sissy."

With the name by which a motherless boy had addressed the sister who mothered him, Troy invoked an intimacy, the only one, up to that point, in his life, and the sole attachment now in Ione's. Her glare wavered. "You're supposed to be in the mountains."

"On my way," Troy said. "Can't insult Miz Waner's hospitality."

Ione's anger with her brother, when it flared, was invariably soon smothered by the frothy wave of tenderness that the sight of him sent surging from her heart. Simply put, she loved him. She softened, visibly.

Jane now smiled a mock confession. "It's my fault."

Ione attended to her brother's hand resting on Jane's shoulder, and then, slowly, as if for the first time, to the presence, to the fact of Jane herself.

"What's that?"

"Troy told me he had to leave early this morning, but I, well – " Jane smiled naughtily: "I made him stay."

"You made him stay." Ione pronounced the words carefully, as if tacking each down so that it could never move or alter. "Tie him to your bed, did you?"

Jane's smile quivered. She glanced at me, as if I could tell her whether Ione was making a joke. "No. Well, I mean – no."

"Then he could of done what he was supposed to if he'd wanted."

Jane looked at me again: she had been misunderstood, had provoked a response totally at odds with her intentions. "Yes, naturally, but – "

"So he's a man, after all." Ione tugged on her soiled gloves, hiding her hands. "He's not a little boy who needs somebody to make excuses for him."

"No," Jane said. "I mean, that really isn't what I mean."

"So what do you mean?" Ione's voice, lowering, had taken on an emotional vibrato out of all proportion to the circumstances. I rested a restraining hand gently on her forearm. She shrugged it off violently. "Just what do you think you're doing – "

Ceasing in mid-sentence, she looked down at her arm, then at me. Her expression changed, and I understood then that Ione was not really angry. Or, more precisely, that her anger masked another, deeper emotion.

"I didn't do anything," Jane said. Then she smiled the smile that allowed into the world only what advanced her purpose. "And it doesn't matter anyhow. You just want to misunderstand."

But Ione looked at her brother, observed how he looked at Jane, and understood perfectly. She fled.

TROY HARDAWAY and Jane Harmon quickly established themselves as a couple, in the evenings shopping together at Foodmart, doing their laundry at the Duds and Suds, sometimes dining at the Silver Sage or dancing at the Elk's Club, making sure that Blue Lake understood that Jane was no longer available.

There were days, too, when Troy managed to slip away from his job to come to her. This was the busiest time of the year at Walden Ranch, and everyone from Ione Hardaway to temporary help was working hard, gathering cattle on BLM and Forest Service leases and trucking or trailing them back to the Rocking W to pregnancy-test cows and doctor and ship calves. Still, Troy sometimes avoided his obligations, and the lovers escaped on horseback.

Troy taught Jane how to ride, not just to sit on and guide the animal but to make the living sinew and muscle beneath her an extension of her own body. Jane took his instruction eagerly, her physical abilities – balance, strength, coordination – such that within a week she seemed to have been riding all her life. He astride Tango, she on a sorrel mare named Virgie, they rode out from the old Hardaway place on Boulder Creek, leaving behind not only his responsibilities but also a wistful old man, still dandyish but now frail and tethered to an oxygen bottle. Or Troy would load the horses into a trailer and drive into the desert or the mountains.

Jane's rides with Troy were the happiest experiences of her stay in Blue Lake. She delighted in the creak of leather and the smell of horse. In the saddle and stirrups she felt her body shaped into a configuration at once natural and inevitable. She returned from these excursions sore, stiff, and radiant, luxuriating in the ache of her muscles. Seeing to Virgie's needs and appearance and comfort, Jane felt, she told me, for the first time in her life fulfilled.

What part she believed Troy to play in this fulfillment I doubt that Jane herself could have said, but certainly she wrapped him in the folds of a gratitude of the sort that women more sensible than herself have confused for love.

Troy, perhaps not quite certain that he had secured Jane's affections, was eager to get her in his own world, in the saddle, in his own world, in country he had ridden all his life. On these rides he showed Jane what he cared for, what, in a very real sense, he was. Desert and mountain, expanse and outcrop and canyon, rock and grit and dust, furtive creature, scaly growth – this was Troy's land, his place. But Jane rode through not land but landscape, scenes and shapes that she took in and transformed into images that expressed her own ideas and aspirations and anxieties.

Her film would show us what she made of it all: the vista and broad prospect, the striking detail, the juxtaposed and complementary textures, and the pleasing or startling arrangement of forms. She was especially adept at isolating the natural image that intimated some elusive meaning just beyond the horizon of human comprehension. But finally her appreciation was merely aesthetic, the desert and mountains only scenery, the setting for a film like those she had been watching since she and her mother saw Under the Mountain. But for Troy Hardaway, land was identity, and identity was history, and history in the desert was a track out of the past marked by places where men and women had been and done.

One day, riding in the Eagle Creek Range, they climbed up to a pretty canyon hayfield in the middle of which sat, as if dropped there, a large basalt boulder. The stone was scratched with images not quite floral, which Jane was at a loss to identify until Troy, without a hint of a smile, told her that they were in Puss Meadow. Jane, understanding, exulted.

Troy showed her other places where the Shoshone had adorned ledge and rock with figures and symbols. He showed her old settlements and the abandoned appliances with which vanished men had excavated for their mines. He showed her roads, worn into the land, that led to the charred remains of a cabin in which two large and three small lives were lost, to a barn built by the first settler in Gull Valley and still in use, to springs and seeps fenced and piped and named after families long moved on. He showed her places where nature had seemed not wholly inimical to agriculture, where men and women still labored to make a life. He showed her places where houses and barns had become the materials for newer buildings on other places, where small farms had become the hay fields and small ranches the pastures and alfalfa fields of the larger, the better financed or managed, the luckier operations like Walden Ranch.

He showed her places and how they came to be: history.

What she saw, her film said, was failure and futility.

Showing her this land, Troy Hardaway said as clearly as he could to Jane Harmon, "This is what I come from. This is who I am."

To which Jane replied, "This should be turned into a refuge."

How Troy Hardaway greeted Jane's announcement I can't quite imagine. Perhaps he smiled past a mild dismay at her seeing, when he showed her himself, only herself. Did he intuit that Jane's notion was at that point both abstract and nebulous, that Jane herself did not know what she meant — refuge for whom or for what, from what? Certainly he did not respond with foreboding, for his beguilement by her was total, his faith in her unwavering. It may also be that Troy thought that this enthusiasm would soon die (as it did).

What he didn't know was that the agent of its eventual resurrection was already on the scene. He didn't know that Jane had another irritant scraping at the soft slick folds of her awareness. Even as she rode with Troy, she had another man, innocently, on her mind.

SNOW IS FALLING. Small dry flakes catch my lamplight, dance against the darkness beyond my window, and disappear. *Ubi Sunt?*

It was not inevitable that Jane Harmon and Carlyle Walden would meet, even if the way they met made it seem so. But for this accident Blue Lake was not inclined to hold Jane responsible. The news that Carlyle Walden had encountered Calamity Jane and broken some bones in his foot surprised no one. Blue Lake assumed that he hadn't been quite sober. He hadn't been sober, quite, for some years.

Months later, when Jane and Carlyle returned to Blue Lake with their new film equipment and ardor for art and one another, they recollected the incident with hopeless innocence. Jane affected despair at her clumsiness, Carlyle invoked awe at her effect on him, and both regaled Blue Lake and themselves with a tale about the assault of a cardboard horse.

That October morning Jane had stopped in Brunson's Liquors for Perrier, a six-pack of which she was removing from a cooler when Carlyle entered and took up a case of Budweiser. Each then angled toward the counter, where the politely formal Harve Brunson greeted first Ms. Harmon and then Mr. Walden.

Jane, at the name, assumed that behind her must be Brock Walden, movie star, the man whom she as child had fantasized was her father, and she excitedly spun in a pretty pirouette, the bottled water in her hand swinging up, slightly, and out. Carlyle, weary after a drive through darkness and dawn from Los Angeles, bleary from the beer he'd sipped along the way, jerked to a halt before the twirling figure. Then the bottles Jane held clipped the corner of a display table where, in precipitous tiers, fifths of scotch rose toward a cardboard silhouette of a white stallion. Bumped, the scotch bottles teetered, the stallion swayed, and then horse and bottles, row by row, fell. Carlyle, panicked, waved ineffectual hands at the cascade even as the case of beer he'd dropped hit and fractured his metatarsi.

Jane, reeking of scotch and babbling regrets, assisted him to his car and drove him to the hospital emergency room.

Harve Brunson, as he cleaned up the mess, determined to add the cost – retail – of his shattered stock to the Walden bill.

Over the following days Carlyle Walden and Jane Harmon, in all innocence, contrived to meet, to inquire and apologize, and more. Say that he wished to see again the grace of line and motion that had arrested him in, of all places, a liquor store in Blue Lake, Nevada. Say that she found herself entertaining the notion that in her fantasy family he would figure as a big brother. Say too that each was pleased to find the other a denizen of the Los Angeles cinema monde, ambitious and eager for applause. An Out There pair, kindred spirits, they seemed. Might they not begin to think that they could become, innocently, something more to one another?

In October, the fancy of men young and old turns to thoughts of venery. Out There hunters come Out Here to sport. Rifle shots rupture the stillness, deer die, and hunters celebrate. Some find pleasure in desert swales or mountain canyons. Some find it on bar-stools in the Adaven and the Silver Spur or in beds in the dim rooms at Darla's.

In his forty-odd years, Carlyle Walden had spent less than half an hour in the willow-shrouded whorehouse on Galena Street. At a callow and feckless sixteen, he had begun there a Rite of Passage, the potency of which his father hoped would make a man of his disappointing son. As Brock Walden engaged in badinage with and stood a round of drinks for the idlers about the place, Carlyle quickly completed his initial ceremonial obligation. Then man and youth set off into the mountains with rifles, soon returning with the carcass of an impressively antlered mule deer. Cletus Rose saw to the skinning and butchering as father and son and assorted well-wishers celebrated into the intoxicated night.

The ritual was without magic, effected no transformation. Young Walden remained callow and feckless.

Brock Walden's only legitimate child – there were rumors of other off-spring, of mothers-to-be married or paid off – Carlyle became the charge of his father when his mother took her life three days before her little boy's seventh birthday. Brock Walden resisted the suggestion of his ex-wife's parents that they raise the boy, whom he had a use for. This was the first season of *Roundup*, the television series that would run more than a decade and secure for its star a place in American popular culture but off to an uncertain start. Now glossy photographs of father and son began to flower in the well-manuered soil of movie fandom. Taken on the *Roundup* set, these carefully composed images of adult strength serving childish devotion were intended to confirm in reality the wholesome values projected by the televised fictions. At the same time they were part of a campaign to cleanse Brock Walden's reputation of the mire of riotous living he'd wallowed in for years. The boy, eager to please, donned boy-sized cowpoke duds and, unaware that his father was playing a role, provided the camera models of an incontestably genuine filial admiration, trust, and love. America approved.

The next ten years, when not in boarding school, Carlyle Walden was often on the set of *Roundup*, trying to help out; serious and well intentioned, he was ever ready to oblige, but he was also easily distracted from the matter at hand by the interests of the mind and impulses of the heart. He grew in feature to favor his sire, had the same expansive brow and aquiline nose and wide mouth, the same breadth of shoulder and depth of chest. But if his father gave him shape, his light-boned mother bequeathed him scale. Compared to the robust father, the slight son appeared insubstantial. He enrolled at UCLA, where he began to write the Great American Western Novel (as he described it to me once, Faulknerian techniques working on Zane Gray materials) and to drink beer. He established no serious relationships, abandoned the novel, dropped out of college, failed as a screenwriter and producer, and settled into writing flak for Brock Walden productions, as well as speeches he delivered in his father's stead at gatherings of those who would preserve what they took to have been the values and virtues of the Old, the Wild, the Real West. He had no lovers, no close friends, no one other in his life but his father. He drank discreetly, not often to obvious inebriation but steadily, maintaining. To Blue Lake he was a man of whom nothing serious would ever be asked or expected.

"Brock Walden is at the ranch," Jane said to me.

I knew that. Three days earlier he had, as was his practice, flown his plane at the rock face behind my house, pulling up and away just in time to avoid crashing in a fiery ball.

"I'll get to meet him, finally."

When Troy Hardaway was showing Jane those desert locations that he was most himself in, he hadn't taken her to the one place in Gull Valley that she was eager to see. In skirting the Rocking W, Troy was of course avoiding a confrontation with his sister: her anger at his gadding about the countryside when work needed doing he could appease, but not while in the company of the woman whose every utterance Ione had determined to take as an insufferable indignity. He met Jane's pleas with the assurance that they could look the place over in the first week of deer season, when she could also meet Brock Walden, whose presence, Troy thought privately, would effectively prevent Ione from objecting to Jane's.

As it happened, however, Jane didn't visit the ranch until the end of October, and not in the company of Troy Hardaway. On opening day of Nevada's deer season, Brock Walden was in a Bel Air hospital after an angina attack. Two weeks passed before he settled his wheelchair into the cockpit of his specially modified aircraft and, against the recommendation of his doctors and all common sense, flew himself and Cletus Rose and a pair of hangers-on to Blue Lake. But Troy was in Salt Lake City, where Ione had sent him to take possession of a new hay baler. It may be that Ione had hoped this separation, brief as it was, would make Troy's heart less fond or Jane's more fickle. In any case, her ploy had consequences she couldn't have foreseen.

Brock Walden and his entourage had been in Gull Valley for three days when, that early Friday evening, Jane came to my kitchen and,

over tea and carrot cake, asked for a favor. Carlyle had invited her to
visit the Rocking W the next morning. He would show her around
and introduce her to his father. Jane had accepted with enthusiasm,
but she now admitted to qualms.

"I'd be out there with all these men, and they'll have guns, and
they probably won't be sober. I've heard that they're… a rough group."

Her concern seemed unwarranted. What was once a horde had
been culled by violence and excess and time. "There are only three
of them, besides Brock Walden, two codgers and Cletus Rose, who
doesn't drink and is a gentleman besides."

"Yes, but…"

"Betty Johnson cooks for them, so she'll be there. Ione too, most
likely."

"I know, but…"

"You don't really have anything to fear," I said.

"Well, yes," she said. "But…"

Gradually it came out. Jane and Carlyle had met several times in
town, over coffee in the Wagon Wheel and lunch at the Silver Sage
talking about film and his father and the Wild West. Troy had shown
no symptoms of jealousy – nor should he, Jane insisted – but she
couldn't predict his reaction when he learned that she'd gone out to
see Carlyle at the ranch.

"You think my company will let Troy know that nothing's going
on with you and Carlyle?"

"Well, I hadn't thought of it quite like that…" She hesitated. "But
it's really not that anyhow. I'd just like you to be with me when I
meet Brock Walden. I don't know why. I just would."

So of course I agreed.

She made to leave but then didn't. "I heard a story, Miz Waner. I –
well, it's gossip, about Carlyle and Ione Hardaway, a long time ago,
when they were teenagers."

"I've heard that story too."

"It seems so… unlikely. They're so different. Do you think it's
true?"

"I don't think about it at all, Jane."

At least, I hadn't, for some time. But after Jane left that day, I sipped tea and remembered.

I met Carlyle Walden when the seventeen-year-old was serving a term at hard labor at Walden Ranch. The elder Walden, after the previous year's sex-and-death ritual had failed, in his estimation, to make a man of his son, came up with another plan, sentencing Carlyle to a summer of long hours of physical exertion in the heat and the wind and the dust and the company of hard-bitten men.

Blue Lake understood early on that this ritual wasn't going to work any magic either. As eager to please as always, the young man donned buckaroo work clothes and an expression of stern resolve and did his time to the satisfaction of no one. He had no feeling for or ability with animals: horses unnerved, cattle baffled him. Machines broke down under his operation. Mucking an irrigation ditch was for him a task of dizzying complexity. He did what he was told as well as he was able, which was, by all accounts including his own, poorly. At the same time he mused, and he asked questions that had nothing to do with the chore he'd been set to. He suffered without complaint the crude humor and derision of many of the men he worked with, and even for this he was faulted. In his favor all that might be said was that he persevered. He kept at it. He didn't quit. All summer he toughed it out.

That summer he also fell hopelessly under the sway of fifteen-year-old Ione Hardaway. So Blue Lake had said, and so I saw for myself the day I met him.

Ione was bringing me a load of manure for the vegetable garden I'd decided to prepare for planting the next spring. Near mid-morning, an old ranch pickup, nose tipped skyward by its load, climbed The Hump and backed to the edge of the plot. Ione emerged from behind the wheel and, after a moment, gestured at the youth who was stepping out of the other side of the cab.

"Miz Waner Ma'am. You can guess who the gawker here is."

I may have gawked myself, such was the teenager's scaled-down resemblance to his father. I thought then that most people would always see Carlyle Walden as I had, second, not as himself but as his father's son.

"I'm pleased to meet you, Mrs. Waner." He spoke slowly, as if holding up for examination each word before using it. "But I feel as if I already know you. I've heard so much about you."

Ione dropped the truck's tailgate with a disgusted bang. Climbing up, she grabbed a long-handled pitchfork, stabbed up a heap of manure, and tossed it, quite deliberately it seemed to me, onto his boots. "Gonna gawk all day here too?"

"No," he said gravely.

As he stepped toward the pickup, Ione pitched more manure, now splattering him at the shins. "Get Miz Waner's shovel and wheelbarrow over there, haul some down to the other end of the garden so she won't have to."

I went inside and, taking my time, prepared a tray of iced tea and small pastries and cookies and fruit, which I then took out and arranged on the patio table as Ione swept out the now empty pickup bed. Between the large neat mound that she had created and the several hillocks of Carlyle's dumping ran a dark, ragged trail of dung.

As I watched, Carlyle knelt, picked up a flaky chunk of manure, and sniffed. "This is pleasantly aromatic when dry and frangible."

"I'll take your word for it," I said, amused. His address was not formal so much as circumspect. Listening to him speak was like watching a cat walk through snow.

"When it's fresh, it's caustic." He crumbled the piece, smelled it. "What would the cattle have consumed to produce this?"

I didn't have to wonder what the local buckaroos and louts would make of a young man who considered cow dung and used words like "aromatic" and "frangible" and "caustic."

"Ione might be able to tell you."

"Oh," he said, standing, brushing his fingers at his jeans. "She already thinks I'm an imbecile." He gave me a glance to see if I might concur. "She's intelligent, more than she lets on."

"A lot of people don't see that," I said.

"She has a temper, too. She got angry when I told her that she made me think of Rousseau's Noble Savage. I meant it as a compliment.

She fits so well with everything around her, like the indigenous peoples before the Europeans arrived. She's at one with this world, you might say."

"You might," I said, managing to suffocate my laugh, "Ione is a remarkable young woman."

He smiled too, an open, ingenuous smile that drove away any after-image of his father. "Remarkable," he said. "That's the word."

Sending him to wash up at the hose beside the patio, I went over to Ione. She slammed shut the tailgate. "I'll whittle this pile down, spread it around for you a bit. The yahoo hardly made a dent."

"This is fine," I said. "Let's refresh ourselves. And you can subject that young man to more abuse."

She glared at me. "He called me a savage!"

When I said nothing, slowly her scowl dissolved. She leaned toward me and half-whispered. "A savage! What did he mean?"

"I don't know, Ione. But he seems quite taken with you."

"That yahoo?" Carefully ignoring him, she removed her gloves and batted them dustily at her jeans, stuffed the gloves in her hip pocket, took off her hat, and ran her fingers through her auburn hair.

This was as close as Ione would ever come to preening. I was again amused, and a bit surprised. Over the previous year Ione had ceased to be a gangly, raw-boned ranch girl: her body had recentered itself, gaining a woman's balance and symmetry, and attracted from both adolescent and adult males long looks, which so far she had ignored. That she would now show an interest in Carlyle Walden suggested to me that there might be something to the young man.

He had dropped the hose and bent to shut off the faucet, evidently turning the handle the wrong way, for the hose suddenly began to whip, spraying water over the dust and the patio brick and his pant legs.

"Jeez Louise!" Ione moaned, dismayed.

"No harm done," I said, watching him bring the hose under control.

Her expression changed. "Now he's wet behind the knees, too."

"Be nice."

"He wet his pants."

"Yes, yes. Let's have some iced tea – "

"Don't know why you worry about me abusing him, Miz Waner. He's the sort that'd be pretty good at that himself."

To keep from laughing I said sternly, "That will do, Ione."

"Oh, don't worry, Miz Waner, he can't hear me," she said. "Wouldn't matter if he did. I say things and he just looks at me like he's got a headache."

Carlyle Walden, she was telling me, had no ear for irony.

Embarrassed at his wet jeans, Carlyle, once seated at the patio table, made of the consumption of food and drink a small ceremony, sampling, appraising, and in solemn tones offering me formulae of approval that he'd learned in boarding school.

Then, as if not to allow silence, he said, "Ione told me about your essay on places in the desert called Crazy Woman. I plan to read it. Crazy Woman is a common nomenclature in the West, isn't it? Nearly every type of topographical feature has the name – creeks and canyons and flats. In Gull Valley there's a Crazy Woman Gulch."

"As you say," I agreed, "it's a common designation."

"These women were so far from the consolations of civilization. They were so far from other women they might talk to about women things. Is this what drove them mad? Loneliness?"

Ione looked at him in wonder. This was a creature new to her experience, a male who spoke of women's loneliness.

"That was part of it, I suppose."

"It was a hard land, and it took hard people to settle it. Maybe some women just weren't hard enough."

He had shifted from insight to cliché. He took my silence as concurrence.

"The people who settled the American West were a special breed. Hardy. Self-reliant. They were tough – physically, emotionally, mentally tough. Like…" His presence of mind kept him from naming, if it could not keep him from glancing sidelong at, the young woman across the table.

Slight as it was, his look nevertheless set her off. "Tough? Savage isn't enough for you? Now I have to be tough too?"

The violence in her tone clearly disturbed him. He didn't try to speak.

"Some ignorant hick who doesn't know how civilized folks behave? Some dumb girl from the sticks who's too tough to have feelings? Loneliness! Did you ever think maybe those women weren't lonely at all, maybe they weren't crazy mad, maybe they were just flat mad! Anyhow, what gives you the right to decide what everybody else is? You think being Brock Walden's kid makes you special? You think – "

I placed my hand lightly on her arm. "He didn't mean anything, Ione."

"Jeez Louise, Miz Waner. He comes waltzin' in and starts all this stuff..." She looked at me, then threw herself back onto the chair in disgust. "What a yahoo."

Carlyle, though shaken by her assault, would not be daunted. After a moment he said, cautiously, "Tough it out. That's the expression everyone uses Out Here. If you experience difficulties, well... you just tough it out, you see it through."

"That's true," I said, smiling at him, then at Ione.

He took what was clearly a preparatory sip of tea. "Except for my father... Ione is the toughest person I've ever met."

At which, astonishingly, Ione Hardaway blushed. Blood darkened her throat, her cheeks, rose to the tip of her ears, crept into her hair. She was mortified and pleased and helpless under her emotion. She turned to me in silent appeal.

I distracted Carlyle with a description of Crazy Woman Gulch, where the wind, blowing at a certain velocity through a rocky aperture, produced a kind of keening. The Shoshone heard the cry of a spirit mother lamenting her lost children. Europeans heard a woman some believed a ghost, others a living, suffering creature they sometimes searched for. That insanity would be a woman's natural response to life in the narrow and barren gouge in the desert no one questioned.

Carlyle listened attentively. "I definitely will read your essay. I – what do you have to do to be a writer."

I offered him my stock answer. "Care about words and sentences."

"I have a large vocabulary for my age, I'm told, and my sentences parse."

"That's a start," I said. "What would you write? Screenplays?"

"Or novels," he said, "I read a lot of them. My favorite writer is Faust."

"Faust?" I was mystified.

"Frederick Faust, yes. You would probably know him as Max Brand. He has other pen names as well. He writes very clearly."

At this point Ione, who had regained her composure and color, began the protocol of departure, folding her napkin, taking out her gloves. Then she seemed to have a change of heart. She poured herself more iced tea.

"I apologize for my manners, Miz Waner Ma'am," she offered.

I smiled and patted her wrist.

"Sorry I yelled at you, Gawker."

Carlyle, flushing faintly, nodded.

She leaned toward him, her smile assuming intimacy. "Been busy lately, rubbed me raw. School, and managing Troy, and figuring out all the things around the ranch that Cletus Rose isn't here to show me – there's ever so many things to take care of."

I held her steadily in my gaze. "Ever so many" had become, after we read *Daisy Miller* in class, Ione's private fanfare introducing irony. The smile she prepared for me was insistently artless.

"Working cattle, you do things when the cows are ready, not when you are. We just turned the herd into the foothills, but before that we had to do the vaccinating and branding – it's noisy and smelly and messy. Then there's the dehorning and cutting."

She sipped at her tea. The cords in her throat tightened as she swallowed. Her lips glistened. She smiled as if to a confidante. "Cutting – that's what we call it Out Here. Castrating, I mean."

The young man colored again.

"It's tricky business, cutting bull calves. You grab the scrotum, but you need to make sure you get both testicles. Then you have to place the knife just right" – Now her hands were in the air, illustrating – "so you whack off only the testes and not the penis."

A sick anxiety had settled in his eyes.

She smiled demurely. "Then you toss them in a jar. Later you can fry them up. They're ever so tasty."

When she sipped again at her tea, I thought that her performance had come to an end. Certainly it had had its effect, she her revenge. Carlyle was flushed, his face a slick sheen. Then, inspired, Ione continued:

"Pretty soon now, when the cows get up higher into the mountains, we'll turn out the bulls. Maybe you'll be helping with that. The cows usually come in in June. Come in — that means the cows are receptive to the bulls."

Carlyle gazed at her. Having taught teenage boys for some years, I knew that glazed-over look. He was responding not to her words but to her presence.

Seated in the warm May sunshine, exuding youthful health, Ione powerfully appealed. Her hair glistened. Her eyes gleamed. Her teeth flashed. Her hands, as she dropped them back into her lap, settled like wings after flight. The small muscles in motion around her mouth seemed agents not of expression but appetite; the slow rhythms of her respiration promised generation, the elemental impulse.

"So we want to be sure the bulls are there to service them. Otherwise the cows get ever so cranky."

Carlyle seemed concussed. Ione smiled wickedly.

At that point, to allow him to recover, I began an outline of my garden plans. Ione listened with exaggerated attention. Then both young people helped me tidy up, and I walked them to the pickup.

"Thank you again, Ione."

"Yes ma'am. Iced tea hit the spot."

"Carlyle, I'm pleased to have met you. Thank you for the help."

"You're welcome, Mrs. Waner, " he said. He seemed newly awakened but uncertain that he was not asleep still.

Then in a gesture that for some reason moved me, he offered his hand and, when I took it, held my own a moment beyond mere politeness.

Did I believe the story about Carlyle and Ione? Of course I did.

Blue Lake knew that Ione had that summer worked her young-womanly wiles on him. How else account for her eructations that fall in the school lavatory, for a ragged attendance record and an otherwise inexplicable trip to the Bay Area (there was a bit of the old man in Carlyle Walden after all, Blue Lake chortled). Whatever the young parents-to-be might have felt, the would-have-been grandfathers apparently struck a deal, evidence of which was the promotion of a dandified horseman to ranch manager and, when the enterprise was incorporated, a ten percent interest – a small price for Brock Walden to pay to keep his son free of a statutory rape charge, but one substantial enough to credit Bill Hardaway with driving a hard bargain. Ione quickly established herself as her father's surrogate, second-in-command, and the de facto boss of the operation, and a few years later, when Bill Hardaway decided to train horses to do tricks on the rodeo circuit, Brock Walden turned over the running of the ranch to her. As was only right, Blue Lake joshed, for she was the best man on the place. Then Blue Lake waited for her to say the word to Carlyle Walden, to secure her future at the ranch by accepting the proposal and person of a man who, it was clear, would always attend on her every wish.

I also believed the story because Carlyle himself had sent me evidence of its truth, which I chose to share with no one.

A STORM SWEPT THROUGH during the night, and the next morning came chill, the mountains white down to the foothills, the desert gray with frost that in the sunlight refused to glitter. As Jane drove silently out of Blue Lake, the air from the car's heater spread the lilac scent of her soap. She wore an old deerskin vest beaded with jet and turquoise at the lapels, a white turtleneck jersey, and designer jeans fitting over the deep sheen of her boots. Her attire argued that she was out to impress, her quiet unease that she was uncertain of success.

"What's he like, really?"

Brock Walden she meant, of course, as always. "He's old, and ill."

"I know, but is he... I realize he isn't the characters he played. And I've heard the stories. Carlyle says they're exaggerations – canards, he called them." She smiled nervously. "He says his father is really a kind and decent man."

"I've seen him be that, Jane, but it was years ago. I didn't know him well, and I don't know what he might have aged into. But we'll learn soon enough."

Then, braking to a stop, she cried: "Oh, look!'

The horses had appeared as if in a vision, climbing up out of a willow-choked swale that fed into Eagle Creek: a stallion, three mares, and a yearling.

Jane took up her camera and threw open her door. As she focused and clicked, the stallion, a heavy-headed, heavily scarred red roan, stopped to gaze stupidly at her. The mares and yearling angled off through the sage at a trot. Then all climbed to the crest of a small hill and disappeared.

"Aren't they beautiful," Jane said.

"Not particularly," I said. Malnourished and unkempt, the mustangs were rather a pitiful sight.

"Oh," she said, "you know what I mean. I – the BLM has several roundups scheduled for next year. Maybe that will improve things for those that are left."

Once we were again underway, we went some miles in silence until, over the hiss of the tires on the macadam, we heard a hum. Jane glanced at me, frowning, and peered anxiously at the dashboard indicators as the sound swelled, until up ahead an airplane dropped into view, white and red and glittering in the sunlight. Jane slowed the car. The plane roared past, dangerously low.

Jane looked at me in silent appeal.

"Brock Walden's saying hello," I told her. "Years ago, he used come so close you could see him grin. They had to go all the way up to the governor to get him to stop terrorizing people."

Jane didn't resume the conversation. Slipping back into herself, she drove and stared out over the land. What she saw I didn't know.

At the Rocking W, what I saw was change.

The waning of autumn had leached the color from the land, bringing into relief neatly geometrical cultivations and constructions. Down the valley, sage flats had been scraped into alfalfa fields, fenced squares confining circles watered by central-pivot irrigation. Nearer the ranch buildings, pasture and more alfalfa fields surrounded the marsh at the head of Molly Creek. Beside the old barn stood a hayrick with sides of canvas and a top of corrugated iron. The road we drove was paved and as straight as the landing strip, beside which was parked the van outfitted to accommodate Brock Walden's wheelchair.

The tidiness took in the ranch yard as well. When in the 1970s Brock Walden brought his television crews out to film at the Rocking W, the debris accumulated over a century had been hauled off, rickety outbuildings dismantled, and reusable materials hidden from sight. The ranch house was made acceptable to the camera by wood-grained aluminum siding and a new, broader porch. Sod was laid over the dust and a picket fence strung, complete with swinging gate that opened to a graveled walkway bordered with whitewashed round rocks. There was a hitching rail. Desert Pastoral.

As we clanked over the cattle guard, Jane floated up out of her funk: "Oh, it's just like *Roundup*, isn't it?"

There was no sign of life about the place. A sedan that I took to be Carlyle's was parked before the house. Across the lot Ione Hardaway's pickup stood at the door of her mobile home.

"I wonder where Carlyle is," Jane worried, pulling in beside the sedan.

As we stepped into the chill, Ione came out of the barn. Above the door, the knobby points of a gargantuan set of elk antlers cast, in the pale sunlight, a grid of shadow within which she seemed confined. Jane aimed her camera. Ione froze.

"I wonder where Carlyle is," Jane said again, her tone suggesting a girding. Ione's attitude as she awaited us suggested the same.

"Miz Waner Ma'am." A slight dip of her hat brim might have acknowledged Jane's presence. "How you fixed for venison?"

The reek of butchering and flecks of fat clung to her clothing; a spot of blood dried like a beauty mark at the edge of her lip.

"Everyone filled his tag this year?"

In answer she opened the barn door and ushered us inside. Here the air was only slightly warmer but the smell of blood stronger. It merged with other, sweeter odors – of horse, cow, manure and leather, hay and dust. From the dimness above came a grumble of pigeons. At the far end of the long space, Ralph Johnson was removing with a bright, thin-bladed knife the skin of the last of the half-dozen headless deer carcasses that hung on hooks from a thick rope strung between posts. Beneath each, a pail or pan collected dribblings of blood. Hides still bearing the shapes of the once-living creatures were draped over a sawhorse. On the floor by the back wall a row of antlered heads stared with dry dead eyes.

The carcasses themselves, dark red and marbled white and traced by sinew, their empty cavities braced open by lengths of lath, bore large, ragged holes. Half the rib cage of the smallest had been blown away. From another a haunch dangled like a thick, storm-torn branch.

"Oh," Jane said, raising her camera to her eye. "Like sculpture."

Ione made a strangled sound.

Ralph Johnson, sweat beading on his forehead, hands and forearms greasy with fat and congealed gore, stopped his knife. "Miz Waner Ma'am."

"Good morning, Ralph. Will any of that be chewable?

He smiled. "These big boys might be better stewed. Even then, the old timers down to the Community Center probably ought to add a extra dab of Dentifix. But the little two-point –" His knife pointed at the smallest of the carcasses – "he won't be too bad. Betty's got hearts and livers in the house."

Then he broadened his smile to include Jane. "Ma'am. Nice vest. Looks like one'a them that Lottie Grimsley makes from B. W.'s kill."

Jane smiled blankly, as if she'd been addressed in a foreign language. "I found this in the Community Center thrift shop. I... B.W. Brock Walden. This was made from a deer he shot?" Her hand caressed the soft leather draped over her breast, the gesture shaped by a tenderness that made Ralph look away.

Beside me Ione snorted. "We'll let you get back to work, Ralph. See that Miz Waner gets a nice roast from the small one."

Jane and I followed her outside. Carlyle Walden, halfway between house and barn, at the sight of us stopped, uncertain as ever. His gaze skittered from Jane to Ione. Then his eyes met and held mine as he came near. "Mrs. Waner, how do you do?"

"I do very well, Carlyle, thank you. And you?"

Not having seen Carlyle Walden for some years, I was struck by how little he now resembled his father. Over the Brock Walden bone structure, Carlyle's flesh had puffed and sagged, softening his features. He looked like what he was: middle aging, alcoholic, vaguely unhappy. And, at the moment, divided in his loyalties.

"I'm improving." He smiled, nodding at the foot fitted in a walking cast. Then he swerved slightly so that, as we three women moved away from the barn, he fell in step beside Jane Harmon.

"Driving in," she addressed him brightly, "it was exactly like *Roundup*. I can't wait to see the inside, the big fireplace and rugs and everything."

"I'm afraid that – "

Ione's grunt of disgust seemed to set the crisp air atremble.

Carlyle waited, but when Ione said nothing, he continued. "The interiors were filmed on a sound stage. The rooms here are – "

"You thought that was real?" Ione couldn't contain herself. "Who'd you suppose could afford to heat a room like that?"

Jane stopped. "I guess I didn't think – "

"You got that right," Ione snapped. "Miz Waner, I'll put the coffee on."

We watched her lean her way across the ranch yard, as if into an angry wind. When she reached the door of her trailer, Jane asked, clearly, herself: "Why does she hate me?"

I touched her arm. "The job wears on her. And she's a bit unsettled when Brock Walden is about the place. Don't take it personally."

"But it is personal. It's been personal since the day I got here, when the trailer wheel… She chose to believe I did that on purpose, just the way she chooses to take everything I say the wrong way. But why? I admire her. I'd like to be her friend. Why won't she let me?"

In his measured fashion, then, Carlyle offered an insight of the sort of which he was sometimes capable: "Mrs. Waner's right. It isn't you, it's what you represent."

"I represent...? What do I represent?"

In the brief silence that followed I noted, for the first time, that Carlyle was sober. "I'm not certain."

He turned to me. But I was feeling guilty about having presumed to excuse Ione Hardaway to Jane Harmon. I said nothing.

"Besides, she's the same with me," Carlyle continued. "Sometimes she's pleasant enough. Other times, she bristles. Her moods are impossible to anticipate."

Jane seemed not to be listening. "Why would I represent something to her?"

As she pondered the notion, Carlyle and I consulted. Brock Walden and his cohorts were scouting deer herds in the newly whitened mountains. Until they landed, Carlyle thought to show Jane around the place. I would enjoy Ione's company, which I looked forward to. Since fleeing my kitchen table weeks before, she had been much on my mind.

Ione had prepared to receive me. The spot of blood was gone from her freshly washed face. Her brushed hair shone. Settling me on her chintz-covered sofa, she served coffee in gilt-edged chinaware. Both chintz and china suited the room, which was decorated in blocks and strips of pale yellows and lavenders and hung with prints of Linda Dufferena's lovely photographs of the Nevada desert. The room belied all that seemed obvious about Ione Hardaway. Seated comfortably in it, I felt my heart touched by a small sadness.

Beside the coffee she had placed butter, jam, and a plate of the plain, delicate biscuits she knew I appreciated. With a skillet or Dutch Oven Ione could make breads as tasty as confections.

Because Ione had no ear for gossip – she had no interest in the affairs of other people, as such – we talked about ranch doings and range conditions and the cattle business. On these subjects as forthcoming as always, she seemed at the same time vaguely disengaged. Beneath her observations yawned the emptiness of the unspoken. I thought she might be regretting her treatment of Jane Harmon, or be taken up with thoughts of her absent brother, but as we were finishing our second cup of coffee, she said, "He's dying."

She could have meant only Brock Walden. "That's a confirmed prognosis?"

"You can see it in his face. He won't last the winter."

Ione tried to will all emotion from her voice, but she couldn't keep her feelings from her gaze, in which I was rather taken aback to discover distress.

"He's an old man, Ione, he's lived a long – "

"No," she said brusquely, "I don't care about that. Not about him."

"I see." What Ione cared about was Walden Ranch and her relation to it.

"I always knew this would come. But..."

"Nothing needs to change," I said. The ranch would come to Carlyle Walden; in fact, he already shared in its ownership, the result of a complex legal and financial maneuver designed to reduce Brock Walden's tax bills.

"You think so?"

I took her meaning. Of course things would change. Things always changed.

"What do you anticipate?"

"If I could anticipate it, I could deal with it. But it'll depend on Carlyle, what he wants. I used to think I knew. Now..." She paused, as if watching where that idea would lead her and choosing not to follow it.

"Even after the lawyers and the feds get through, Carlyle will be set up pretty well – the place in Malibu and some other property, that annuity from his mother, the TV residuals. He doesn't need Walden Ranch."

"Neither did his father."

"B. W.'s got a feel for the place. But Carlyle...?"

I didn't ask where she got her information about the Walden finances. She wouldn't have offered it if it weren't true. "So you think he'll sell?"

She might have sighed. "We make a profit, Miz Waner, but not a lot. He could do better investing in something that'd give him a larger return."

"You've talked to Carlyle about this?"

The question sparked her anger. "How am I supposed to do that, with him off sniffin' around – "

I replaced my cup on its saucer, folded my hands in my lap, and asked her, quietly, "Do you really need to hold Jane responsible for all of your difficulties?"

Ione flushed. "You're gonna tell me this's my own fault?"

"You know I'm not."

As quickly as it had appeared, her anger vanished. "Well, you could."

Still speaking quietly, I said: "But I might remind you that you're perfectly capable of dealing with whatever the situation brings."

We sat in silence. Then the air about us quivered with a disturbance that slowly deepened into the sound of an airplane engine.

"That'll be the yahoos," she said, rising. "At least there won't be any more of them every hunting season, their rifle in one hand and their... bottle in the other."

I helped her straighten up. In her small bathroom I discovered that I was straightening myself up as well.

Ione and I stepped outside just as the white van rattled recklessly over the cattle guard. Dust struggled up against the still chill air. Jane and Carlyle appeared on the ranch house porch and made their way to and through the gate. As if acolytes in some obscure ceremony, three old men stood before the front door of the van, from which Brock Walden, overflowing the aluminum wheelchair clamped to a mechanical lift, descended to earth.

He seemed a gargoyle, a huge head on an amorphous swell of flesh. Even at a distance I could see what had led Ione to surmise that his end was near. Brock Walden suffered, I knew, from diabetes, congestive heart trouble, and emphysema, but it was a series of small strokes that had put him in the wheelchair. All showed on his face, in the bloated flesh, the blotched skin, the pinkish-gray pallor. But if death lay on his features, Jane didn't seem to notice.

Presented, she stood before him fulgent, animate, vocal. Beside her Carlyle hovered. Brock Walden sat unmoving. Jane's gesticulations seemed illustrations of some story. Then, beaming, she extended her hand in mock formality.

I found myself trembling with premonition, yet even as I started across the hard dirt toward them, I knew that I was too late.

Brock Walden reached out with a clawed hand and, drawing her closer, his eyes never leaving her face, he raised her hand to his mouth.

Was it then that I truly took Jane Harmon to my heart? When the radiance of her innocent delight slowly dimmed? When her expression emptied? When she cried out, softly, the cry of the violated? When Brock Walden forced his fat, wet, obscene tongue between her fingers?

IN A RECENT issue of *People*, a large photograph poses Jane Harmon before a movie poster on which Brock Walden reins in a rearing stallion while under threat of a blue-jawed bad man's six-shooter and a blonde ingénue's décolletage. The accompanying article confirms the success of *The Last Roundup* and Jane's status as an important young independent filmmaker. She is just finishing a film about wild horses in Nevada, she says, and her next project will deal with women and the West and madness. She also plans a treatment of an original script by her co-producer, Carlyle Walden, whose biography of his father will soon be published. The two are scouting sites and talking to money people.

In a smaller, companion photo Jane wears a dark jersey and jaunty beret, very much the auteur. Beside her, Carlyle holds in one hand galley proofs of his book; the other hand dangles limply from the sling that eases pressure on his arm or shoulder, an injury that gets no mention.

No mention is made, either, anywhere in the article, of Walden Ranch, of Blue Lake, Nevada, or of injuries or absences suffered Out Here.

That chill October day at the Rocking W, Jane recovered from Brock Walden's assault on her sensibility far more quickly than she did from what she deemed my betrayal. For the rest of my visit, she swaddled herself in grievance and wouldn't look at me.

In the house that morning, after Carlyle had given us a tour of the ranch workings, we found the four old men arranged around a table dressed with bottles and cards and currency.

"Hey, uh...." Brock Walden would flirt, but he'd already forgotten Jane's name. "Girlie – how about you set in a hand. Pretty thing like yourself got all sorts of tricks up her sleeve, I'd guess, but we'll risk it."

The drawl with which Brock Walden had charmed moviegoers and mocked, gently, his own image seemed now a thin, wheezy caricature.

The two men I didn't know offered sycophantic snickers. The third man, Cletus Rose, he alone hatless in the house, rose from his chair as he nodded to me.

"Win – persuade her." Brock Walden grinned. Before I could respond, he went on: "Still looks good, don't she, Clete? Give a man a good ride."

I felt my flush. Cletus Rose's squint deepened. "No call for that kind of talk."

Brock Walden laughed, at which Cletus picked up his hat and left the room.

Jane could only stare at the creature that was Brock Walden, not so much shocked or angry as bereft, as if she'd been orphaned anew.

Carlyle hovered. When he proposed a drive out to look at the mustangs that ranged around Mud Springs, I went to find Cletus Rose and a ride back to town. Jane did not deign to notice my departure.

For some days, I didn't see her. Then one morning, stepping out of Hasweldt's Drugs into a cold, slanting wind, I nearly fell as I literally ran into her, an accident for once not her fault. Steadying me out of my stumble, she offered polite but remote concern, as if I had ceased to be a person of any consequence to her.

Back at my kitchen table, I brooded. Jane was holding me to account for Brock Walden's outrageous behavior. Considering everything,

I was ready to admit at least some culpability: I should have warned her what he could be, yes. But what specifically could I have told her?

Eleanor Broadhurst's appraisal of Brock Walden had not taken in the whole man. Nor had it considered his complex relations with Blue Lake. As for her warning, that seemed misguided. Three years passed before I even saw him again.

Wild West Days had drawn people from as far away as Reno that summer, the fair had brought good prices, the carnival new rides, the rodeo abundant excitements but no serious injuries, and Blue Lake was, at the dance in the armory, in the mood to celebrate. Spirits were high, even without assistance from bottles tucked in the glove compartments of vehicles parked outside. Inside, the Sagebrush Songbirds kept good time as they worked through tunes of the day, and, in the heat of the July evening and the crowded room, we whirled and waltzed or clung and shuffled, drank the punch served to us by the VFW Auxiliary, and congratulated one another on the success of our efforts. Then, just as the day began to weigh and the night to lengthen, something like an electrical charge surged across the room, and everything got even better when in came Brock Walden.

After riding in the parade that morning, he had begged off from the big dance, business calling him back to Los Angeles. Blue Lake had accepted his absence. Yet now here he was, preferring our fellowship to Out There opportunities. The hall crackled with new energy as, while Cletus Rose soberly watched, Ol' Bee-Dub-Ya worked the crowd, chatted up officials, teased and flattered women, chaffed and glad-handed men. He danced with a County Commissioner's wife and the daughter of a Gull Valley rancher and the morning waitress at the Wagon Wheel Café. He danced with Eleanor Broadhurst, whose throaty laugh rang out over the music like a gong. Then, as John Broadhurst led me through a sedate foxtrot, Brock Walden tapped his shoulder. ""You mind, Parson?"

The minister smiled, and Brock Walden put his hands on me.

"Win," he said. He grinned, his face flushed with something more than heat. Whisky tainted his breath, although he was not drunk. His hand was heavy. "This's a long time coming."

"What's that?"

"Custom. Buckaroos welcoming the new schoolmarm."

"You're not a buckaroo," I said.

"Pretend."

He danced disdaining rhythm, powerfully, with his shoulders and hips, as if in a restrictive, ritualized combat. Struggling to stay with him, I missed a step, at which he slid his arm farther around my waist, drawing me to him, close.

Too close.

He pressed his aroused self against me. "Welcome to Blue Lake, Miz Waner Ma'am."

For a moment, in my shock, I felt faint. My resistance in his embrace, his grip, had no effect on him. Helpless, I could do only what I did: I stopped dancing.

He dragged me a few steps before he too stopped. "Too much for you, Win?"

And my husband was there.

I hadn't seen him cross the floor, hadn't seen him tap Brock Walden's shoulder. But I heard what he said. He said, "I'm cutting in."

The two men confronted one another. In the crowded, noisy hall, as the music played and the dancers danced, we three became a still silent center of attention, or so it seemed. The moment lengthened. Then Brock Walden took his hands from me. He adjusted his front. "Heat got her, seems like."

He smiled his movie smile as he turned to me. "Win. Been a real pleasure."

We watched him make his way through the crowd and out the door.

By the next day Blue Lake had made the incident an epic encounter: Henry Waner had faced down Brock Walden, called him out, run him off. That of course was not quite what had happened, but rumors built like thunderheads, swelling into the outrageous ozone, so that much rode on the two men's next meeting. It was as if someone had finally questioned the figure that Brock Walden presented to Blue Lake. What was he like, really? What would he do?

He would do nothing. Brock Walden and Henry Waner didn't meet until that autumn, when they greeted one another with a nod and passed on, no issue between them, neither suffering under an affront in need of satisfaction. Blue Lake, allowing for the possibility of misunderstanding, let it go. If the truth of Brock Walden was other than what they had committed to, they didn't want to know it.

I didn't speak to Brock Walden again for ten years, by which time my husband was dead.

So what could I have told Jane? About a whisky-warm man pressing his erection against me at a festive dance? About an obscene joke of a kiss long forgotten?

Besides, I guessed that Brock Walden's kiss bothered her less than what followed. Was I also to blame when Jane, stunned, miserable, turned away from the old man's leer to bury her face in the nearest shoulder, which happened to be not mine but Carlyle Walden's, this under the mindful eye of Ione Hardaway?

Jane's absence was one that I couldn't fill with reading and writing. I missed her visits, her stories, her take on Blue Lake, her talk of art and movies and herself: she had engaged me and made me laugh and given my days, as I awaited her arrival, a tang of anticipation. Now I could find consolation only in my sense that our estrangement had to be temporary. Who else, in Blue Lake, had she?

So I watched from my window as she came and went. Roaming town and countryside, I knew, she took photographs and conducted interviews — local weavers and potters and basket makers, teachers and ministers, cribbage players at the Community Center, 4-H kids. One Friday night she went with Troy to a high school football game. She spent a morning with the women at Darla's, a day tracing the old wagon road that had borne families through Dead Horse Canyon to a shortcut to California; she shot footage of a BLM mustang gather, and she filmed modern mining operations, where huge machines chewed away desert mountains and excreted tidy geometric piles.

She searched for a subject. She sought too a foundation for a relationship with Troy Hardaway.

They rode when they could, and some nights went out, but mostly, the pale flickering light in Jane's window suggested, they watched the western films she rented at Video Shack. I imagined her explaining technical or artistic points of filmmaking, or asking about cattle and horses and cowboy paraphernalia and customs. She was, I was sure, in her fashion, working. Then the window would go dark.

Much was made of these dark windows and what Blue Lake supposed was going on behind them. This was, after all, a woman so bold as to buy her own condoms at Hasweldt's Drug Store: surely she had initiated Troy into arcane Out There sexual practices. What else could account for his desire – his almost desperate need – to see and to be with her? This did not square with my sense of either of them, however. For Jane, their beddings were, I was sure, a matter of pleasure, physical, emotional, and aesthetic (no doubt unkindly, I imagined that making love was for Jane a composing, an arranging for effect). For Troy the issue was different. He was in love, utterly. He loved Jane as he would a well-favored, gracefully gaited mare, loved to look at and to admire and to care for her. He loved her person and her personality. He loved the fact of her. He wished Blue Lake to witness his inexplicable good fortune, his undeserved happiness.

To this end they sometimes went dancing. Jane, uncomfortable in bars, would rather have watched again The Big Country or Red River or High Noon, but she acquiesced to these outings, Troy's only request of her. Which at last brought her back to my kitchen and tea and sympathy.

Attaching herself to Troy Hardaway, Jane had reduced but not erased the peril she felt in Blue Lake. Threat still prowled at the edge of her awareness, Norman Casteel still slunk about the streets, and Pete Haas still lurked – she saw him, in the distance, watching her, and felt him nearby, an oppressive male malevolence. Awaking in the night to dread, she heard the grumbling of a pickup, might have heard scratchings at her locked doors and shufflings before her windows. But against this she had Troy, ready to challenge all presumptions, repel all advances. She felt, if edgy, ultimately safe. Until the Nevada Day dance at the VFW Club.

The next morning, Jane, telling me, still trembled.

They had stayed later than usual in the crowded hall, Troy being in such high spirits that Jane too had begun to enjoy herself, warming to dampness, adjusting to the din of voices and music, suffering with equanimity the bumps and jostlings of the crowd. "It got rowdy, a little," she said, "but it was just everybody having a good time."

Then, coming out of the ladies' room, she saw as if in a nightmare Pete Haas, dead-eyed, sneering, and Troy turning from him, and Haas slamming his fist into the side of Troy's face.

"I was horrified," Jane said. "It was like…"

Jane had no vocabulary to describe what followed. Her only frame of reference here, as elsewhere, was movies, but this sudden, shattering violence had none of the choreographed heroics of *Shane* or the comic flailing in *The Searchers*. This seemed a combustion of the very air into ferocity. It ended when Haas brandished a jagged-edged beer bottle, and sensible hands took hold of him. Snarls and curses followed, but the fight was over. It had not lasted a minute. Troy's cheekbone was gashed. Haas' mouth dripped blood.

Blue Lake would judge the affair a draw but award Troy, not known to be a bar brawler, a moral victory for having survived a sucker punch to hold his own.

Jane had no interest in such determinations. "They went at each other like animals."

I poured her more tea.

"Not just… him. Troy too. I – they would have killed one another, Miz Waner."

I might have said a number of things but none to any effect on her. She hadn't come to my door to listen.

"They were fighting over me. Like I was… spoil. I – the Haas person, I understand, that's what he is, but Troy…"

"He was attacked, Jane. He had to defend himself."

"Why? He could have called the police."

"Men don't, Out Here," I said.

"Men in bars, you mean. They go at one another like beasts, and then they blame us. Like it's our fault, when it's not even about us, it's just them." She seemed to have tapped into a reservoir, deep and cold, of old animus. "Sometimes I hate men."

I broke off a small piece of macaroon.

"After I took him to get his cheek stitched, he wanted to have sex. He acted like I should be grateful, like I should reward him."

After a moment, I said: "When you committed yourself to him, you must have anticipated something like this, Jane. It had to happen, eventually."

She picked up her teacup but didn't drink. Then she made one of her skips.

"In western films, at dances the community comes together as a, well, a community. And the violence, the fights and shootings, they're… hopeful, they make things safe, they secure the future. Out Here there is no future, no hope. There's no community either – just a herd working itself up for sex and…" She searched for a word, found it: "brutality."

And then somehow we were speaking of Brock Walden.

I apologized for not having told her that he was capable of the coarsest vulgarities. "Maybe I didn't want to ruin your family fantasy. I enjoyed the idea of being your mother."

"I never imagined he could be so… ugly."

"That despicable kiss – he did that to me at the parade your mother remembered. I suppose your little tale reminded him."

After a moment, she said. "I thought he had to be nice. Otherwise you would never have been his mistress."

I stirred my tea before I spoke: "I was not Brock Walden's mistress, Jane."

"Everybody says you were." She measured me from under her narrowed brow, as if she would take me in again, from another angle.

"Everybody is mistaken."

"Why would they say that if it isn't true?"

"Because they think it is," I said. "Or they want it to be. And because I never tried to discourage them from thinking it."

"I don't understand."

"You of all people should," I said. "As long as they thought I was Brock Walden's mistress, they left me alone."

But even to Jane I had to explain.

Blue Lake had allowed me a year to mourn Henry Waner.

He was on his way back from a hunt in the Eagle Range when his pickup hit a patch of black ice and spun wildly to the lip of the embankment and, then, slipped over – down twelve hundred feet, bouncing off rock and pinon to a burying, upside down, among willows at the edge of Cress Creek. So the sheriff reconstructed the accident. The pickup was not going fast when it tipped over the precipice, apparently: Henry might have been able to escape. Perhaps he believed that he could stop it, or that he could somehow drive it through the fall, that this was but one more ride to stay with, one more situation to tough out. He didn't jump.

When he hadn't returned by midnight, I notified the sheriff. The searchers knew where to look, but even in daylight the skid marks were barely noticeable, and the pickup, crunched up and nosed into creek willows, was largely hidden from sight. On the third day, Brock Walden, appealed to, flew over the area for hours until Cletus Rose caught a glint of sunlight on metal.

His sternum crushed, Henry died of internal injuries. The mountain cold precluded a precise determination of the time of his death. That he might have lain a long time at the bottom of a wild ravine, broken but conscious, added anguish to my grief.

I buried my husband. Then I saw to what was left of my life.

When Consolidated Mining shut down their Blue Lake operation and Henry lost his job, he and I had decided to remain. We were both Nevadans. We belonged Out Here. So we bought the company house, before the door of which I planted a lilac bush, and I continued to teach, and he started doing geological consulting. We saved and planned and bought the property on The Hump, and that summer we had begun to build. Only finish work remained, and after his death, to keep busy, I oversaw it. When I could move in, I did.

Why, Jane wanted to know, had I stayed Out Here? Blue Lake too was curious. I was only thirty-five, an experienced teacher, and a published writer — the university press had just issued in a single volume a collection of my essays on local history and desert matters. I could, it was assumed, go wherever I wanted, do whatever I wished with whomever I chose, make another, a different life. After thirteen years in Blue Lake, I had friends here but no compelling intimacies, a grave to tend but no blood relations, domestic habits and small social rituals to order my existence but no obligations. Finally, however, I was still a Nevadan, still the bookish girl from the Amargosa Valley. Out Here in the desert I had all that I wanted. I chose to remain where and who I was, to do what I had been doing and to do it by myself.

This last would become an issue. Blue Lake allowed me to mourn and to finish the house. But when I moved in, when I met my classes, when my year was up, I was made aware that my single state was no longer acceptable. Over the next months I was beset, as Jane Harmon would be thirty-five years later. Men I had known only to nod to now assumed familiarity; they seemed to feel themselves owed, due. Women I had thought friends now regarded me from under wary brows. I felt the pressure, I knew what was expected of me, but I would not be driven out or into another marriage.

I had always understood why Western heroes rode off into the sunset. As a girl and young woman, orphaned, I envisioned a future that did not easily admit another. Meeting Henry Waner, I was stunned to discover that I must have him, even though I really shouldn't have anyone. Married, I was surprised to find myself happy, so that our childlessness sometimes seemed a reproach. We were a pair, sharing a love of the desert and plans for a life in it; he had his rocks, I had my words, and we had one another. Now Henry was dead and I was alone and content to remains so.

But in Blue Lake I was besieged, until Brock Walden came to my rescue.

At Henry's funeral, in the church and at the graveyard, he and Cletus Rose remained, as much as Blue Lake would allow, at the edge of things. With others they came to the house, two big men filling with their shoulders my small living room and sipping the coffee Eleanor served. While Cletus Rose, after quietly offering his kind-eyed condolences, spoke with John Broadhurst about, it seemed, Camus, Brock Walden freed himself from men who talked about deer or cattle or women, coming up to take my hand. "I'm sorry about Henry."

"Thank you for helping us find him," I said. "I'm grateful."

"He had sand. I liked him. The notion of him laying out there alone, I – "

"Yes. Yes." Tears blurred my gaze.

He raised my hand, enclosed it in both of his. "That was stupid of me, Win – a dumb thing to say. I just wanted to tell you how sorry I was."

"I understand," I said. "We're all... overwrought."

I found a handkerchief. Other men found him, as I, even in my grief, thought how very different this Brock Walden was from the lout who had pressed against me a decade earlier. Soon he and Cletus were gone.

Eighteen months later, I returned home from school to find a Walden Ranch pickup in my driveway and Brock Walden on my patio, ostensibly to talk about Wild West Days – he planned to par-ticipate, and that year I chaired the volunteers' committee. Inside, he admired my home, drank the coffee I served him, and talked about himself, which was his way of wooing. He talked for over an hour. Then he left.

"And," Jane asked, "he didn't try...?"

"Of course he did," I said. "Brock Walden always tried. At one point he even put his hands on me."

Jane leaned forward, as if to get a better view. "What happened?"

I could think of no way to convey the emotional truth of the experience: the abrupt move of his big body to corner me on my own sofa, the groping heavy hands, the wet mouth. I wasn't so much shocked or surprised as I was disappointed. It was all so com-monplace and clumsy and vaguely adolescent.

"I didn't respond the way he expected."

"And he didn't... insist?"

"That wasn't Brock Walden's style," I said, "He couldn't believe that I wasn't desperate to sleep with him, so we had an exchange. He said, 'You want love, is that it?' and I said, 'I want you to leave'."

"That was all?"

"I was never alone with Brock Walden again."

Then I told her the rest of it. How that evening in the Community Center Thrift Store, to the silent inquiries of Ruby Blascovitch and the knowing smirks of Irene Walters, in a fit of perversity, I merely smiled. How Blue Lake, perhaps recalling the incident on the dance floor ten years earlier, soon inflated the hour behind a closed door into an adultery of longstanding. Now Brock Walden and I were imagined in an on-going affair made of hours in Blue Lake when I wasn't to be found, afternoons in Reno or Las Vegas where I was supposed to be shopping, and weeks each Christmas when I told everyone I was visiting Eleanor Broadhurst in Los Angeles.

I assumed the ploy would gain me only a respite, that the truth would eventually out, but time passed and I was never directly called to confirm the story, and Brock Walden didn't deny it. Why he didn't was a mystery. And Blue Lake let me be. More time passed, and the story became commonly accepted fact, and the fact came to be of little interest, and we all aged, and none of it mattered anymore.

After her husband's suicide, Sheila Brenner and her daughters left Blue Lake. In Los Angeles, so it was said, Brock Walden helped her find a job in a studio commissary. Eventually she remarried, unhappily according to her mother. Her elder daughter became an elementary school teacher and remained single. Her younger girl was lost to drugs and sex and dreams.

When Sheila returned to Blue Lake to attend to her dead mother's affairs, I happened on her coming out of the courthouse. She was thinner, hollow-eyed and older than her years. She accepted my sympathies but didn't seem deeply grieved – her mother had lived a long life. But as she spoke of selling the house she'd grown up in, of the various final chores that she was about, of the changes in the town, of the people who were no longer here, her voice took on a tremolo. I thought she was about to mourn the loss of an old life, a younger and still hopeful self. Instead, eyes glistening, she said: "You killed him."

She could only have been speaking of Jim Brenner.

"All of you in Blue Lake, you and your ugly talk. Stories and gossip and lies. You took the heart right out of him."

"I'm sorry, Sheila," I said.

"Brock Walden and me – he never touched me. Never!"

There was nothing more I could say.

"I hate this place," she said, brushing at her eyes. "You all think you're so tough, but you're just shriveled up and cruel."

She pushed past me. I watched her down the steps and out onto the sidewalk and down the street.

OUT THERE WITS sometimes joke that Out Here we have only two seasons: brown and browner. The jest is often meant as a metaphor for our inner lives, the charge being that we are insensitive to the richness of human endeavor and intercourse, that we pass our days in the dull indifference of the poor in spirit.

Some of us object, insisting that our quiet, contained, stoic demeanor is the mark of the far-seeing. Others argue that the desert palette is primarily one of pastels, but these range across the spectrum, finely discriminated if faded, like the feelings of aging lovers.

And others observe simply that there is brown and then there is brown.

November advanced into deeper cold, grayer frost. Snow sometimes flurried, the wind pushing white wisps over the streets. Jane and Troy continued to ride, and to huddle behind windows eerily flickering or suggestively dark, but they no longer danced. Troy wore the small scar on his cheekbone like a decoration for valor. And Jane, quite unknowingly I believe, began working on their separation.

As if totaling Troy's virtues against an unspoken charge of inadequacy, she praised him.

Troy was really more intelligent than he let on, wasn't he?

He was nearly as capable as his sister, as good with horses as his father, and he got along easily with almost everyone, he didn't need to remain a hired hand, a Nevada buckaroo, didn't I think? He could do much better for himself in Southern California, in the movie industry or on one of the boutique ranches of the rich and famous, couldn't he?

He had a nice sense of humor and laugh and smile. He was a good man, a kind person. He had no vices.

And she spoke of leaving.

She might return to Los Angeles at Christmas, when the friend to whom she had sublet her apartment would be out of town. She had financial and professional matters to see to, and a report on her grant activities that she really should deliver in person. It wouldn't be for long, a week, maybe two.

And she acknowledged twinges of uncertainty. She and Troy didn't really know each other that well, their relationship had been rushed into, each could use some time to…

All of which said only that Jane was trying to find a place for Troy in her real, her Out There life, trying and failing.

At the same time, Jane and Carlyle Walden were, innocently, corresponding.

That day at the Rocking W, Carlyle had hobbled eagerly about with her, and when he drove her to outlying Walden Ranch pastures and hayfields, she had recalled her sense that the land might offer refuge. For mustangs, he asked, or wildlife? Unprepared to admit that she had thought refuge for, actually, somehow, herself, she allowed that it was just a thought, she didn't know what it meant, really. But Carlyle too had had a thought. Once back in Los Angeles, he wrote to her, expressing his feeling that a wildlife refuge might make a fitting memorial to his father. He then contacted Nature Conservancy and similar organizations and got information about tax advantages and benefits for the range and the community. Then he asked for her opinion, which he seemed genuinely to value.

In return, Jane asked Carlyle about Brock Walden and his movies, about Roundup and the availability of tapes of the show, her questions spinning from her sense that an actor would somehow figure centrally in a film about the Real Wild West. Carlyle told her of his recent decision to write a biography of his father. Their projects sharing a principal, they might labor to mutual benefit, he said – at the same time giving her to understand that he understood her and that they had common interests enough to support a weightier consideration of one another.

Carlyle, I believe, knew that he had begun a courtship, although I doubt he anticipated success. Jane, if she didn't know herself sued, should have. Troy knew of the letters but thought nothing of them, Carlyle Walden being, after all, Carlyle Walden.

Others in Blue Lake now got letters from him. Mine I took to be typical: a brief personal greeting, an explanation of his biographical project, and a request for impressions, memories, anecdotes, and reminiscences to freshen and color the studio version of Brock Walden's life. What came back to him was something at once dark and enlightening.

Proposing Brock Walden, post-war fan magazines and public relations handouts had told a story that, much like the roles he would play on screen, sought easy effects and underscored simpleminded moralities, with but sidelong glances at truth. Fade in on mean, mid-1920s, urban New Jersey streets and a boy, the sole offspring of a restaurant hostess and a long-distance truck driver, she often too ill to work, he on the road for weeks and months and at last swallowed up by the Great Depression. To the boy, dutiful Walter, the pleasures of school give way before the responsibility for his loving and beloved mother – montage: selling newspapers and shining shoes and running errands and other Ragged Dick enterprises. Alas, funereal organ tones in somber rain announce the thirteen-year old alone. Crisis: passing a school yard crowded with former playfellows, the boy enters a neighborhood grocery, simulates a pistol, and demands money from the elderly proprietor who smiles and gives him bread and beans and advice: Go West, Young Man. In the best American tradition, Our Hero lights out for The Territory.

Open roads and blue skies, freight yards in starry nights, small towns and fruited plains. Adventures accumulate as young Walter drifts, working at what jobs he can charm or cajole, learning to use tools and machines and animals, dodging grim authorities and warding off dangerous men and enjoying the meals and sympathy of kindly women, growing into a muscular young roughneck, discovering America. December 7, 1941 finds him mucking irrigation ditches in California's Big Valley. Strings and fife, "The Marine Corps Hymn," and sharp cuts: courage, carnage, and camaraderie in the jungle. At war's end, Walter Broekenworth, medals clinking on his manly chest, in Los Angeles seeks out a dead buddy's family, one of whom is female and works in the office of an agent, who studies the young Marine's physique and profile and smile and wrangles a screen test for Brock Walden.

The camera likes him. His on-screen presence in walk-ons commands attention and demands larger roles; women tingle in sexual anticipation at his drawled utterances; men admire his insouciant competence and swift sure violence; and Brock Walden becomes a B-picture fixture, while off-screen activities – barroom fisticuffs and sexual set-tos – keep studio flacks busy quieting and covering up. He gains the reputation of one in every sense careless. He is, Hollywood later has it, a man roughed by life into ragged, snagging edges around an obdurate core, a man misdirected and wasting his talent and life as he descends into ruin until...

Violins: sunlight splits grim clouds, and the tragedy of an ex-wife's suicide brings into his life a boy. Awww. And Brock Walden, finding in the face of his son his own lost innocence, becomes a real father. More violins, reeds, muted brass in a swell of arpeggios: Giving of himself brings redemption. Now *Roundup* secures finances, film performances surprise, one earning an academy award nomination, and all is forgiven. His career thriving, Brock Walden lends his distinctive intonations to truck commercials, becomes a spokesman for a firearms company, makes recruiting ads for the Marine Corps, and takes up the cause of veterans, testifying before congress on the problems of the warrior readjusting to peacetime life, offering as an example his own earlier riotousness. He ages and begins to ail, becomes valued and venerable and, in the parlance of the day, iconic, a symbol of what is great about America and the West, which – we are not told exactly how – shaped and saved him. At last, in wheelchair and lap rug, he sits by the fire in his Nevada ranch house and tells this story to the dutiful son who will share it with the world. Violins. Flames die to coals. Fade out.

This was the story, more or less, that Carlyle Walden thought basically true, much as he thought the novels of Zane Grey and the films of John Ford to be aligned with if not always to record history. And in fact Hollywood had merely refashioned and slathered with sentiment another version of Brock Walden's life, a sort of anti-story long whispered, which was never denied by its protagonist. Some of it Brock Walden told to me that afternoon in my living room.

He was born Walter Broekenworth in Camden, New Jersey, yes. But his mother was an alcoholic fry cook who drank herself into a coronary while her son, whom she had heard neither of nor from for ten years, was fighting in the South Pacific. His father was an armed robber and hijacker dead in a prison yard knifing. His only pleasure from school came in truancy, and that ended when he dropped out of sixth grade and took to the streets, to conning and thievery and, his growth coming early, the strong-arm trades. He knew women young, fleeing, at fourteen, from the consequences of a conjunction with a shop girl. Abroad the country, he worked and hustled and stole – these to him requiring roughly the same physical and moral energy. He came to know the comfort of jails, the blows of truncheons and boots, the adrenaline rush of flight into darkness. He might have killed a man whose attack he met with a fist wrapped around a load of lead. He did not want for sexual release.

Shortly after Pearl Harbor, Walter Broekenworth, arrested drunk and disorderly in a Bakersfield park, took the judge's option and joined the Marines. To his surprise, he liked the Corps, understood the purposeful discipline, and respected the men he fought alongside. He found war a challenge to body and mind and spirit and will, one for which he had long if unknowingly prepared. He was good at killing and not being killed. Later his life would seem to him preface and afterword to that brief, intense time in the island jungles of the South Pacific.

His sixty years in Hollywood was a long confidence game. He brawled for pleasure and for the confirmation by blood and bone that he was actually alive. He was kind or cruel as the impulse moved him. He had many women but loved none and preferred the company of men like himself. He felt no lack in his life, no absence. He had had his way with the world, and he didn't care that he was dying.

Carlyle Walden, hearing all this now, still wished to find Brock Walden heroic. But corresponding with Jane Harmon, he began to sense that his image of his father was colored with sentiments from his childhood and shaped by the force of his own emotional need. Looking as it were through Jane's eyes, he began to see what the lens of innocence had distorted. He began to see himself more clearly as well.

For Jane, on the other hand, all this was material. But after our visit to the Rocking W, in the dwindling November days she grew grim, for she couldn't find in or make from what she had a story. Brock Walden would center her project, somehow — that was her only point of reckoning. From this certainty, again and again, she set out imagining, trying to find her way when she didn't know where she was going. She spent hours at her computer, perusing the photographs she'd taken, seeking the informing image, the shape, the jar to place upon the hill and bring all around it into order.

Appealed to, I tried to console her. "The creative process has its frustrations. We all experience it."

"Yes, I know, I know." She furrowed her brow at the pen and notebook that I'd put down when she appeared. "But this isn't like writing a little essay."

I let that pass, watching as, absently, she hazarded her tea mug at the table's edge.

"This is so much more..." She made as if to snare a word, her elbow nicking the mug into a tremble. "...important. It's my big chance, my last chance, really. My career hangs on it. If I can't get this done, I'll be back in L.A. raising money for other people to make films with."

Rescuing her mug, I filled it from the teapot. "I'm sure you feel that way now, but – "

"No. It's now or never."

Her dramatic gloom irritated me. "You can only keep at it, Jane. Tough it out, as we say Out Here. Inspiration will come. Or it won't."

Then she made one of her leaps. "It's because of Troy."

"I'm sorry, I don't – "

"That's why Ione doesn't like me. I thought it was the accident, getting off on the wrong foot – but it isn't. It's Troy. He sneaks off to see me, and she thinks I... entice him. But I don't. I haven't done anything."

Jane's repeated claim of innocence served only to bring it into question.

"It's like she thinks I want to lure him away from here, from her."

"I really don't think – "

"She's so... I try to concentrate on Brock Walden and movies and the desert, on everything I've seen and heard Out Here, but I keep coming back to Ione, to her and Walden Ranch. There's a story there."

Jane was talking to herself now, articulating inner apprehensions.

"It's another women's issues story, I know, and I wanted to move beyond those, or at least place them in a broader context – it isn't the story I've felt Out Here, but it's one I could tell, I know I could, I have the vision and the art..." Petulance pursed her lips. "It could be a wonderful film, only she won't let me make it. She refuses to even talk to me."

Her tone held an unattractive whining. "You almost seem be saying that you think Ione is morally obliged to help you make your movie."

"Morally obliged? No, I didn't mean..." She frowned. "But why wouldn't she, except for spite, when it would tell her story?"

"Maybe she doesn't want her story told." After a moment, I added: "Or maybe she's afraid that what will get told is not her story but yours."

Jane's expression made clear that she didn't have the slightest idea what I was talking about.

"You speak of your film," I said. "Your vision, your artistry, your career. What has all this to do with Ione Hardaway?"

"Everything, Miz Waner. After all, it would be about her. It would show her strength of character. It would celebrate her achievement in what's supposed to be a man's world. Think of all the girls and young women who would benefit from knowing Ione's story, who could take her for a role model."

"Even if she doesn't want to be taken as such?"

"Of course. Why should she have a choice?"

"Jane, you can't – "

"No, Miz Waner, she is morally obliged," Jane said with sudden conviction. "If she didn't want other people to appreciate how extraordinary she is, she shouldn't be so, so... so extraordinary."

As was often the case, Jane's claim constituted its own evidence and was thus irrefutable.

Nothing came of this conversation. Jane continued to wring her imagination, as if to press from it the essence of the Wild West, but to no avail. She needn't have concerned herself, however, for her instincts were unerring, bringing her always and inevitably to a consideration of the intricate complexities of Ione Hardaway.

I had long flattered myself that, among all in Blue Lake, I alone really knew Ione, I alone appreciated an intelligence given vent in jest, often sharp, and an irony keen-edged or rough-surfaced. Out of that intelligence arose Ione's ire, for all its fierceness oddly cold, almost abstract – a response not to people and acts and events so much as to the idea of these, to the perception that life allowed the outrageous. How else but with jest and irony and anger should a thinking woman reply to such an offense?

What Ione's affections embraced, however, I couldn't say with certainly. She loved her brother and her father. She loved, I believed, in her way, me. If pressed, I would have said that Ione Hardaway loved most of all herself, loved her life on the land, loved the day-to-day effort to defend Walden Ranch against the encroachments of Out Here elements and vicissitudes, the assaults of Out There opinions and legislation. In this labor, this maintenance, idea and actuality somehow merged. For Ione, life held little else but work. Self-contained, self-sustained, she came to care for people only with effort, through an act of will. She assessed, evaluated, judged, and chose – only then did she give of herself, usually to her rue. Ultimately, invariably, people failed Ione. Perhaps the first to do so was her mother, whose death imposed on a young girl's awareness the inevitability of endings.

Blue Lake would say that all this meant that Ione Hardaway was hard, tough. I think rather that she was deep. If in nothing else, Ione was like her long dead mother exactly what she appeared to be but somehow more.

She was also a woman on the edge, which Blue Lake had long suspected but had no notion of how perilously.

THANKSGIVING EVE brought a cold rain that near midnight turned to snow. Heavy wet flakes fell for two hours and, as the temperature sank, set into a white crust on which the sunlight glittered icily when the day came cold and bright. As Troy Hardaway parked before Jane's house, he at once noted in the snow the imprint of boots coming and going between the street and her bedroom window. George Burleigh, summoned at Jane's insistence, found the tracks ominous, even as he assured her that they had not been made by Pete Haas, who had been in Reno, under the eye of ATF agents, for a week. This news did not ease Jane's distress. Neither did George's promise to urge the police into regular surveillance.

At my door some time later, Jane, still stiff with anxiety, spoke in ragged huffs – she felt tired, head achy, unsociable. While the night before she had been pleased by my invitation to Thanksgiving dinner at the Community Center, she thought now she might just have a bowl of soup and a nap. As Troy kindly loaded my car with baking, I brewed tea and, persuaded that other people were precisely what Jane needed, encouraged her to join us, stumbling onto, at last, the only cause in which she was inclined to enlist.

"Everybody contributes, Jane, if not food then help of one sort or another."

"I'd just spill something." Such a remark gauged her depression.

"Just your being there would be helpful," I replied. "To chat with folks, make sure that no one is alone."

"I'm not very good at that kind of thing," she said.

But she was good at taking pictures. "Or you could photograph the affair. Everybody would appreciate that."

"Well…" Interest lightened her gloom.

"You have that digital camera. You could take photos and then show them around. And print copies – the center has the necessary machines, I believe."

"I suppose I could…"

"You could – could you put the pictures on a computer and create a slide show?"

"I could do better than that." Jane smiled now, as if in recognition of her own virtue. "I could make a little film for them. And it would give me…"

She didn't need to finish her sentence. The photographs would give her more material, more images, among which she might find a story. She rose, telling Troy they would need to stop at the house and pick up some equipment.

I bathed and dressed and drove to the Community Center, in the kitchen made my cookies and cakes presentable, and then stepped into the dining room. The hall was crowded with those in Blue Lake who could or would share the holiday meal with no one else. Among them, sitting with her father, was Ione Hardaway. Her shirt and jeans freshly laundered, her auburn hair brushed into luster, her hands hiding in her lap, Ione appeared, as she watched the old people, softer, more feminine, hinting at another woman she might have become.

A few high school girls set tables while their parents banged about in the kitchen, but most in the room were of my generation, most coupled, some otherwise attached, as Shirley Casteel to her nephew Norman, and all dressed for company: pearls and shantung, such as I wore, or bright blouses and pantsuits; ties or bolos and fancy belt buckles and boots polished to a high gloss. They exchanged hugs and handshakes, jibes and platitudes; they shared sympathies, carped about weather or politics; and they posed for Jane Harmon. Moving among them, Jane drew them out as she took them in. Her lens met anticipatory smiles or theatrical protests or real shyness and not a little amusement as she posed Blue Lake seniors at tables draped with shiny white cloths, beneath orange crepe streamers, before the cut-out or crayoned gobblers and squash and Pilgrims and Pequots rendered by Blue Lake second graders. To all appearances having a wonderful time, Jane coaxed and cajoled and accommodated, with her photographs pleasing, with her personality charming all.

"Got a way with old folks, ain't she." Bill Hardaway's words seemed to float on bubbles of oxygen. His once dandyish mustache had grown out into a dark smear beneath the clear plastic tubes jutting from his nostrils. "And horses."

"And yahoos." Ione feigned a frown as her brother slipped into a chair beside his father. "You know this one, Miz Waner? Reminds me of somebody used to buckaroo on the Rocking W, almost."

"You're awful handsome today, Sissy."

Ione's scowl failed. "Spreads cow flop like him, too."

Jane approached, her camera winking as if in code. "Can we do the family?"

"Not till I get out of this contraption." Bill Hardaway reached for the valve on the small oxygen tank dollied on the floor beside him.

His daughter slapped his hand. "Leave that alone or you'll be riding shank's mare back to the place."

"I ain't having my picture took looking like no walrus," he blustered.

"On really good looking men," Jane said, "those tubes are an accessory."

"Yeah, well..." His vanity nourished, Bill Hardaway set his mouth in a strained, serious smile.

Jane posed them: father, brother and sister, father flanked by children, father and son, father and daughter. The images she offered us insisted that another old man would not last the winter.

"If we're doin' family, we need one more," Ione said.

She placed a hand on my shoulder, bringing her face near to my own. Jane's camera flashed. In the captured image Ione's smile brought back to me the girl she once had been. My own smile was unmistakably maternal.

As the meal was served, Jane continued to take pictures, now candid shots of diners intent on food and drink and one another. Then she moved to the computer and, nibbling at the plate of hors d'oeuvres Troy had fixed, occupied herself. Irene Walters, who never ate at these affairs, pulled up a chair to watch, murmuring encouragement. Troy looked on, smiling.

I ate and listened to Ione, today unusually voluble. The roads were too icy to let her father drive, so she'd decided to join us at our meal. Nothing was happening at the ranch that couldn't wait – a mare was due, but not for a day or so, the cows were pregnant and healthy, the winter feed was stacked and dry, and the books were up to date. She was plotting pasture cycles to test an intensive grazing system, but there was no hurry about it. She'd spent the morning, as I had, baking.

Bill Hardaway, having eaten little, was up and tugging his oxygen bottle from table to table. I remarked to his daughter: "I suppose he doesn't see much of his friends these days."

"Not many left to see." After a moment she said: "B. W. had a dizzy spell and landed in the hospital. Next morning he up and walked out. Cletus found him in a bar down the street."

"That would be his way, wouldn't it?"

She watched her father talking with Jane Harmon. "You get one of Carlyle's letters too?"

"I did." That she had as well surprised me.

"You gonna give him the low-down on your long, hot romance with his dad?" Irony edged her tone. "He's heard all the rumors, Miz Waner."

"No doubt." I spread chokecherry jam onto one of the rolls she'd brought in.

"Years ago I told him you might of been curious enough to try B. W. on for size, but once would be all you'd need." She threatened to smile. "He gave me that headache look."

"What about you? What does Carlyle imagine you could tell him about his father?"

Her gaze emptied for a moment. "Who knows what that yahoo'd imagine? I – you know what he's doing down in L.A? He's having Cletus teach him to handle horses."

I didn't try to mask my confusion. "Horses?"

"Yeah. Why? He can already ride – not good, horses still spook him some, so Cletus can help him, I guess, he's a good teacher. But I don't see the point of it. Unless…"

She turned from me to look across the room where Jane, flanked by Troy and Irene, clipped cables from a computer to a small projector.

"You got any idea what's going on, Miz Waner?"

"No," I said. But I did have a sudden intuition about why Ione was present.

Tables were cleared, coffee served. Irene Walters and several men stepped out to smoke, while a few women slipped in pairs toward the ladies room. Ruby Blascovitch rose and, joking that she'd have to talk fast before everybody fell asleep, thanked the volunteers for their efforts, ending with an announcement that Jane Harmon had fashioned a memento of the occasion.

Troy dimmed a bank of lights, Jane flicked a switch, and on a wall appeared an image of the room, empty but for white tablecloths and orange streamers and the art of children. Then the shadows faded and reformed into a procession of old friends meeting in ritual fellowship, breaking bread and giving thanks, offering sober stares or comic smiles, in formal postures seeking certainty, or with foolery fronting affection, as they celebrated life and labor and one another. Blue Lake was shown itself as it wished to be seen.

For all the bonhomie, however, the final effect was subtly, insistently plaintive. The faces were worn, scarred by years and weather and care. The good clothes did not quite fit bodies now stooped or swollen, beaten down. The still images, as they measured and fixed a moment, in succession suggested transience, men and women dissolving in mid-gesture, ghost-like. Blue Lake looked and saw those no longer there, smiled past the unavoidable that lurked in every sag and seam of flesh, that looked out from the dying eyes of Bill Hardaway. Then white light emptied the wall.

Jane accepted Blue Lake's applause, thanked those expressing appreciation, assured those enquiring after copies. She reran the film, setting it to loop, then moved through the room, savoring the last drops of approval from those who gathered into small chatting groups, some beginning their goodbyes, others lingering over coffee. The room was still half full when she joined us.

"It's really quite wonderful, Jane," I said, meaning it.

"Yes, I know." Her smile lit her face the way the projector lit the faces appearing and vanishing on the wall. She turned her smile toward Ione, and she waited.

Ione wrapped her hands around her coffee cup, interlacing her fingers in a deliberate gesture that clearly constituted a care-taking. "Nice thing to do for everybody."

Jane of course had made her film for herself, but it was not my place to correct Ione's mistaken impression.

"It's good."

"I know," Jane said again. "Imagine what I could do with your story, if you'd let me."

Ione's mouth tightened against her irritation. "I don't know how else I can say it. I don't want to be in your movie."

Jane's smile didn't waver. "But you and your situation, it's all so…inspirational. Everybody says so. Miz Waner too."

Obliquely appealed to, I said nothing. Ione scowled.

"You're a very special woman."

The declaration was so open, so innocent, so guileless, that as opposition to it Ione's glare was useless.

"She's got'cha there, Sissy," Troy grinned.

Jane sensed her advantage. "I could make a film about you alone, there's all the conflict with men, the challenge and achievement – but what I really sense, what I'm after, is much larger. It's…well, I don't know exactly how you'll fit into it, but you will, you and Blue Lake, all Troy's showed me, the old folks here today – somehow it will all come together. And Brock Walden and his TV show and the big sign outside of town – the horses and the Wild West."

Ione managed a grimace. "Whatever that is."

"If it's anything," Jane said then, "it's you."

Ione was caught between anger and bewilderment. "I – what's that supposed to mean?"

"I don't know," Jane admitted, seeming to marvel at her own insight. "I only know it's true. It is, isn't it, Miz Waner?"

"'The natives of the rain are rainy men.'"

Everyone at the table stared at me.

"Never mind," I said quickly. "How does Brock Walden fit into this?"

"I don't know that for sure either," Jane admitted. "But his story has to be part of it, somehow. I can just… *feel* how it all has to come together."

For a moment, silent, she quivered with anticipation. Then her tone altered.

"Of course, I have a lot of research to do yet. There's so much I don't… but Carlyle has been a big help – our projects overlap, my film and the biography he's writing, and his idea about turning the ranch into a memorial."

"Memorial?" Ione was suddenly still. "What kind of memorial?"

"Oh, he thinks maybe a wildlife refuge named after his father," Jane said blithely.

"The Rocking W?"

"Or a museum for all Brock Walden's memorabilia, or a colony for artists and writers and filmmakers who work with western themes – he isn't really sure, he has a number of possibilities in mind. "

Ione's hands throttled her coffee cup. She spoke softly to her brother, restraint clipping her words. "You know about this?"

Troy, always alert to his sister's moods, now anxiously fingered the small scar on his cheekbone. "No. I mean, not really…"

Ione leveled her gaze at Jane. "Whose bright idea was all this?"

"His, Carlyle's." Jane took Ione's silence as doubt, which it was. "Well, not the refuge, that occurred to me once when Troy and I were out riding. Carlyle understood right away."

"Understood what, exactly?" The words came as if from a great distance, through an emptiness that would engulf and so buffer her anger.

"It's just that there's so much land Out Here, maybe we should let some of it alone, set it aside for the wild horses and deer and creatures that are natural to it. Where they could be safe."

"We?"

"Well…" She looked to Troy, seeking a complicity that might justify the pronoun. "You know what I mean."

"Wild horses?"

"Yes, and a bird sanctuary, and – "

"Walden Ranch? The Rocking W?" Ione stared down at her hands, as if willing them to remain clasped and harmless. Her voice trembled with rage. "You think – you got Carlyle to think – we should quit ranching?"

"Well, you have to admit it's… inefficient, all this land, all the hard work, for so little." Jane smiled her smile, denying all dispute. "The whole idea of a ranch is so old fashioned, isn't it? Nostalgic, almost. I mean, a refuge and museum, they'd conserve – "

"We produce food. We get all there is to get out of the land, and we take care of it, keep it alive."

"Well yes, but how much food – "

"We keep this town alive, too. Every penny Walden Ranch earns gets spent, one way or another, in Blue Lake. Without us, the town starts to die."

Ione spoke in a strange sort of quiet fierce futility, her mouth tight, her gaze hard and unseeing. She was angry to despair.

"You give the land to wild horses and you'll kill a way of life."

"It's a… picturesque way of life, I'll grant you that," Jane chirped with sudden enthusiasm. "Like all these old people in their ill-fitting clothes. Wonderful background. Quaint, even."

"Quaint." Ione slowly shook her head in furious disbelief.

Jane, refusing to allow Ione's anger a consequence, continued. "As far as the town dying, well, a refuge will draw tourists. So will a museum."

"Tourists. Quaint. Nostalgia." Ione now spoke so softly I had to strain to hear. "Turn us into a fucking theme park."

It was the obscenity that persuaded Jane, finally, to silence.

Ione too sat silently, enraged, finished with words. For a moment I feared. Then she shuddered, her body shedding tension. I watched her subdue her impulse to violence as she might an angry horse.

"It's all right, Sissy." Troy brushed his hand over her shoulder.

"Does B. W. know about this?"

"No," Jane said. "Not yet."

Ione shuddered again, less roughly. "Figures."

"Carlyle wants to keep it a surprise."

Ione pried her hands from her cup, let them rest on the table. "Yeah, well, we'll have to see about that."

Jane again smiled the smile that would bring the world into an alliance with her every inclination. "I'm sure it will all work out."

The spat might have ended there. Jane didn't seem to know that they had quarreled, and Ione, still deeply upset, had nevertheless ridden out her anger. Looking to her father, who stood with two other old men watching the faces flicker on the wall, she snapped at her brother: "Tell Dad it's time to go."

Jane, suddenly taking up her camera, brightened her smile: "You have lovely hands, Ione. Let me just..."

The camera flashed. Ione sat, stunned. The camera flashed again.

Ione sent her chair crashing to the floor as she leaped up, trembling. For a moment she seemed to strain against invisible fetters. Then she wheeled and made for the door.

Jane watched her leave. "What's wrong? Why is she...?"

"She's real touchy about her hands," Troy said. "Embarrassed."

"I didn't know. I'm sorry," Jane said, for some reason addressing me.

I rose: "Excuse me. I have to see to my plates."

So I was in the kitchen when I heard the gunshots – three sharp, carefully spaced pops, unmistakable.

In a dream of dread, I hastened into the dining room. Ione stood in the center of the stillness. Her small pistol was aimed at the film projector, from which no light shone. She seemed utterly forlorn.

I was moving to her, stepping past Jane, when Ione, seeing me, turned toward us, the pistol still in her hand, and Jane with a sudden squeaky gasp stumbled back into me, and, tottering after balance, I tripped over Bill Hardaway's oxygen bottle and fell, hard, onto my back and lay, sprawled and breathless, on the floor as faces gathered above me.

Gasping for air, unable to move, I became aware of the disarray of my clothes, and my face filled with heat. Only Ione Hardaway registered my mortification. She bent and tugged down the hem of my dress, which had bunched up at the middle of my thighs. Then she was gone.

BLUE LAKE didn't see Ione for two weeks.

When she hadn't returned to the ranch by the next morning, chores were seen to, critters tended: the mare foaled, with Troy's assistance, as Jane, fascinated, filmed. No one was alarmed at Ione's absence, for she'd gone off before after rage had brought her to violence – shooting out the front tire of the pickup of a trespassing hunter; quirting a drunken buckaroo who'd left a gate open; dragging out of the saddle a high school boy she'd caught abusing his horse. She was in the desert or the mountains, we assumed at first, refitting herself for human intercourse.

After a couple of days, however, Blue Lake began to talk, from which emerged the realization that over the past few months Ione had been driving in the dark again. Her pickup had been seen at odd hours, it was now recalled, on the highway south, on the highway north, unaccountable comings and goings. Come to think of it, she had some mornings seemed emotionally bruised, some afternoons distant and dazed with weariness. This could only mean, to Blue Lake, that, as before, Ione was looking for love.

Blue Lake takes especial interest in romantic relationships, love lives – sex – and Ione Hardaway had long been a study. She had, Blue Lake was persuaded, at fifteen seduced Carlyle Walden, conceiving and then aborting his child, and only waited for the right moment to satisfy his yearning for her and her own for Walden Ranch. Meanwhile, through high school and for a time after, she connected with men as she chose, now a buckaroo, now a townie, now a self-styled stud, now a shy surprise, but always at her own inclination and never for long. She lasted a year with a NDOT surveyor but seemed not to mind when he departed for Seattle and graduate school. She spent six weeks dancing and driving and camping in the mountains with George Burleigh, newly returned from Desert Storm, but nothing came of it. Then, managing Walden Ranch, she rebuffed the advances of locals, taking up long distance love with a brand inspector from Winnemucca, a banker from Fallon, a rancher from Independence Valley. When this last affair ended, Ione, now thirty, began driving.

Once or twice a month, usually in mid-week, always after the day's work was done, Ione fueled her pickup at the ranch pump and drove off, two hundred or three hundred or five hundred miles, perhaps to return by morning but perhaps not. Her pickup might be seen parked before a Fallon bar or a Tonopah motel or a trailer on the outskirts of Eureka. She herself was espied in Reno, in Las Vegas, in Elko. Once she was ticketed for speeding in Beatty. Once in a bar in Mesquite she broke a man's nose. Once, after a tie-rod snapped and her pickup careened into a Smith Valley ditch, she spent the next seventy-two hours in the Winnebago of a newly retired Air Force colonel. Once she picked up a Sausalito time-share salesman in a Sparks truck stop, circumstances making me a witness.

Those circumstances – a delayed doctor, a long editorial meeting, a raw February wind flinging snow – brought me to the restaurant for a late supper. I had just started my salad when, through the wide archway into the adjoining lounge, I saw Ione Hardaway slide onto a barstool. For a moment I thought to make her aware of my presence, but something in the set of her shoulders and cinch of her waist restrained me. Instead I watched as, shortly, she was approached by a man I took to be a trucker, middle-aged and paunchy, wearing muttonchops and an Oakland Raider cap, who leaned against the bar and spoke with a crooked grin that straightened grimly at Ione's response. Departed, he was succeeded by a young ersatz buckaroo, lean and languorous in stiff jeans and boots and Stetson; after only a few minutes, he sauntered off. Then came a blond block of a man, his blue suit suggesting sales, his smile success, which was quickly confirmed by Ione's laughter. I was waiting for dessert when they prepared to leave. Ione saw me then, spoke to her companion of the moment, and came over.

"You won't try to make it home tonight, will you, Miz Waner?"

I enjoyed her self-possession. "I've already taken a room."

"Me too. Breakfast?"

I couldn't resist: "Will we be three?"

"Not unless you got a mouse in your pocket," she said, and returned to her new friend.

The next morning we ate and talked about the weather – cold, nasty wind, but no snow – and the drive to Blue Lake and the medical question that had brought me to Reno and the urging of the editors at the university press that I write more essays. Ione didn't trouble to account for her own presence until, over coffee, she said: "None of my business, but don't you ever miss it, Miz Waner? Men, I mean."

"From time to time," I said.

"And you never do anything about it?"

"I don't?"

"The stuff about you and Brock Walden, I know that's all hooey."

"Yes," I said, "it certainly is."

"Even if you really want folks to think it isn't."

Then, over a second cup of coffee, although I hadn't asked, Ione explained herself. When she "came in," she went looking for a bull. Otherwise she had no time for a man, no use for one really. Men were fine, better than women, mostly. Some she liked, and she thought well of Cletus Rose, who'd taught her much of what she knew about ranching, and George Burleigh. But except for a phallus, a man had nothing she needed. She didn't want a family, her father and brother occasioned enough affection and fuss, and she wouldn't have children. She had friends – me, Ruby Blascovitch, Irene Walters, a few others – and didn't need a companion. All she went out into the night after, on occasion, was a scratch for an itch.

"Since you brought up his name, " I said, "what ever happened with George?" I had thought them well matched, he the kind of big man, in body and spirit, with whom she could sometimes be small. But after a short fling, she moved on, and he soon married the recently arrived girls' physical education teacher.

"He wanted kids."

"I see." I remembered then a bit of talk that had drifted through Blue Lake a few years after Ione graduated high school: she was unconcerned, word had it, with contraception.

"Yeah," she said. "And then him and Anita – nothing."

She sought sexual relief out of town because she liked the drive in darkness into anonymity, where she could keep her encounters basic, physical and impersonal.

"Last night's beau, to him I'm a woman he ran into on the road, that's all. No expectations. No obligations."

"Just sex."

Ione threatened to smile. "You say that like it's a bad thing, Miz Waner."

"I'm not judging. I've just never been able to have it that casual. Love has always seemed to me unavoidably complex and intimate."

"You mean romantic? Hearts and flowers? Soul mates – that's what you want?"

"No, not that," I said. "But we're men and women, Ione, not brutes."

"Maybe not brutes, but we are animals." An edge sharpened her tone. "Too bad that's not all we are."

Too bad we couldn't just eat, drink, mate – bed strangers rather than involve ourselves with the hopes and fears and demands and desires of a familiar. Which is what Ione Hardaway did, scratching her itch. But finally it was not enough.

Ione drove for nearly ten years. Then she stopped. Why Blue Lake couldn't say. She had been looking for love, in her own tough, angry, isolate fashion, but what she found was, somehow, inadequate. The sex had been good enough, on the whole, but what these couplings satisfied – desire, longing, loneliness – was not what had nagged and shoved and harried her out into the desert night. At least not only these. Ione would satisfy the elemental urge, yes. And she would connect, come together with another. But she was after more.

Sometimes when Ione drove through the night, she didn't stop for love. She just drove – highways and state routes and back roads of gravel and dirt – headlights hollowing a yellow space in the darkness, shadowing the empty desert, catching a flash of nocturnal eye in a mountain ravine, sending a rabbit on an erratic bounding, an owl into a sudden flap. Or she idled up and down the streets of desert towns, past neon enticements and dark doors and the occasional pale light, in the ambient glow of the pickup cab presenting a profile fit for a mountaintop. She didn't want a man these nights. In a different kind of anonymity, she was after, I think now, assurance. She wanted to believe that what she was driving through – the land, the town – would endure, would go on without her. She wished to be sure that the living desert was not, as it sometimes seemed, merely her own imaginative creation, her own work of art, which would turn to dust when she was gone from it.

Perhaps she persuaded herself. Perhaps she simply wearied. In either case, she stopped driving at night. Then came Jane Harmon, the Out There filmmaker whose presence in Blue Lake somehow argued against Ione's hope. She again took to dark desert roads in the dead of night.

Such I sifted from what Ione had to tell me the afternoon in early December when she reappeared at my door. By then, Blue Lake knew that she'd been to Los Angeles. Three days gone, she had called Troy from Cletus Rose's apartment, enquiring after my condition and promising a return; a few days later Carlyle Walden in a letter to Jane confirmed that Ione had spoken to him and to his father. Then we heard nothing. Now she told me that she'd been in Monterey, looking at the ocean, which was never the same and never changing.

"It seems to have done you some good."

She sat across from me, composed, open, at an unusual ease. As the soft light of late afternoon warmed her features, I caught, in small movements of mouth and brow, a glimpse of the girl who had endeared herself to me.

"Strange, sitting around gawking."

But of course she hadn't gawked. She had studied the sea.

"I'll start my apologies with you, Miz Waner. I'm sorry. You could of been hurt bad."

I was surprised. Apology didn't come naturally to Ione. "It was an accident."

"Maybe so. But it was my fault. I know better than to point a gun at people when I don't plan to shoot them."

I looked at her hands, smooth, still, no longer a girl's. "You were upset."

"No excuse."

I assured her that my fall hadn't done any real damage. "And thank you for your concern for my modesty."

"Some of those old yahoos were getting ever so excited."

We were at my kitchen table, over tea and ginger cookies, so we saw Jane Harmon pull her car into her driveway and go into the house.

"She's next. Won't be easy." But Ione's grimace seemed ironic, almost as if, the decision to approach Jane having been made, the apology would be a mere matter of form.

She gently swilled the tea in her cup. "Carlyle says you're helping him with his book about B. W."

"He sent me a note. He had a question about citation."

"Nothing else?"

"No," I said; then I added: "Not yet."

As she so often did, Ione understood. "He's working up to something? You and B. W?"

"I don't know," I said. "Maybe."

Then she said, carefully: "He's different."

I had sensed change, reading his letter. He was learning a lot about his father that he hadn't known. He wasn't quite sure what to think of it all. In his prose I could hear Jane Harmon's voice.

"He always idolized B. W., like a little kid would," Ione said. "And he's still in awe of him, maybe half afraid of him, the way he is of horses. He loves him but it's more complicated now, not... pure, I guess is the word I want. It isn't pure any more."

"Maybe he's developing a sense of irony," I said.

Ione registered my own irony. "Yeah. But I can't talk to him any more, Miz Waner."

"Do you mean you can't order him around any more?"

Her smile came small, rueful. "Maybe. Had my chance and didn't take it?"

I sipped my tea.

"He's dead set on turning the ranch, or some part of it, into some kind of memorial to B. W. Which doesn't make a whole lot of sense, now that he's coming to see the old man isn't all that heroic. But then not much of what's going on lately makes sense." She sighed deeply, as if she'd been holding her breath for a long time. "He's doing it for her."

"For Jane? Maybe," I said. "But she hasn't asked him to, remember."

"I know. But it's like the horses thing. He wants to be able to handle horses well enough that she'll respect him."

I said nothing.

"Strange words to use about Carlyle, huh? Pure. Respect." Ione spoke as if to herself. "Except I always did respect him, Miz Waner. In a way. Even though I never really could quite figure him out. He was hopeless, but he never got mad, never blamed anybody else, never quit. He'd stumble around and the yahoos would hoot but he'd just keep on trying, keep at it."

Ione was telling me something important. "Is that why you didn't... take advantage of his feelings for you?"

"Getting tangled up with me would have ruined him," she said quietly. "He needs somebody better."

"Not better. Different, maybe," I said, thinking that I understood. It wasn't that Ione hadn't cared for Carlyle. It was that she had.

"She – Jane – seems to be doing him some good."

It was the first time I had heard Ione speak the name of her nemesis. "Yes."

"Is she getting ready to dump Troy?"

"I have no idea, Ione."

After a moment she said, again quietly: "The thing is, Miz Waner, she doesn't care."

"Care? About what?"

"Anything. Anybody. Her world has a population of one."

"I see."

"No, I don't think you do," Ione said. "She's bright and nice and friendly, you know, but finally she doesn't care. When she breaks things, when she ruins things and people, she doesn't care because they don't matter. She's a gawker. She looks and she fits everybody into this movie that's running in her head and that's all we mean to her. That's just the way she is."

That was as long a speech, and as deep a consideration of another person, as Ione ever made.

"What people has Jane Harmon ruined?"

"You seen my brother lately? He's scared to death she's about to throw him over. If she does, he'll take it hard. He's never been dumped before. Never denied."

I couldn't tell if she was holding Jane or herself at fault.

"He asked Cletus to check out the job situation for him in L.A."

There was nothing I could say that Ione didn't already know.

After a moment, she smiled: "Cletus says hey."

"He's a gentleman."

"He's that. Gave me his bed for the weekend. Wouldn't have it any other way."

Ione couldn't have heard but perhaps anticipated Blue Lake's muttering at the news that she spent the weekend at the apartment of Cletus Rose. Why, Blue Lake wondered. Why not at Brock Walden's place, with all its rooms, or a motel? Had something been going on there that Blue Lake wasn't unaware of? And for how long? You don't suppose...?

"He has a copy of your book beside his chair."

"I was happy to sign one for him," I said, then shifted the subject. "You didn't have any luck with Brock Walden?"

"Thinks it's a joke. He doesn't care what Carlyle does. Not his affair. He'll be dead."

I hesitated. Then I said: "There was an agreement."

It was a question, one I had never asked, should she take it so.

Ione looked out the window, at the bare treetops, the bare playa. "A place at Walden Ranch, Miz Waner. I'd always be a part of it. That's all I ever wanted. That was the deal."

After a silence I said, "And Carlyle won't honor it?"

"He thinks he is," she said. "He talks some kind of caretaker position, at least. Maybe still run a few cows, or do a dude ranch thing. I'd still be there, have a job, but…" Her gaze went distant. "It wouldn't be the same. Living on a ranch and not ranching would be worse than nothing."

Ione told me then about driving in darkness, about the strange sense she had of being a fixed point in an ever-changing landscape, a still speck of awareness beneath the wheeling of the stars. She felt, she said, two hundred years old in an America born yesterday.

"I know things change, Miz Waner. Time passes, old ways die off. It's always been that way. But it isn't just what's bad or doesn't work or causes problems and pain that goes. I – all I want is to hang onto what's worthwhile."

"And how do you propose to do that?"

She smiled then, the old, ironic, Ione smile. "I'm going to do what you're always telling me to do, Miz Waner. I'm going to be ever so nice to Jane Harmon."

MORE THAN ONE reviewer of *The Last Roundup* linked Brock Walden's obituary with the demise, actual or anticipated, of the Western as a narrative and dramatic genre. His generation was the last to take the form seriously, it was said; tales of men and women on horseback taming the wild in the land and in themselves no longer resonated with American audiences. Like Chivalric Romance and Revenge Tragedy, the Western had outlived its relevance.

Brock Walden, had he heard that he had participated in the death of the story that brought him fame and fortune, surely would have laughed.

December. Daylight paled, and nights grew long. No snow fell, but cold came, and wind, and the desert went hard with frost, the air sour with wood smoke that grayed the day and at night smeared the colored lights on the Christmas tree in Cottonwood Creek Park. The rhythms of life slowed in Blue Lake as the year plodded toward an ending.

At Walden Ranch, work went on as usual – animals were tended, and tools oiled and sharpened, and machines greased and tuned and repaired; fences were mended and irrigation pipes patched and weirs shored up. Ione Hardaway did some of this work, and she oversaw the rest, often in the company of Jane Harmon, for whom, it became evident, Ione was conducting a tutorial on ranching in the high desert. She showed Jane how the ranch worked, who worked it and when and how and with what tools, showed her what it produced and what it contributed to the lives of men and women in and around Blue Lake, Nevada. Riding or driving about Gull Valley, the two women visited places that to Troy Hardaway were names and tales and history but to his sister were the frame and vital organs and fluids of a living body. As Jane shot film and asked questions and took it all in, Ione noted how the range was used, where and how it was improved. Unfurling maps, she traced activities of the seasons, of wet years and dry. She gave Jane a peek into the ranch books, followed the money that flowed into Blue Lake tills. She posed for still photographs, she rode and drove and worked and, in her Dutch oven, she baked for the movie camera and didn't hide her hands. She sat for interviews. With Jane she drank coffee, in her trailer, in her pickup, once or twice in the Wagon Wheel Café, and she talked, quietly, patiently, and she listened, and she was nice.

So far as I could see, Ione wasn't feigning her pleasantness. Though irony now and then nudged up her eyebrow, she seemed actually to enjoy instructing Jane. It was as if in explaining the operation of the ranch, Ione came to a new appreciation of what she had wrought through a labor of twenty-plus years. And despite herself, she came, as so many of us did, to be pleased with Jane's presence.

Blue Lake looked on this development with perplexity. How account for Ione's sudden generosity of spirit? How explain her openness to the woman who represented everything for which Ione had unalloyed scorn? How explain her coffee-drinking coziness with the Out There vamp who threatened the emotional stability of her brother? Ione Hardaway was allowing – no, was assisting – Jane Harmon to make a movie about herself? Why?

"Because, Miz Waner," Ione had told me the day of her return, "a story about me has to be a story about the ranch. To tell it, she'll have to see the ranch the way we do."

"You want to make Jane into an advocate for ranching in the high desert?"

"Sounds pretty farfetched when you put it that way, I admit, but that's the idea. If I can get her to see, really see – well, she'll have to change her mind."

"And your ultimate goal is…?"

"If she changes her mind, she won't want the ranch broken up, which is what a refuge or memorial would do. And Carlyle got the idea from her, didn't he? Maybe her movie will show him how that isn't a great idea."

Such was her hope. And such was Jane's enthusiastic response to Ione's tutelage that Ione could sometimes allow herself to believe that her efforts would achieve success.

She, who knew that Jane didn't care, should have known better.

But like many of us, Ione fell victim to Jane's innocent, solipsistic charm. She admired Jane's riding and approved of her handling of the horse, never suspecting that, reins or curry brush in hand, Jane experienced a pleasure nearly as sensual as sex. Ione was surprised too by Jane's willingness, when called on, to lend a hand, to wield a tool, to get her face dirty – she wasn't merely a gawker. She found Jane's questions, as the days passed, increasingly pertinent, so she could begin to think that Jane actually got it. She ceased scoffing at Jane's blind smiling certitude that all would arrange itself in accordance with her wishes. Ione began to feel that maybe, somehow, it might.

At the same time, Ione's attention wedged wider the split between Jane and Troy. The lovers saw little of each other in daylight, for he could hardly slip off to meet her when she was in the company of his boss. When, evenings, he came to town, he found Jane at work and not especially interested in his company.

All this took its toll. Troy Hardaway was not, as his sister had said, ruined, but he was drained, which I perceived the day I met him coming out of Merritt's Jewelry store. He held up a small, beautifully wrapped box that contained, he said, Nevada turquoise and silver, and he seemed to ask me for assurance that his gift would be properly appreciated. His smile was nearly a grimace to which the small scar on his cheekbone was a pale accent. He seemed thinner, anxious, no longer young.

Jane, meanwhile, was thrilled by Ione's attention.

"I'm just thrilled, Miz Waner," she said to me one morning. She was waiting for Ione; the two were going to look at captured mustangs at the BLM pens in Paradise Valley. Ione wanted to improve the ranch stock and hoped to find a mare of satisfactory size and agility and configuration. "I've never had a friend like Ione."

"I'm glad that the two of you are finally getting along," I replied.

"She doesn't have many close friends, does she? That makes me feel really... privileged. Even though – she doesn't talk much about herself, about her personal life, but I admire the way she does without... relationships. I wish I could. She just says she's too busy, but I know there must be more to it than that."

Her inflection angled for an explanation, but I didn't comment.

"Do you know why she's alone, Miz Waner?"

"Ione lives as she chooses, Jane. Her reasons are her own and none of my business."

"Yes, yes," Jane waved away my implicit criticism. "But she's so central to everything Out Here, the ranch, Blue Lake – her personal life really is more than just... personal."

Her intensity alerted me. "What have you heard?"

"That story about her and Carlyle – it's true, Miz Waner. He says when he was a teenager, and for a long time after that, he was in love with Ione, but after they... were together that one time, she ignored him."

"That should be the end of it, then, shouldn't it?"

"But it isn't. Everybody knows about all the boyfriends she's had since, and the… other men. People wonder if back then she might have been with someone else, too. Now everyone is talking about her spending the weekend with that man, Brock Walden's body-guard or stand-in or gofer or whatever he is, Cletus Rose – "

"That's ridiculous." I felt my angry flush. "Cletus Rose is Ione's friend. Years ago he was her mentor, showing her what her father didn't know about ranching. His affection for her has always been avuncular. He's a good man, and a gentleman."

"But back then he was a sort of a wild man?"

"When he was young and drank, he got wild, yes. He hasn't had a drink in fifty years." Then I made myself clear. "Cletus Rose is also my friend, Jane, and this particular bit of Blue Lake gossip I find deeply offensive. As would Ione. If you value your new friendship with her, you won't not repeat this slander."

"I see," she said. But of course she didn't see at all.

Jane and Ione went off that day to film captured mustangs and to look for a suitable mare. The next morning Jane showed me pictures of a handsome gray. "Ione thinks she has Morgan blood. She's really wild and skittish, though. Ione talked about having her dad work to settle her down a little."

I was preparing clothes for my annual month-long visit in Southern California, which Jane took as occasion to announce her plan to return to Los Angeles over Christmas and New Year's. She suggested that we meet for dinner there, expressing an eagerness to meet Eleanor Broadhurst. Then she asked if I would introduce her to Cletus Rose – they hadn't actually met formally that day at the ranch. At my hesitation, she gushed: "Don't worry, Miz Waner. Ione says he's a gentle man, like you did. That's good enough for me."

The next evening Jane's knock interrupted my packing. Over tea she told me that Troy would dine with us in L.A. "He needs a vaca-tion, he says. And I'll be able to introduce him to people I know, people who can help him. I think he'll be surprised at the opportu-nities there."

Her smile was bright enough, but it argued with the doubt that shadowed her gaze.

I had been looking forward to a stay in Southern California. The mere sight of Eleanor Broadhurst, of the glint in her blue eyes and the crooked slant of her grin, had for decades raised my spirits. This year, however, over the first hours after my arrival, I grew concerned. Eleanor had always been thin, but she now seemed shrunken, wizened and bony and frail. On her balcony, smoking a Virginia Slim, she stilled into uncharacteristic contemplation. Moving, she was stiff, wheezy, and slow. Her mind, however, was still agile, her wit quick, and her company bracing, so that what I had begun to fear I was finally able to put out of my mind.

In the days before Christmas we shopped leisurely, saw *Oklahoma!* at a community theatre, and enjoyed a string quartet performing Mozart; we dined at decent restaurants near her West Hollywood condo or nibbled at cheeses and vegetables at her dining room table; and, as always over the first days of our get-togethers, we talked of Blue Lake and the years we had shared there, of old friends gone and husbands dead nearly forty years. Christmas Eve we spent with her eldest son and his family, who for years had made me one of them. Christmas Day we worshiped at the nearby Episcopal church, where, singing familiar hymns, I felt a stiffness slide from my spine. I'd become involved, deeply, in the goings-on of Jane and Ione and the others, and I was happy now to be away from the blasts of feeling, free from the snarl of gossip and speculation. For a few days, at least, I could relax.

Eleanor knew generally of Jane's doings in Nevada, but she made no inquiries, her lack of interest serving to further distance me from Blue Lake, as did the day I spent at the beach with an old friend. What in the empty desert seemed large and urgent issues became in the busy city beside the expansive sea of little moment, a stirring in small lives.

Jane called three days after Christmas to tell me she'd made dinner reservations for the following evening. She offered neither a reason nor an apology for the short notice, but with her tone she turned a proposal into a pleading. Eleanor, when I named the restaurant that Jane had chosen, raised a brow. "I'll run right out and buy something to be seen in."

"It's fashionable?"

Eleanor grinned. "Let's say that it has aspirations, as does its clientele."

The next dawn brought rain, which till mid-morning fell fine and soft but by sundown was battering the streets and filling the gutters. Eleanor and I were late getting to the restaurant, where in a dim hush, at subtly lighted tables, diners offered attitudes, posing. All but Troy Hardaway, who at our arrival rose to his feet like an old man, his smile a clenching as if against pain.

After introductions, Jane gushed. "I'm so glad we could do this. Being with you, Miz Waner, here in Los Angeles, makes my experience in Nevada so much more... authentic."

In his western-cut suit and bolo tie, Troy, an authentic Out Here Nevada buckaroo, seemed an oater extra wandered onto the wrong set. As he took up his glass of beer, his gaze, falling on me, threatened to splinter.

After we ordered, Jane began to chatter. She would meet with the grant committee next week, they were already enthusiastic about her new focus on Ione Hardaway and Walden Ranch, she was preparing a presentation and portfolio that would surely earn their approval and might even reopen their wallets. She was especially happy to meet Mrs. Broadhurst, who was still remembered in Blue Lake: the widow of an Episcopalian vicar must have wonderful stories to tell. As for stories, she and Troy had been to Brock Walden's Malibu ranch, hoping to find the old man more helpful – Carlyle said that B. W. was medicating himself with bourbon and marijuana, which encouraged him to rambling and vivid tales of his wild, wicked ways – but he was asleep when they arrived, so Carlyle took them to see Cletus Rose, Miz Waner wouldn't have to do that now, although Jane couldn't quite see what was so special about a beat-up old cowboy who lived with a bunch of books over a garage and who hardly said a word, let alone told stories, although from what she'd heard he must have a lot to tell.

"You have no idea," Eleanor murmured. When she dared meet my frown, she smiled impishly.

Well, anyway, Jane went on, otherwise she and Troy had lunched and dined and networked – her friends loved Troy, he was so handsome and smart and funny and authentic. His anecdotes about cows and horses and his sister charmed everybody, they were so... authentic. Everybody admired the authentic Nevada turquoise and silver earrings he'd bought her, and they gave him lots of names of people to talk to and places to inquire at, agreeing that he could easily find a suitable position if he really wanted one.

Troy listened as if Jane spoke of someone he couldn't quite place. His fingers found the scar on his cheekbone. He signaled the waiter for another beer. As I had on the street in Blue Lake, I sensed him spent.

When Eleanor asked him how he liked Los Angeles, his humor was forced: "Quite a town. Everybody's rich and nobody works. Magic."

Jane frowned. "Troy thinks that if you aren't using a tool you can't be working."

He rubbed his scar. "Can't get much work done with a drink in your hand, nitwitting."

"It's called networking," Jane said severely, quietly, as if to herself.

"Saloons serve ambience with their beer," he said, raising his glass. "Lets them charge eighteen dollars for a Bud."

Jane now ignored him.

We ate. The silence deepened. At last Eleanor ended it by asking after Troy's father.

"He's hanging on. Barely. Ione's got him working with an adopted mustang mare, but I don't know how much he'll be able to get done."

"And Ione?"

"Same as always. She – " He gave her what he could manage of a smile. "You hear about the Thanksgiving Day Film Projector Murder?"

I had told her, which Eleanor now cleverly forbore from mentioning.

He ordered another beer and then told a tale, beginning not with Thanksgiving dinner at the Blue Lake Community Center but with the meeting of Jane and Ione in the ditch outside of town months earlier. Something of his old, easy-going good humor returned as he recounted The Hundred Dollar Dance and the picnic in the park, Jane's departure and return, their failed plot to enlist Ione in Jane's cause, the confrontation in my kitchen, his dodging his sister in order to see Jane. He made light of the fisticuffs on the dance floor and didn't mention the tracks in the snow. He spoke warmly of old faces on the wall and proudly of Jane's triumph. Then he described her spat with Ione, Ione's reaction to having her hands photographed, Ione's rage and outlandish revenge.

Eleanor listened with delight, as did I. Even Jane seemed to take pleasure from his telling, with its tall-tale timing and emphases and elaborations. She seemed, at least as long as he spoke, to take pleasure in Troy himself. At the same time, we women understood that this was not merely buckaroo raconteurship. It was lovemaking, compelled by a throat-tightening desperation. Now, finished with his tale, his devotions, his wooing, Troy rested anxious eyes on Jane, who looked at him and looked away.

"It's too bad Ione and your dad couldn't come down here with you," Eleanor proposed.

For a long moment, Troy continued to look at Jane. Then, finally, he turned from her. "Somebody's got to feed the cows," he said. "If it keeps snowing, it's gonna be me."

The rain outside was part of a large storm that had brought heavy snow to Nevada, he told us. If it kept up, as was forecast, he'd have to go home and help out. He was surprised Ione hadn't called him back already.

Jane looked pained, but not at the prospect of his departure. Rather, it seemed as if Troy's stay constituted an ordeal she was suffering through, this dinner with Eleanor and me providing brief relief from his unrelenting presence.

Troy casually took up the bill when it came, then stiffened in shock. He pretended to study it as he regained his composure.

"May I?" I gently slid it from his grip. "Merry Christmas, all."

When we came to leave the restaurant, after an exchange of phatic phrases with Eleanor, Jane turned to me. "I'm glad we could do this, Miz Waner. It's so nice to see you in my world."

"When are you going back to Blue Lake?"

"I – it sort of depends."

She avoided my eyes, and Troy's. I didn't enquire further.

Saying goodbye to Troy, I recognized that he was not wholly sober. "You'll let Jane drive, won't you?"

"I'm fine, Miz Waner," he said.

"Please, Troy. For my sake."

He looked at me, suddenly lost. Then he took out his truck keys and handed them to Jane. His smile was an attempt at gallantry in a language he could no longer speak.

Impulsively I embraced him. "If I don't see you again, have a safe trip home."

I didn't know if he heard what I understood myself to be saying to him.

Eleanor and I drove back to her condo in silence. There, settled over a glass of wine, as the rain lashed her balcony window, she grinned: "Here's to authenticity."

I smiled.

Eleanor's grin faded. "She's pretty much sucked all the fluids out of him, hasn't she? "

I found myself, surprisingly, rising to Jane's defense. "She didn't ask him to fall in love with her."

"Of course she did, Winnefred. She asks everyone to fall in love with her."

I was watching the Weather Channel the next afternoon when Jane called to pass on Troy's goodbyes. He had returned to Nevada, with what understanding between Jane and himself she didn't say. She made no mention of when she might herself return.

Snow fell in Nevada that day, and the next. In and around Blue Lake, traffic slowed, finally ceasing as county plows proved too few to keep roads passable, and only snowmobiles like loud mutant bugs moved over the land. Several bunches of cattle were known to be in jeopardy, and authorities expressed concern for deer and elk herds. Then, on the last day of the year, the clouds broke, but the blue sky merely teased: the following morning brought more snow and fierce winds and much lower temperatures. The blow lasted three days, and high desert creatures came to misery. Deer and antelope populations were ravaged. Mustangs died beside iced-over waterholes. Cattle froze in sight of ranch houses. At Walden Ranch, men and a woman worked into bleary, flesh-quivering fatigue, saving what they could.

In Los Angeles, after a day's torrent flooded ravines and sent a few houses sliding down hillsides, the rain subsided to showers and fog; eventually the overcast thinned and lifted and fell apart, and the storm was over.

In Nevada, finally, all was white and still.

I didn't hear from Jane. When a call finally came, it was Carlyle Walden inviting me to lunch at Malibu. Cletus Rose would be happy to pick me up. Although I knew the way to the ranch, I agreed to be conveyed.

We were nearly there when he spoke. "Seem to be making a habit of this."

I smiled. Cletus and I had come to know one another in similar circumstances some thirty-five years earlier. "Will people talk?"

"Good chance of it."

I touched his forearm. "Let them."

Brock Walden's Malibu ranch was little more than a pair of pastures and a stable set in acres of gullies choked with chaparral. At the house, an unattractive sprawl of fifties brick set off from a huge garage, Carlyle Walden awaited us at the front door. When Cletus declined an invitation to lunch, as we knew he would, and, with a tip of his hat, hobbled off toward his garage apartment, Carlyle escorted me into a dining room with rough adobe walls and exposed beams and beautiful rugs, where a large mahogany table was set intimately for two.

Over soup we talked about his healed foot, about Evelyn Broadhurst's health, and about the storm. Nevada was digging out, he said. Stock losses at Walden Ranch had been minimal, mostly because of the unflagging effort of Ione Hardaway. Here the rain had most days not been heavy enough to deter him and Jane from riding into the Malibu hills.

"I know she enjoys being on horseback," I said.

"As I have learned to do," he replied. "I've finally come to terms with equines. They're powerful brutes, and they can be malicious and devious, but, as Cletus observes, I'm more intelligent than they are. Usually."

His wry smile bespoke an incipient assurance. Carlyle was not actually changing, I thought – he was, finally, developing. His diffidence shaded into modesty; his cautious courtesy and elevated diction were tinted with the hues of play. Still serious of mien and tone, he seemed not to take himself quite so seriously.

He then ventured an account of Cletus Rose's first lesson in handling horses. At a San Diego stud farm, they had watched a thoroughbred stallion cover a mare. The coupling was awful in its violence, the huge ugly phallus like a weapon of assault. Hooves thudded, teeth flashed, both animals screaming with what seemed fury as the human handlers, all caution and alertness and quick reactions, guided the mating. Carlyle's appreciation of their skill turned to wonder when he heard stories of what horses had done to men. Limbs had been lost to stallions' teeth. Lives had been lost under stallions' hooves.

"An experience like that could wipe out a person's interest in horses altogether," I said.

"Cletus wanted me to see that fear is natural, even necessary. But it's where one begins with beasts, not where one ends. It didn't purge my interest in horses, but it did nearly finish my interest in sex."

It took me a moment to understand that Carlyle Walden had actually made a joke.

He spoke then, as we ate crab salad, of his father, whose imminent death caused the son no distress. "He's lived a full life. He looks upon death without trepidation."

But Brock Walden wouldn't die just yet. He had good days, when he went out to play cards or, as today, to eat with his pals. Other days, not so good, he lazed about the house, sipping bourbon and sometimes smoking hash and telling stories. The bad days, infrequent, he suffered coughing attacks, shortness of breath, and chest pains, drifted in and out of drugged dozes, and cried out in dreams.

On occasion he didn't know who or where he was. He could continue like this for some time, the doctor said.

"I'm sorry, Carlyle," I said.

"Thank you," he said, "but I'm not in need of sympathy. What I do hope to get from you, Mrs. Waner, is your indulgence. I have a theory."

"About your father?

"He's done bad things, but he's not a bad man."

His tone had shifted. His pause was a preamble.

"I've received letters, many letters, Mrs. Waner, that say he's violent and cruel, that he has a total disregard for the feelings and persons and careers of other people. He's done terrible things. He doesn't deny any of it. In fact, he tells me scandalous stories, and he laughs at my shock. He wants everyone to be shocked, which is the reason he's cooperating with me on the biography. He wants the world to know that he doesn't give a damn about it."

His expression had grown glum. As he had with horses, he was coming to terms with his father — at what cost to himself I couldn't tell.

"Except…"

I expected then a mitigating list of Brock Walden's virtues, of his kindnesses and unaccountable charities and good works, his unsolicited favors. What came was quite different.

"He's angry, Mrs. Waner. He's been angry all his life."

I thought that might be true.

"I've been rereading accounts of the exploits of scouts and trappers, the mountain men who blazed the trail across the continent. What they did in the West was noble, but they, as men, weren't. They were mean, ignorant, and vicious. They dressed in animal skins, they bred like animals, they fought like animals, biting and gouging over a fur or a jug of whisky or a woman. They weren't Jeremiah Johnson, they were the miners in *Ride The High Country* or the ranch hands in *Shane*."

His references, I thought, came from Jane Harmon.

"Crevecouer and Jefferson and Tocqueville and Turner all make the same point. The frontier, the West was a safety valve, a violent, dangerous place to which society shunted violent, dangerous men. Men found unfit for civilized intercourse."

Carlyle paused. I waited as he chose language.

"My father believes that he was found unfit for 'decent society'."

"That's why he's angry? Because he was rejected?" I was deeply dubious.

"No. His anger comes from his own conviction that he deserved to be cast out."

This was either the keenest of insights or sheer nonsense. Perhaps my ambivalence registered in my expression.

"I'm not trying to excuse him, Mrs. Waner," Carlyle said. "I know that none of this matters to the people he injured. I'm only offering an accounting."

That he would attempt such an accounting said much about Carlyle himself.

He elaborated on his theory over a fruity dessert. He had the settling of the West a heroic adventure, even if undertaken mostly by thugs. He had his father reenacting the story, as a youth working his way across the continent, as a Marine in the jungles of the South Pacific, and as an actor in film after film ringing subtle changes on an epic tune. All the while, Carlyle proposed, be he Walter Broekenworth or Brock Walden, he felt himself unwanted, unacceptable, stained, Cain wandering in exile. His life had been one long combat – battles and depredations – with the world that would not have him.

He offered one last example from films. "He's Ringo, in *Stagecoach*, with his prostitute girlfriend driven off by the town biddies. Except my father didn't have a woman to depend on."

"He had hookers galore," I said dryly. "Apparently none met his specifications."

Carlyle smiled. I was impressed. He would not have smiled even three months before.

He continued to talk, mostly, I suspected, because I continued to listen. I had the feeling that no one, not even Jane Harmon, had heard all that Carlyle had to say.

Now he explained how a memorial to his father would honor too those early stockmen, of the sort Brock Walden had played on television, whose efforts were indispensable in establishing America as a continental nation. Again he cited *Shane*. "Their time was past long ago, the ranchers. But even though the Rykers were on the wrong side of history, history would have taken a very different turn without them."

"Ione once argued in a sophomore English essay that Shane fought on the wrong side."

"Ione, yes," he said, and finally, over coffee, we spoke of her. Whatever he decided to do with the property, she would be in charge. She would always have a home at the Rocking W. He could not fathom her resistance.

"Maybe Cletus Rose could explain it for you," I proposed

"Cletus," he repeated. "When Ione drove in a month ago, we offered our hospitality. She chose to stay with Cletus, over the garage, although he had to give up his bed."

Carlyle had taken Ione's choice as a rejection, from which he yet smarted. I wondered if he was still pained by her rejection of him nearly thirty years earlier.

"I suppose Cletus could explain that as well," I said.

"The Out Here ethos? Independence?" He frowned. "The kind of pride that keeps Cletus from living in the house with us?"

It wasn't independence, or at least not that alone. But it was pride.

We lingered over coffee, Carlyle discussing the various ideas he was researching, with the help of Jane Harmon. "She knows people in the not-for-profit sector, and they've given me good counsel about tax write-offs and other matters. She's remarkable, isn't she, Mrs. Waner."

I remembered the occasion on which he had said exactly that about Ione Hardaway.

Something of his old uncertainty rose into his voice then as he spoke of Jane, as if his esteem might be a presumption. He enjoyed her physical grace, admired her vision and talent, and envied her spontaneity, her willingness to respond immediately if not always wisely to life. He recognized, he said, that no man could ever be more than a minor moon in orbit around her. "She's an artist. Her art will always take precedence over the needs of those of us without gifts."

"That's Romantic claptrap, Carlyle," I said. "Artists aren't morally privileged. They aren't excused from basic human obligations."

He smiled his new smile. "I don't want to excuse Jane, Mrs. Waner, only explain her."

"Next you'll be telling me that you're in love with her."

"Maybe I am," he said. He was suddenly somber. "But I won't tell you so, or her, not while she's in another relationship."

"That's an extremely delicate scruple, Carlyle," I said.

"But such as it is," he smiled again, "mine own."

On that note our meal and my visit ended. While I freshened up, Cletus Rose returned. Soon we were in heavy traffic, talking of what Cletus had been able to teach Carlyle about horses. He'd never be much more than competent as a working buckaroo, Cletus allowed, but he now knew to use his fear, how to establish and maintain control. Then Cletus asked after Ione. When I had explained what she was trying to do with Jane, he said. "Jane'll never get it."

I nodded. "But she'll get Carlyle, if she wants him."

"Wouldn't be the worst thing could happen to him."

I smiled. "He seems to know how their relationship must work – he spoke of being a small satellite in orbit around her."

After a moment he said: "Learned that from me too."

Shortly before I returned to Blue Lake, I received a call from Jane. She had clothing that Troy had left at her apartment, which I agreed to take back with me. Soon she was at Eleanor's door, two shirts in a plastic laundry cover dangling from her finger. She was rushed but had time for a quick cup of tea.

She was hardly inside when, as if fulfilling an obligation, she spoke of Troy. Her friends had found him wonderfully authentic, she repeated. Everyone liked him, especially her women friends. Everyone was eager to help him. There were excellent opportunities for him here, good jobs he could have, but he'd gone stubborn. He'd been willing to check out possibilities, at first, until he decided that he hated Southern California. It was crowded and frenzied, ugly and malodorous, shoddy and expensive, full of affected, artificial idiots.

"This can all be a bit overwhelming to us Out Here types," I said.

"Oh, I know. And he's right — I mean, all that's so obvious it's a cliché, isn't it?" Jane said. "But even so, it's my world, Miz Waner. He can't accept that. He thinks because I'm an artist I can live anywhere. But I need to maintain contacts, and I need stimulation, the company of creative people. I've enjoyed Blue Lake, but I could no more live there permanently than I could on Mars."

Conviction buttressed her claim, which offered her an out. Her affair with Troy Hardaway, I thought, was over.

Then, as if now done with an unpleasant duty, she smiled her smile. The foundation people were delighted with her portfolio and the footage she'd shown them of Ione.

"She's been wonderful, Miz Waner. And this spring, I'll be able to shoot during calving, and then at the fall gather. Carlyle is providing clips from Brock Walden's movies and the television show, and he may even write a narration. It's all... coming together."

"You've found a story, then?"

"No, not exactly. Not yet. But it's there. I — Brock Walden, his films and life and ranch will provide structure and background and some of the recurring images. I've had a chance to talk to him, and he was charming. He's... complicated, sort of sophisticated and primitive at the same time?"

Carlyle had shown her some of the letters he'd received, and he'd run past her at least part of his theory.

"My refuge idea, it's coming to seem... inspired. It turns out the whole West was a refuge, from civilization. That explains so much, doesn't it? Men without women, on the frontier or in war or in gangs, they live like animals. That's what they do. That's what they are."

I wasn't sure that that explained anything, but I didn't say so.

"And then women come along and ruin everything. And get blamed. We're all Eve."

It was an old argument, one I was not prepared to contest. I thought of Shane, of wedding dresses and begonias blooming in pots on windowsills.

But Jane added a new twist. "Until Ione Hardaway avenged us all."

IN A GOOD POEM, image and idea and emotion meet in a moment of language, illuminating life. But in a story, I am discovering, ideas secret themselves behind actions, words order emotions, and narration reduces and alters experience. So much does not get told. What was is immersed and diluted in what might have been.

Writing this story, I would account for my unease, my sense of loss at the passing not of a man but of an attitude toward life, as well as my uncertainty about what happened when so many urges and injuries came together and Brock Walden died in the ranch yard of the Rocking W.

I feel in what I have written the weight of omissions, the sway from veering around gaps, and the uneven pressures of the imprecisely said.

I can't recreate the past. I can only remember and gesture.

I didn't see Jane again until the day of Bill Hardaway's funeral.

Troy found his father bent into awkward angles on the barn floor, beneath him the now empty oxygen canister, strewn about him the oats intended for Tango and Virgie. The horses, disturbed by death, burred and thumped nervously. After calming them with strokings and soft words, Troy went into the house and called his sister.

Somewhat later, Ione neared tears when she discovered hanging on the old man's bedroom door the freshly laundered twill slacks and pearl-buttoned shirt he was to have worn to the upcoming Valentine's Day dance at the Community Center. From a desk drawer she retrieved a will copied out in his fastidious hand: he wished to be buried beside his wife in the family plot, a square of desert, fenced with leaning wrought iron, on a knoll overlooking the cluttered ranch yard and slumped buildings that had once belonged to the Hardaways.

The next day Troy guided a backhoe around shade-held patches of snow to the gravesite. The frozen earth gave before the teeth of the machine, so that soon the desert bore the darkness of dirt and hole. He finished the grave by hand, in shirtsleeves working up a sweat as the chill February sunlight flashed on his shovel.

"I'd of hired it done, but Troy claimed the job," Ione told me. "Dug like there was something down there he wanted to get at and kill."

I poured her more tea.

"I admit I got an ache when I found those dancing duds. Dude to the end." She offered a small smile. "But Dad and Troy – they were close, two of a kind, some ways. I was always the odd one out."

"Your father loved you dearly, Ione," I said.

She seemed not to have heard me. "Dad's going wasn't the only thing Troy was working off with that shovel."

By then Blue Lake knew that Jane Harmon and Troy Hardaway were no longer a couple. She had sent him a letter. He had hastened to Southern California, returning three days later exhausted and alone.

"He's unhappy, yes," I said.

"More'n that," she said. "Something's gone out of him."

Blue Lake had noticed that Troy Hardaway was moody these days, anxious and grim; he drank more, although never to inebriation; he angered more easily and often; he drove faster, except when cruising at night past Jane's dark house, afflicting himself with her absence. Because he had Loved and Lost, Blue Lake pronounced. But he'd get over it. Already book was being made as to which local body would console him.

Ione had come to discuss the funeral. There would be no service – Bill Hardaway hadn't been churchy – but Blue Lake must have its obsequies, so the next day, following a viewing at the mortuary, she and Troy and pallbearers would see the body into the ground. After the interment, Blue Lake was invited to the Community Center for rituals of refreshment and sentiment.

"Irene and Ruby will take down the decorations for tonight's dance," she said. "But tomorrow folks are bringing food. It needs coordinating, so we don't end up with ten tables of lime jello and carrot-shavings salad."

"I'll be happy to organize the effort," I volunteered.

I thought she might leave then – she wanted to get back to the Rocking W, where a heifer was having difficulty delivering a calf – but instead, after a moment's distraction, she spoke in a different tone.

"Dad hardly had enough to warrant a will. Most stuff goes to the Community Center. He left buckles and such, and his rifles and good tack, to Troy, the ten percent of Walden Ranch to me." She shifted in her chair, as away from a soreness. "The only horse he still had was Virgie. He gave her to Jane Harmon."

I was not greatly surprised.

"What'll she do with a horse?" It was less a question than a challenge.

"I don't know, but I'm sure she'll see that she's looked after properly."

"You bet she will," Ione said with something of her old anger. "She'll dump her on Troy. And he'll jump at the chance to prolong his misery."

Troy would feed and exercise and groom the horse, she meant, in order to maintain contact with Jane, so that he might continue to suffer hope.

"He'll get past this, Ione," I said. "He'll tough it out."

"Legally, the Hardaway graveyard is part of the Walden Ranch. When I called down to get an okay to bury Dad, B. W. was out somewhere, so I talked to Carlyle." I thought that she had changed the subject, until she added tonelessly, "Jane was there."

I had heard nothing from Jane. Had I not known that her equipment and much of the film and photographs she'd shot for her project were still in Blue Lake, I might have doubted her return.

"They're collaborating, she told me."

"I'll bet they are."

"Be nice, now."

Ione took up her gloves. "Jane owning Virgie. The will isn't witnessed or recorded, Miz Waner. Nobody's even seen it. I'm the only one who knows about it."

I knew then what she wanted. I couldn't give it to her.

"You'll do what's right, Ione. You always do, when it matters."

"No," she said with a small smile, "not always."

That Valentine's Day evening at the Blue Lake Community Center, friends of Bill Hardaway danced. At the Rocking W, Ione soothed a distressed heifer carrying a large calf. In town, Troy, as his sister once had, drove dark streets. At my kitchen table, I plied my pen.

I also kept a kind of watch. Since Thanksgiving I had, in the still of the night, looking up from my work, looked down. The house below seemed empty; the thinning snow beneath the windows remained smooth. The police reported no unusual activity in the neighborhood, and I noticed no increase in traffic. The only vehicle creeping along the street at a pace to reconnoiter was Troy Hardaway's pickup. I thought, once or twice, that I detected movement, or saw shadows where none had been before, but in the late hour, weary from words, I could be sure of little.

But I was sure when, near the end of that Valentine's Day, as I washed my cup and saucer, I saw Jane Harmon's car pull into her driveway.

The next morning, Troy Hardaway's pickup was parked outside Jane's house. I didn't realize that Troy was in the cab until, the day well begun, he emerged stiffly and, stretching the cramp from his body, approached her door. It opened immediately to his knock, and he disappeared inside. Breakfasting on coffee and a bun, I pondered these events. Then I made my ablutions and dressed for the day's solemn assemblies, by which time Troy's pickup was gone.

I was on the telephone, scheduling the delivery of a cheese platter, when Jane appeared. She wore beige silk under the rich black wool of her pantsuit jacket – an Out There outfit I suspected she had purchased for the occasion. She looked fresh, even after the previous day's long late drive, full of energy and wonderfully alive.

She had a rent check and an apology for its tardiness. She couldn't stay to chat, for she was off to the visitation, and then the burial, at which she was going to take both still and moving pictures. "It's something I can do for Troy and Ione."

"Ione approved?"

"Of course." She smiled her smile. "I mean, Troy did, and how could she object? It's for her, for them."

I though she might offer an account of her meeting with Troy. Had they entered into a new understanding? Or had she simply found a way to make use of his pain?

She perceived, if she misconstrued, my concern: "Don't worry, Miz Waner. I'll be... discreet."

She might have said more but for the airplane. We fell silent as the engine noise swelled to deafening, its reverberations battering the rock wall behind the house, setting my shelved crockery into a shaking. The plane passed overhead, engine straining as it climbed to avoid the cliff; then the air smoothed and the sound grew small and soft and was gone.

"He's half dead. How can he fly a plane like that?" Jane frowned. "He's come for the funeral. Were they close, he and Bill Hardaway?"

"Not that I know of."

"Then why...?"

I had no answer to that question.

Neither had Blue Lake. That was ol' B. W. for you, apt to do what-ever came to mind. Hadn't been to a funeral Out Here since Henry Waner drove off a cliff. Before that it was Jim Brenner blowing his brains out. Remember that, and the talk about B.W. and Brenner's wife? Course there was that old business with Ione and Carlyle — Bill got the best of B. W. in that, didn't he? — but that couldn't have anything to do with his showing up now, could it? Anyhow, B. W. never needed a reason — he was like one of them old Greek gods, swooping down from the mountaintop on a whim or a letch.

Such was the murmuring at the Community Center. I had stopped only briefly at the funeral home, where Bill Hardaway, laid out, looked like a poor effigy done in wax. Then I hastened to oversee the arrival of foods that began long before the hearse led the small cortege off to the Hardaway Place. Many of those who had viewed the body came to the Center, where they helped or idled or gossiped, admired the flowers and wreaths, picked and sipped at what was still being spread out on the tables, and awaited the family. They awaited too Brock Walden.

Out in the desert, six old men dug their boot heels into a low hillside, cautiously seeking footing as they balanced a casket. Another older man pulled a wheelchair up the slope, while two younger supported the weight and struggle up of a large, angry cripple. A pair of mourners waited at the grave. All gathered under the late morning sun, and the pallbearers maneuvered the casket onto the cloth bands stretched over the dark hole, and hats were doffed, heads bowed, and the cloth bands slowly unwound, and the long box settled into the earth. No one had spoken. Now Ione offered a word and her hand to each of the pallbearers, old friends of her father's, and to Brock Walden and Carlyle Walden and Cletus Rose and George Burleigh. All made their way down to their parked vehicles.

Many months later, Blue Lake would be moved by what Jane Harmon, cropping and cutting and arranging, had made of this, seeing in her film what she had taken in that cold February day in the desert.

Nevada in winter, sage and snow and bare earth. Incoherent tracks frozen into the ranch yard mud. Bricks fallen from the house chimney, and curtains hanging limply behind smeared glass, and a nail pulling out from the warp of a windowsill, and paint cracked and flaked to bare wood. Stacks of lumber and hay gone to waste and jumbles of machinery to ruin. The contours of sag and bow and collapse, the colors of rust and rot. Old men laboring under the dead weight of a friend, and the gleam of sunlight on the wheelchair, and the freshly dug darkness in the earth, and the faces like the land, and the bared heads bowed in anticipation of the final descent. Images before which Blue Lake could only silently nod.

An hour later, when the Walden Ranch van pulled up outside the Community Center, inside Blue Lake voices tightened with excitement. On his visits to the ranch, Brock Walden rarely came to town anymore, and he had long ceased attending functions, so that many now gathered had not seen him for several years. When he rolled through the door, aged and ill – his face, pouched and cut and blotched, looked like the rough splashing of an Expressionist brush – some were uncertain that they were seeing him yet. Then he laughed, and Blue Lake fit the sound to memories and found under the puffed and mottled flesh familiar configurations. Men and women pressed around him.

Carlyle, nudged aside, caught my glance, came over, and accepted coffee. He described the interment. "Out Here minimalism."

"That would be Ione's way," I said.

"Ione – one never knows quite what she really feels." He seemed for a moment to hope that I might explain her to him. Then he smiled. "Bill was such a showman, with his trick horses and satin shirts, he might have wished for more ostentation. A last Grand Parade of some sort."

"A moment of desert silence ought to do for each of us," I said.

He looked at his father, whose grin radiated affability. A line of old men and women, knotted and gnarled, wound around the room to his wheelchair as if he were the bereaved, receiving. "He doesn't want even that. We'll spread his ashes on the ranch."

"I wouldn't have thought he cared what you did with his ashes," I said.

"He doesn't care, Mrs. Waner. But I do."

"As with the ranch itself? "

"Yes." He fell silent, watching his father. Then he said, seriousness weighting the Out Here idiom: "I'll do right by her."

He was speaking of Ione. She had been on his mind all along.

Mingling and serving, taking care to avoid Brock Walden, I eventually made my way to Cletus Rose, who had found a piece of wall to lean on. Just above his shoulder, partially hidden by a coat-rack and missed by Irene and Ruby, was taped a small heart of red construction paper. I offered him a plate of the fig cookies he liked: "To keep up your strength."

He was, at eighty, still a powerful man. He smiled. "Not much call for it these days."

In the center of the big room, Brock Walden spun his wheelchair about as if in a dance, his laughter echoing off the walls. He was momentarily revitalized, by what I couldn't tell. "Why is he here?"

"Last rites."

Troy Hardaway came in then, alone. Ione had planned to stop at the Rocking W and check on the heifer, Cletus said.

Someone else was missing. "And Jane?"

Cletus shrugged and bit into a cookie.

We watched Troy stiffen under the words and hands of those who would console him. He seemed wary now of men and women he had known all his life, as if their motives were suddenly inscrutable, as if they might be agents of the malice that had wrecked his life.

"You advised Troy on job prospects in Southern California," I said to Cletus. "I know he went down there with serious intentions. What happened?"

"Too much."

"Too much what?"

"Scurry. Fuss."

Most people thought Cletus Rose ignorant and dull. Because he showed no interest in their prattle, they expected little from him. That is what he gave them. To a few of us he was more forthcoming.

"He blames L.A. for his girl trouble – all that Out There business you Nevadans talk about. He thinks she can't see him in Los Angeles for the distraction of her friends and the tearing around and the glitz. He figured out quick enough his only chance was to get her back Out Here."

"Well, she's here." I said. "But his chances are pretty slim, I'd say."

Then Carlyle Walden was beside us. "I hope you'll excuse us, Mrs. Waner. Cletus and I have an engagement."

It was noon, so I knew where Cletus was going. His small smile confirmed my suspicion that he was helping Carlyle with something besides horses.

Energized by Brock Walden's presence and a fruit punch surreptitiously made strong with rum, the gathering took on a festive air. The room warmed as faces grew flushed and voices rose. A few mourners went back to their lives, but for most the occasion became a holiday of sorts, and they remained, enjoying the tales of Brock Walden, telling their own stories of Bill Hardaway and Blue Lake, prolonging this pause in an otherwise inexorable advance to an inescapable ending.

By the time I was able to offer my condolences to Troy, he was worn out, eyes glassy from fatigue and the punch. He responded with jittery nods and grunts, until I asked about his plans: "You'll stay on at the place? It would be good to have a Hardaway there."

"Till B. W. goes, anyhow. After that, I don't know that I'll have a job or a place either one." He winced against his own bitterness. "He's ruining it all, Carlyle. Him and his refuge or memorial or whatever."

"Nothing is certain at this point," I said.

"But why do anything?" He didn't allow an answer. As if too tired to take up the burden of understanding, he could only repeat the question. "Why?"

"I'm sure he'll do right by everyone involved," I said, echoing Carlyle's own words. "And you have skills. If it came to that, you could hire on with another rancher."

"Not in Blue Lake, things the way they are."

"Maybe not, but – "

"I'd have to go, leave the place I've lived all my life. Why? Why me? Why doesn't he leave? Why doesn't he leave us alone?"

My sympathy for his plight was dulled by the petulance that turned his questions nearly to screeches.

"She's just as bad. Thinks I should go to L.A. and let rich men pay me to smile at their wives. Or at least she did. Now she just wants me to go away."

"Jane? Troy, I'm sure she – "

I was silenced in mid-utterance by an obscenity, the first Troy Hardaway ever uttered in my presence. But I saw that remonstration would be pointless. Troy now was aware only of Jane Harmon coming in, flushed, excited, bright and vital. Behind her, smiling happily, Carlyle Walden carried her movie camera, just as Troy had three months and another lifetime before. He watched them advance into the room, and, at last, he saw.

He straightened his spine as Jane came over, smiling: "You should have seen Ione. She sliced the poor thing open and pulled out the calf and then sewed her up again, just like that. There wasn't even that much blood. She saved them both. She was…wonderful."

Troy, jaw clenched, did not, perhaps could not speak.

"The heifer," I said.

"There wasn't time to wait for the vet, so Ione did the caesarian herself. I got it all on film. It's perfect, isn't it – death and birth. I mean, it's only cows, but still…"

Jane at last sensed Troy's unhappiness. Her smile softened. "She's wonderful, your sister."

Troy looked at her with such naked need that she turned away.

"We've all known that for a long time," Carlyle said with a smile.

Troy's expression went slowly, deliberately mean. "You think my sister's great too, do you?"

"I do indeed."

"I know you did thirty years ago, when she had something you wanted."

The life went out of Carlyle's smile.

"Now you're getting it from somebody else, you don't need her anymore."

"Troy, I understand that you're – "

"That's why you're planning to get rid of her. Of all of us. For what?" This time he answered his question. "A game refuge. A museum. A memorial."

Others might have taken the rasp in his voice for menace. I heard only despair, even as I saw the recognition that seeped into Carlyle's eyes: this was a matter of form, this hostility, a preamble to violence.

"I have no plans – "

"The hell you don't. You've got big plans for the Rocking W, for me and my sister, for my…" He coughed, as if strangling on the words. "For my all of a sudden ex-girlfriend. You think you can come Out Here and do what you want, take what you want, ruin everything for everybody."

"You're upset, Troy. This is a difficult time for you. " Carlyle spoke lifelessly, as if in an empty ritual. He knew that words now meant nothing. He knew what was coming. He handed Jane her movie camera.

Psychic currents had eddied the crowd into a loose circle around us. Cletus Rose looked on impassively. Brock Walden seemed amused.

"I'm sorry about your dad, Troy, and I want you to know – "

"I don't care what you want me to know. It'd be a lie anyhow. You're a liar and pompous bastard and a coward. If you say I'm wrong, let's step outside and settle it." His color deepened.

Carlyle took a deep breath. "No thanks."

Murmurs rippled through the crowd. At the same time, I became aware of another sound, faint, whirring, mechanical.

"Come on," Troy said, frustration fanning his anger, "Get out from behind Daddy's knees and be a man."

Silent, Carlyle seemed like the rest of us a spectator as Troy stepped forward and shoved. The assault was childish, the sort seen on school playgrounds. Carlyle stumbled back but didn't fall. Whirr.

"Outside."

I put a hand on his arm. "This doesn't become you, Troy. This isn't – "

He jerked away from my touch. "Leave me alone, Miz Waner. You're part of this, the three of you drinking tea and laughing – "

Then, looking at me, he lost himself. Past making sense, past protesting injustice, he had come, in his exhaustion, hopeless and helpless, to his last resort. He wheeled and hit Carlyle in the mouth. Whirr.

Carlyle made no move to avoid the blow. Struck, he stumbled back, caught himself, and sank to one knee. A line of blood appeared on his lip.

Jane Harmon moved into my vision, her movie camera whirring.

"Outside." Troy's voice scraped in his throat.

For a moment Carlyle didn't move. Then he got to his feet. "Yes, all right."

"No!"

Ione Hardaway shoved her way through the ring of on-lookers.

"Stay out of this, Sissy. He's been – "

The sound of Ione's bare hand on her brother's face rang in the room as sharply as the shots from her pistol had three months before.

"Sissy…" His voice went small and plaintive, his pleading gaze tearful.

"You think this is a fit way to send dad off?"

"He's got it coming, you know he – "

"So you'll go outside and knock him down, and you'll have to keep knocking him down because he'll keep getting up, like some dumb animal, because that's the only thing he knows how to do, and finally he won't get up because he can't, and then they'll cart him off to the hospital or the morgue and you to jail."

Ione's quiet passion stilled the room.

Then Brock Walden clapped, slow and mocking. Someone laughed.

Cletus Rose put his hand on Troy's shoulder. "Let's get some air."

It was over, we thought, until Ione turned angrily to Brock Walden. "Glad we could provide you with a little entertainment."

He cocked his head, inspecting her as he might a mare in the auction ring. "Pretty tame. West ain't so wild any more."

"I could of let my brother beat your son to death, I guess."

"Didn't, though," the old actor said. "You always were a tad too civilized."

"You could of stopped it. You could stop all of it."

Brock Walden smiled. "You got a problem, Miss, take care of it yourself."

"Maybe I will." Ione smiled faintly, ironically, and turned away.

Jane filmed this altercation too, and its witnesses, and the room with its wreathes and flowers, even aligning within the frame of her lens the small red heart forgotten on the wall. She caught again many of the faces she had photographed on Thanksgiving, many of her subjects in the same dressy clothes. Another ritual enacted, another passage marked.

For the next hour, Jane hid behind her camera, avoiding my eye. I wondered if she thought that I would hold her accountable for the violence. I should have known better: a woman who lived on her nerve ends, on the breath and pulse of the moment, she rarely subjected her actions or emotions to real scrutiny. When we finally spoke, she could dismiss it all. "It wasn't brutal, Miz Waner. It was just silly."

Ione did her duty that day, drank coffee and chewed on cheese-stuffed celery and absorbed the sentiments of Blue Lake. Brock Walden gathered with a group of men from which there issued gonadal huffs and windy guffaws. Cletus and Troy remained out on the sidewalk, the older man listening patiently to the younger, while Carlyle stayed inside alone, watching Jane, watching his father, watching the mourners avoid him – not because of his response to Troy, with which, finally, Blue Lake did not find fault, but rather because of a general uncertainty. Refuge? Memorial?

People began, eventually, slowly, to take their leave, and I retreated to the kitchen to sort out plates and dishes and to make arrangements for their return. In a moment of calm, I visited the ladies room. Stepping back into the hallway, I met Brock Walden, who was struggling out of his wheelchair.

He waved off my move to assist him: "Time comes I can't get up and walk into the jakes, I'll pack it in."

"How are you feeling?"

"Some days better than others, you know."

The occasion summoned civility. "You've given your friends here a good deal of pleasure today."

"Consolation," he grinned. "They see the shape I'm in, they feel better about their own corruption."

"In any case," I said, "they have a great deal of affection for you."

The notion didn't interest him. "They had fun watching men fight over a woman, huh? And watching the woman. Not much of a fracas, but she loved it."

"I didn't see that," I said.

"Must not of been looking." He grinned again. "Not that long since men fought over you."

"I don't know that anyone ever – "

"You don't know," he snorted. "You know only what you want to know, Win. But that husband of yours was a protective cuss. Pugnacious too. I liked that about him, how he was ready to fight me for you."

"You don't care enough about women to fight over them," I said.

"Ah, Winnefred. I'd surely have fought for you."

Something of his old charm lurked in the words, foolish and false though they were, and in his smile.

"I'd fight for you now, if it wasn't pointless, what with diabetes, and the meds, and plain old getting old."

His admission of impotence surprised me, although it shouldn't have, being merely something else he didn't care about. This he immediately confirmed.

"Wasted a lot of time fooling with women. Did some dumb things."

He seemed to expect a response. When none came, he continued: "I don't regret much. Maybe I should, but it never seemed like a useful activity. Doing it over, though, I'd change a couple things. Let his grandparents raise the boy, like they wanted. Spend more time Out Here. Treat some people a little better. And the thing with your husband."

I didn't know how Henry Waner came to figure in a sick old man's accounting. Then he added: "I'd of liked us to have been friends, Winnefred."

My conversations with Brock Walden, fewer than a half-dozen over the years, had not prepared me for this sort of undecorated declaration. Whether this was the leading edge of a real humanity or merely part of the confidence game I couldn't tell.

"I never saw much evidence of that," I said.

But he wasn't listening. "That day at the Rocking W, you all bright eyes and big words, I thought you might be a woman a man could talk to. I thought…"

He drifted off into, I assumed, memory. I didn't care to wait for his return. But when I moved past him, he reached out his old man's hand and, gently, stayed my step. "You don't know what kind of friend I've been all these years, do you?"

I had no idea what he was talking about. "Apparently not."

"I kept your poor little secrets, Winnefred. Just like he kept mine. Cletus."

"Cletus?"

"Cletus!"

The echo, harsh and loud, came from not Brock Walden but his son, who was suddenly there, distraught. "Cletus! He's down!"

ONE MORNING months later, Jane, over coffee and sweet rolls, gave me an old photograph. "We were going through B. W.'s stuff, things he's picked up on various shoots," she said. "He thought you might like to have this."

I looked. The Brock Walden of thirty-five years before, in a beautifully cut suit, grinned at the world, very much as if he were on top of it. Attached to his arm, wearing a new party frock too bold and a hair-do, I now saw, too young for her, my nearly forty-year-old self smiled at the camera.

"That was thoughtful of him," I said. "And uncharacteristic."

"Well, it was really my idea. I mean, you said you weren't his mistress. You told me that. But there you are, the two of you. When I asked him about it, he just laughed."

"I happened to be visiting Eleanor when one of his films was about to open," I said. "He invited me to a party hosted by the producer. We went, and I had a nice time, and then Cletus Rose drove me home."

"I — your dress, Miz Waner. It's..." She paused, searching for language.

"A mistake." The black sheath seemed, in its simplicity, scanty, barely there.

"Claire Trevor, in *Stagecoach* — that's who you remind me of here."

I smiled. "She played a harlot, as I recall."

"No, I didn't mean... but you and B. W. — nothing happened?"

Disappointment etched her features so deeply that I had to smile. "At the party he met another, younger, more likely opportunity."

Jane looked at the photograph. Then she slid it aside, as if it were nothing she might make something of. Once she had gone, I took it up, smiling, remembering my date with Brock Walden.

Knowing that I would spend the winter break in Southern California, Blue Lake had charged me with persuading Brock Walden to take part in Wild West Days that year. I intended merely to go through the motions, by phone, but when I called the Malibu ranch, he proposed that we talk about it on our way to a public relations hawking of his new movie.

"They'll be folks as far Out There as you can get," he drawled. "But you might want to take a gander at them, and give me somebody to talk to."

I admit to ambivalence. Not two years earlier, Brock Walden had put his hands on me in my own home. But I was curious about the Hollywood world, and this would put me, briefly, at its edge. Finally I avoided a decision by telling him that I'd think about it and that he could call me the next day. I was certain he wouldn't.

Eleanor was amused at my hesitation. "What's the problem?"

"You're the one who warned me about him," I said.

"He's not the man he was at thirty-five, Winnefred."

I knew what she meant. Brock Walden's career, and his life, had run down. Decent movie roles came infrequently, as did guest appearances on television shows. At the same time, his finances had grown shaky, his entourage seedy, his barroom escapades rare, and his sexual predations half-hearted. He was not so much old, in his early fifties, as passé. There was now little call for the character he played, little interest in or indulgence of the man he was. And I had to admit that his pass at me had been less than vigorous.

"It doesn't matter, though," I said. "He's still basically the lout you said he was."

"But you haven't stayed a naïve, innocent, twenty-two-year-old, have you?"

I smiled. "You mean I'm so worn and haggard he won't give me a second look?"

"I mean you won't shiver when he gives you the slow grin and the slower drawl and hangs onto your hand just a little longer than he ought to."

I tried to get past her with jokes. "What? No fission? Forget it then."

"As for second looks, Winnefred, you could have him ogling, with a little effort. A new dress, one with lots of bare back and décolletage, a new hairdo, my seed pearls, maybe a little more blush – you'd have him helpless."

"Eleanor," I said, "I won't – "

"What is the matter with you, Winnefred?" Her eyes sparkled. "It'll be fun!"

"Maybe," I said. "But the question's moot. He isn't going to call."

But he did. And I accepted. And Eleanor and I went to work.

The Brock Walden who appeared at Eleanor's door at the appointed hour was not at all the worn-out profligate we had convinced ourselves he had become. Tanned and healthy looking, his grin crinkling his face, his suit fit smoothly over his wedge-shaped torso, he seemed no less vital than he had years before in his ranch yard.

"You'll put the biddies to shame tonight, Win," he said.

I was afraid that I might appear not biddy but bawd. My dress showed less skin than Eleanor had urged but more than I was comfortable with. I felt exposed.

He spent some minutes joshing with Eleanor. Leaving, he took her hand, leaning to press a kiss on her cheek. Her expression made me laugh.

At the curb waited an automobile, from which, as we approached, a man got out of the driver's seat. He was large and bald. I greeted him: "Good evening, Mr. Rose."

Opening the door, he returned my greeting but not my smile. "Mrs. Waner."

The lights of L.A. and environs glittered. The night was cold with damp, but beside me Brock Walden was warm, scented with talc and a musky aftershave and a hint of bourbon. "I want you to have a good time tonight, Win."

"I'm sure I will," I said.

He quickly agreed to show up for Wild West Days, should his schedule permit (it didn't). Then he began to talk about the movie the producer would be pushing at the party. He thought it was better than anything he'd yet played in, due to a good script, intelligent direction, and the work of his costars, serious actors who forced him into, he felt, his best work. (This was the movie that would win him award nominations and revitalize his career. That night, on the way to the party, it was clear that Brock Walden himself already had a renewed vitality.)

"Been mailing it in for years. They wouldn't let me get away with that this time."

Cletus Rose drove us into the Hollywood hills and a cold mist that thickened to fog as we climbed through twisting canyons, at last arriving at a mass of brick and glass spread over a sheered-off hilltop. Lights glowed eerily in the murk. Cletus dropped us at the door, which opened with a rush of warm air and muted voices, and soon we were with the host, offering a champagne toast to the success of the upcoming film. Brock Walden introduced me to two auxiliary producers, the screenwriter, and a nice looking young man whose name I'd heard before, one of his costars. Then, with a grin, he set off, he said, to get a real drink and take care of the business at hand. I was to mingle.

Instead, I observed. I recognized few faces, but most of those attending seemed, by expression and bearing, not aspirants but achievers. The men reminded me of seals, sleek and slippery. The women seemed objets d'art, some got up like rock stars, others like restaurant hostesses. My outfit, at this gathering, was not daring, although men seemed fascinated with my front. At one point I was approached by a tipsy elderly man who looked down my dress and assured me that I had been an extra in a beach party film he had co-produced twenty years earlier. A rather aggressively effete young man wondered if I might possibly be a scandal rag reporter. A woman with a thirty-year-old face and a fifty-year-old throat was certain that we had met at a similar fete some months before and brought me up to date on the affairs of people I'd never heard of. The film's young costar joined me, and we chatted pleasantly about Blue Lake, which he had once passed through, and Billings, Montana, which he had left to study acting in New York, and Brock Walden. "He isn't bad," he said, as if assessing a wine. "He could be better, good in fact, but he doesn't want to be."

"He doesn't want to work at it?"

"It's not that," he said. "He just doesn't want to be really good. That would argue with who he thinks he is."

Through all this I had caught glimpses of Brock Walden attending to business, all grin and pat and grasp, his laughter a rich bass chord in the chorus of voices. I had also seen Cletus Rose, not as I had thought mere chauffeur for the evening but clearly a guest on familiar terms with many in the room, comfortable in his suit and skin. Quietly, coffee cup in hand, he let come to him those who would. When the actor went off after another flute of champagne, I became one of these.

I had noticed him watching me once or twice, his expression oddly blank. Now he greeted me with only a nod. For a moment we stood silent, his reserve obliging me to wait for him to speak. But he said nothing until we were joined by an aged actor, who once had played the sidekick of a singing cowboy, and his middle-aged wife.

Cletus introduced me: "This a friend of B. W.'s, Mrs. Waner." Then he amplified, curiously. "Winnefred Westrom Waner." Then he added, "The poet."

Astounded, I could only nod, press hands, and mutter conventionalities.

The young actor, back with my champagne, smiled broadly. "I don't know your work, Mrs. Waner. Should I?"

"No," I said, struggling to repossess myself. "Not really."

That was true. My verse had been published under my initials and maiden name, mostly in small journals whose readership was limited nearly to those listed on the masthead or contributors' page.

"I have a friend," said the sidekick's wife, "who wrote a poem that was accepted by Hallmark. The card company? We bought a box of them."

Across the room, Brock Walden leaned his ear toward the lips of a woman with flames of hair who gripped his arm like a raptor clutching carrion.

"Richard Hugo, do I like him because he writes about Montana," the actor asked, "or are his poems really good?"

I was preparing to offer an opinion, until I realized that the question had been directed not to me but to Cletus Rose.

He shrugged. "He hits and misses. The hits are pretty good."

"The last hit I took damn near got me hoosegow time," the old actor grinned.

The conversation drifted, our small circle gaining and losing members, as did the party. The young actor trudged off with his agent. Cletus Rose excused himself. Brock Walden and the redhead had disappeared.

Cletus soon returned to tell me that B. W. was tied up in negotiations that would take some time to settle. Cletus would drive me home. B. W. would call me. By the time I had thanked the host, who had no idea who I was, and retrieved my coat, the car was idling at the doorstep. When Cletus made to open a rear door, I said: "I'd rather sit in front, if you don't mind."

A stiffness in his shoulders suggested that he did mind, but he didn't say so. He saw me to my seat, settled into his, and we started down the canyons. The fog may have accounted for his rigidity over the steering wheel, and his silence.

Finally I asked: "How did you know that I wrote verse, Mr. Rose?"

"Reader's Guide."

There was more to say on the subject – why would he have been looking me up in a library reference publication? How did he know to look under my maiden name? – but he didn't say it.

Fog hung in the headlights like an elemental uncertainty. The silence grew oppressive. His expression, in the faint light from the dashboard instruments, was grim, nearly a scowl. And I'd had enough.

"I don't know what I've done to earn your disdain, Mr. Rose," I said, "but if I've offended you, I'm sorry."

"Disdain?" He seemed genuinely startled.

"That might be too strong a word. Say disapproval. You radiate censure." Suddenly, inexplicably flustered, I blurted: "Is it the dress?"

"The dress? What about the dress?"

"I look like a floozy in it."

"No, no," he said. "The dress is fine. You look – "

He leaned over the wheel, peering into the fog for a moment as, at a sharp curve, the headlights yellowed treetops, beneath which was only darkness.

"It's not for me to disapprove, Mrs. Waner," he said finally, carefully. "I admit I'm a little disappointed. I didn't think it showed. If I've been rude, I'm sorry."

"I've disappointed you? May I ask how?"

His response took so long that I thought perhaps one would not come. Then he took a resolute breath and said, "I thought there was more to you. I didn't think you'd fall for his line."

Brock Walden's, he meant. "I see."

The fog thickened. He slowed the car. Yet at the same time he looked over at me, looked at me really for the first time that evening.

"I've watched B. W. and the ladies for years. I know the pattern. When I heard about the agenda for tonight, the party and then back to Malibu – "

"I don't know anything about that. My plans were to attend a party, period."

"Maybe," he said, 'but then there's the wine, and the excitement, and he is Brock Walden, isn't he? It's easy to get interested. And he's hard to put off."

"I've put him off before, Mr. Rose." Then I said, on an impulse inexplicably playful. "And I'm sure, had it come to that, you would have defended my virtue."

The quality of the silence changed.

Finally he said, "Maybe I made a mistake. I'm sorry."

"Malibu – that must be where he is now, he and the woman with her head on fire," I said. "Ne-go-ti-a-tin'."

Cletus Rose smiled and drove down the canyon.

After a while he said: "It was the poem about ruts. The old wheel tracks that become tire tracks, and then the condom – and the way it ends: 'The desert makes us lonely/So much space to be small in.'"

I was flattered. And something more.

"I assumed W. A. Westrom was male, but the next time I was in the library I did a little checking. W. A. Westrom wrote a lot of desert poems, but a lot of food poems, too, even a very funny one about road apples and cow pies. I did some more checking and came up with you. Had to be."

"I've had more champagne than I'm accustomed to, Mr. Rose," I said then. "Could we stop somewhere for coffee?"

"I know an all-night diner." He smiled again. "The clientele this time of night will be colorful."

"I could use some color," I said.

So we had coffee, Cletus Rose and I, in the company of other eccentrics and outcasts, and we talked.

Three hours later, Eleanor struggled up from sleep on the couch, yawned, stretched, grinned, and said: "Have you anything to confess?"

"No," I said. Then I smiled. "Not yet."

CLETUS REMEMBERED only a sudden painful blow to the chest, as if, he said, he'd been kicked by a horse. Troy Hardaway offered details: Cletus scowling and scratching at his sternum, slurring words and staring wide-eyed before toppling onto the fender of a parked pickup and sliding down to the sidewalk. Dr. Carson would make the official diagnosis: myocardial infarction. Blue Lake would deem Cletus fortunate: Flo Eddys, it happened, was inside paying her respects to Bill Hardaway before taking the evening shift at the hospital; the EMTs arrived within minutes; and Dale Carson was making rounds when Cletus was brought in. The timely ministrations of all prevented more damage to the heart. Even so, Cletus was not out of danger for some time, most of which I spent in the waiting room, sipping tepid coffee and urging on myself calm and hope.

In those first critical hours, everything seemed distorted. Nurses and orderlies crept down halls as if mute emissaries from mysterious potentates. Brock Walden wheeled about like a child, now loud and bullying, now lost, his demands swollen with confusion and laced with what sounded like real fear. Carlyle, lip puffed out, and Troy shouldered shamefaced past one another as if in a dance to which neither knew the steps. Troy at one point stood before me and stammered out a nearly incomprehensible apology. Ione held my hand. Departing, she smiled. "Now it all figures, Miz Waner."

Jane was absent. Someone, Troy I think, said that she hated hospitals.

The crisis passed. Cletus came back to us, somewhat abashed at the commotion he'd caused. He'd been in excellent shape, so while the prognosis for a man his age must be guarded, he was soon out of bed and undergoing tests. However, as he would only gradually rebuild strength, the question became where he should convalesce. Brock Walden said Los Angeles, with him and Carlyle. To the astonishment of nearly everyone, I said Blue Lake, with me. Cletus said that he had confidence in Dale Carson and could hire whatever nursing help he needed and for the moment preferred my company. Brock Walden shrugged and flew off, and Cletus moved into my guest bedroom.

And Blue Lake talked: Miz Waner and Cletus Rose — all these years. No wonder they slipped around on the sly. A schoolmarm sleeping with Brock Walden, well, such an affair could be regarded as nearly providential, for who could deny Him? But Cletus Rose? Blue Lake had nothing to say against Cletus, knew him to be, in his calm, Twelve-Step manner a man to be counted on, but finally he was a hired hand, no one to make allowances for. News of our coupling, out of wedlock, would have raised a censorious clamor in school board meetings. No wonder.

So I sank in the esteem of some who greeted me with disapprobative sniffs and frowns. Others — men, mostly — puzzled at what Cletus Rose had hidden of person or personality that I would risk my job for. A few others — women — thought me fortunate.

Not that any of this mattered now. Actually, it had never mattered very much, for, had it come to that, I could probably have handled any school board. As I would explain to Jane, Cletus and I kept our relationship to ourselves not because it was a secret but because it was private. We had never considered marriage, except of our true minds. For all our basic similarity — we were essentially solitaries, children of empty spaces — we were different enough, led different

enough lives that we could never share more than the moment: a
night, a weekend, a week here and there. We took these and were
grateful.

Now, however, we had time to enjoy one another at our leisure.
No nurturer, I left his care to those whose business it was, but I
accompanied him on his walks, which gradually lengthened, and
I prepared and shared the meals his diet dictated, through both
shedding a few of my own pounds. I read to him, or he read or
rested while I wrote. He attended his thrice-weekly AA meetings.
We entertained the visits of well-wishers – Ione, Troy, George and
Anita Burleigh, Ruby and Irene, and two or three friends of Bill, as
Cletus called them. And as we always had, we talked about what he
read and what I wrote and most of what we thought.

What we didn't talk about, what neither of us wished to say, was
that while Cletus might get better he would not get well. For all his
hardiness, he had become an old man, irreparably weakened and
slowed, who warded off awareness of mortality with jests: "I woke up
this morning and didn't hurt anywhere and thought I must be dead."

When he joked about racing Brock Walden to the pearly gates, I
told him about the odd conversation I'd had with his boss in the
Community Center hallway.

"That's part of him," Cletus said. "Not a big part."

"He was a bit cryptic. He spoke of Henry – did the two of them
actually fight?"

"No."

Something in his voice – a faint quaver, a tiny scratch – gave me the
sense that he was not telling me the truth, at least not the whole truth.

"He must have been angry at the way Henry confronted him publicly at the dance that night."

"He isn't a small man, Winnefred. He doesn't hold grudges. At the
funeral, when he told you he liked Henry and was sorry he died, he
was telling you the truth."

Still suspecting that I had not heard all there was to hear, I let it
go. "And he knew about us?"

"Guessed, right off. Never asked."

"He said that you kept his secrets."

"He's got a bunch."

I let that go as well. I had little interest in Brock Walden and his secrets, not when the man he pretended to be on screen was sitting, in the old and injured but still living flesh, across from me.

Those days I spoke only briefly with Jane. She dropped off a rent check for March but, seeing Cletus in slippers at my kitchen table, she hurried off as if from a sanctuary no longer secure. She was filming at the Rocking W, where Ione, busy calving, took the time to explain what was going on. The two women rode on occasion, minding the cattle that followed the greening grass toward the foot-hills, and Jane for nearly a week lurked about Mud Springs, where three mustang bands watered, and where she endured long hours of boredom for the chance to get onto film the animals in breeding season, a fascinating and sometimes frightening exercise. And she tended Virgie, feeding and grooming her and mucking out her stall, when she knew Troy would not be about the place. Otherwise, after her morning run, she worked at home with the film she had shot or clips from Brock Walden movies, scratching out notes for cuts and splices, and drawing diagrams of possible story lines that began from the circled initials B. W. or I. H. but always came to nothing. And she read the letters from Carlyle. She often worked late into the night, but she didn't notice when Troy guided his pickup slowly past or parked for a while a block away to watch her door and the light flickering in her window.

So Blue Lake had a great deal to occupy tongues. But no conversa-tion could long continue before coming to questions about what Carlyle Walden was up to. Troy could offer little illumination, and Jane with remarks about artist colonies and wild horses only thick-ened the murk. Carlyle would celebrate the career of his father – Blue Lake got that. A memorial to Brock Walden might also recognize the heroism of pioneers. But wasn't Walden Ranch already a memorial, of sorts? And Brock Walden had a star on the famous Hollywood sidewalk: why not leave it at that? Or put up a statue in Cottonwood Creek Park? In any case, what did a memorial have to do with a wildlife refuge? And how did artists figure into all of this?

Many of the answers Blue Lake came to were fanciful, expressed in tones varying from the dreamy to the hysterical: Carlyle would turn Walden Ranch into a haven for all wild horses gathered by the BLM in Nevada, or donate the property to the state for a park into which wolves would be reintroduced to keep the mustang population in check, or found a school dedicated to the preservation and production of Western films, or establish a treatment center where emotionally disturbed military veterans trained and cared for and painted pictures of horses, or a camp that provided healthy, hard, outdoor ranch work and military discipline for troubled youth, or deed the ranch to a university for artistic and intellectual conferences, or start a dude ranch catering to those who celebrated free range beef and platonic love.

Blue Lake's concerns eventually reached Carlyle, who wrote in conciliatory tones to the local newspaper, acknowledging his intention to make at least part of the property a memorial to his father and the intrepid spirit of those who settled the Great Basin and Intermountain West. Some sort of wildlife refuge would no doubt be part of the project. There were other possibilities, those designed to entice tourists to celebrate Western art and history. He was flexible, open to – indeed solicitous of – community suggestions. He would set up a foundation and establish a board of Out There bankers and lawyers and accountants and Out Here ranchers and business owners. He vowed that no economic damage would be done to Blue Lake. Anyone who lost employment or income would be resituated or compensated. Nothing would be decided in haste. All would be carefully thought out. No one need be disturbed.

Disturbed, however, Blue Lake remained. Everything was iffy, maybe, might. Who knew what would come, Carlyle being Carlyle? Calculations were penciled on napkins at the Wagon Wheel Café. How much money did Walden Ranch put into the economy? Which Gull Valley places could actually serve as wildlife refuges and what would their doing so take from the cattle operation? What increase in tourism would come from a museum or art gallery or refuge? If Blue Lake business people benefited, would the folks who grew hay for and leased land to Walden Ranch? Factions developed. People spoke of refuge refugees. They parried with bumper sticker epithets – Out There Idiots, Californicators – assertions that a community must evolve to survive, must keep up with the times, must change. What no one asked was: Where is Brock Walden when we really need him?

He was in Los Angeles, refusing to die. Carlyle reported to Jane that his father, as if to defy doctors, was somewhat improved in health – he was still ill, terminally, but momentarily invigorated and talking of flying up to Blue Lake to fetch Cletus.

Cletus was ready to be fetched. As April arrived and advanced, he began to speak of chores he needed to attend to, affairs he needed to see to, jobs he needed to start or to finish. He, like Ione Hardaway, must be doing, and there was in my life little that needed to be done. He had lived alone for sixty years, he had his rooms and books and chair and routine, his horse, his tasks, and he would return to them. Knowing this, I'd anticipated and so was not injured by his restlessness. Yet I persuaded him to remain with me a while longer. Eleanor would arrive for her annual visit in mid-May, and we agreed that he would depart a week earlier. Carlyle, with or without his father, would fly him home.

So he puttered about, and we walked, and we talked as the days lengthened and our time together diminished. One afternoon, when Jane came to my door seeking the name of a reliable plumber to unstop a drain, Cletus insisted on taking a look; a half-hour later the blockage was cleared and he and Jane were drinking my tea. After that she came to us from time to time, gleaning bits of information about him. He had been a champion high school bull dogger, and a Korean War soldier court-martialed for a drunken fight with his sergeant. He had been jailed in Bisbee, several times, on drunk and disorderly charges. He had once, as an extra in a Western being filmed locally, brawled in a bar with the movie's star, Brock Walden, who bought both of them out of the consequences and got Cletus sober and put him to work, watching his back.

Jane saw Cletus only as one of Brock Walden's projects. If she didn't see the real man yet (she once asked me if the books in his apartment were mine) it was partly because she had other things on her mind, foremost her film. But she was also troubled by the tension between Troy and Carlyle and, now, again, the presence of Pete Haas.

One result of Jane's split with Troy was the renewed attention of Blue Lake men. Jane being better assessed, the approaches were fewer and subtler; nevertheless, several aspiring swains offered her their interest. While Blue Lake saw that George Burleigh took a special interest in Jane's welfare, all understood that she no longer had an official protector, as it were, which emboldened certain louts. Men who had watched her dance with Troy now presumed an acquaintance and offered unwanted attentions. There were overtures, mild enough, and some ambiguous propositions, and proposals laced with lasciviousness. Norman Casteel began to boast of his plans to sweep Jane off her feet, so that one afternoon Mina Pasco banged on Jane's door to demand that she leave her boyfriend alone. And Pete Haas came again to perch at the edge of her life – watching, waiting.

Another man was watching too, and at last they came together.

Cletus had put out my patio furniture that afternoon, and we three were enjoying the twilight, the soft April air scented with budding sage, the last light lingering on the horizon, when Jane announced that the evening was indeed beauteous. She felt, she said, like Shakespeare's sister, spiritual. She decided to stroll through the holy time down to the drug store.

We watched her walk down the hill.

"Shakespeare?"

"Wordsworth." I said. "The sister I assume is the 'Nun, breathless in adoration'."

Darkness fell on Jane's devotions. As she entered Hasweldt's, Blue Lake would later calculate, Pete Haas was coming out of the Adaven. He climbed into his pickup, where he sat until Jane was back on the street. When she was a block away, he started to pull back from the curb, only to find his progress suddenly obstructed as another pickup swung in behind him.

Precisely where Troy Hardaway had been watching from Blue Lake never agreed. But now he was there, and he and Haas were out of their vehicles and casting conflicting shadows in the light from shop windows and neon signs and streetlamps. The altercation was angry but not loud, so that what was said Blue Lake could only conjecture: bravado, obscenities, challenges and threats and chest-beatings – the usual courtesies preliminary to a scrap. As often happens, however, no blows were struck. In the account that became Blue Lake lore, Troy warned Haas away from Jane, Haas protested his rights as a free American, Troy offered to settle the question with fists, Haas pled a recent probation that forbade fighting, and Troy avowed that such wouldn't matter if Haas ever troubled Jane Harmon again. Troy got back in his pickup and drove off. Haas went back into the Adaven (also a violation of his probation, Blue Lake noted).

Jane, meanwhile, made her way home, finding familiarity in the neighborhoods, sensing new growth everywhere about her, feeling, she would say later, for the first time a resident of rather than a visitor in the desert, feeling too in the darkness an immanence, as if the night were filled with the reality she thought she sought.

She soon heard about what had happened, as Troy knew she would. She was not pleased. "Now there are two of them," she told me.

"You don't mean that," I said.

"No, you're right, I don't. But that's what it feels like, sometimes. I wish they'd just leave me be."

That wasn't going to happen. I knew it. Jane knew it. Blue Lake knew it. And Blue Lake knew something else. Pete Haas had chosen not to fight in the street, but not from fear. Like Brock Walden, he enjoyed a brawl – the more savage, the more pleasure he took in it – but he preferred to fight when he had an advantage, which, insofar as Troy Hardaway was concerned, Blue Lake knew, he would eventually create.

BLUE LAKE HAD a blue lake that spring. The playa shimmered in the breeze, a few inches of run-off in the bright sunlight reflecting the sky. The winter's big snow and a series of wet storms brought the desert beautifully to bloom – grasses flourished, shrubs blossomed, and flowers annual and ephemeral colored the otherwise drab earth – and Jane, delighting, imagined that nature had assumed such finery to adorn her film.

Of course she still had no film, only images and intuitions. So when the L.A. group underwriting her project again enquired about progress, Jane vacillated. She hadn't been able to make the Ione Hardaway-Walden Ranch-Brock Walden link. Maybe she would do wild horses after all, but do them differently, say something new, work out something with free range and fenced ranch. To that end, she rented and watched movies about horses – thoroughbreds, cow ponies, wild stallions – and, no longer able to make use of Troy's expertise, she asked questions of and floated impressions before Ione, who had no time to listen, and myself, who had no knowledge to exploit, and, finally, Cletus.

Jane had grown more comfortable with Cletus, but she'd failed to get past the placid surface to his quick intelligence and quirky humor. As did Blue Lake, she assumed that for me the gratifications of an affair with this beat-up, alcoholic cowboy must have been primarily sexual. I marveled at how she who sought the real Wild West could be so blind.

Then she watched The Misfits.

The next evening, on my patio, she waxed wistful. "If only I could make a film like that. The scenes with the mustangs are powerful."

"Those animals Clark Gable chased across the playa weren't mustangs." Cletus, having wrangled wild horses as a young man on his father's Arizona ranch, spoke with some authority. "Too big and pretty. Mustangs are ugly, most of them. Broomtailed runts. Shaggy. Beat up."

"But Hop is a beautiful horse."

Hop was the mare with Morgan blood that Ione had adopted from the BLM, so named for her skittishness, which the skills of Bill and Troy Hardaway had not overcome.

"Hop isn't a mustang either. She's an expensive horse somebody abused and abandoned." His voice softened, inviting her attention. "You saw real mustangs at the BLM corrals. Not a Trigger or Black Beauty in the lot, was there."

Jane couldn't argue that point. She chose another. "What they represent, though – the idea of them. Freedom. America. You know…"

"That's your idea, not theirs. With plenty of food and water, a penned up horse, wild or feral or tame, is just fine, thank you, ma'am."

"But…" Her expression pled for an explanation.

"A horse has brute needs and urges," Cletus said with the same soft voice. "When these are satisfied, he, or she, is satisfied."

Jane sipped her tea, taking him in.

The next morning she appeared, early, with a small, battery-powered film viewer. Ignoring my offer of coffee, she clicked on the machine and held it out to Cletus. "What do I have here?"

He looked and frowned. "Evidence of your insanity, I'd say. You could have been hurt, getting in among them like that. These beasts are dangerous."

He was looking at the footage she'd shot of the mustangs around Mud Springs. The images and action would, in her film, have a powerful effect, but even now, raw, they were forceful. Her camera rendered the foals' bony configurations and the mares' matted coats and the stallions' scars with as much care as Cézanne's brush gave to fruit.

"I've read," Jane said cautiously, offering Cletus a new regard, "of a social structure and hierarchies in bands – lead mares and all that."

Cletus smiled. "I've heard feminists talk about lead mares. Ought to take that show on the road."

He observed the order in the animals' behavior, the bands' security arrangements, the studs' assertions of dominance. He didn't need to explain the stallions' clashes with teeth and hooves or their mounting of and thrusting at mares.

"But their behavior is social?" Jane asked.

"You seem to want to make that moral," he said, again smiling.

"Well, not exactly, I suppose…"

"It's just a way to stay alive, keep the band safe, the mares protected."

"But it's all so elaborate, so… familial."

"All to the purpose," he said. "A stud's job is to pass on his genes. He's a near-ton of testosterone. He'll mate with any female that comes in, his own daughters under certain circumstances, and he'll maim or kill anything that gets in his way. You're lucky one of them didn't come after you."

Jane involuntarily cringed. "You make it all so... vicious."

"It's no ballroom out there," Cletus said. "Especially during mating season."

"Sex," Jane said softly, after a moment, "and violence."

Her tone of voice might have alerted me. But, interested in her altering attitude toward Cletus, I missed its import.

He nodded. "Pretty much."

"And food," I said, pushing forward a plate of toast triangles.

Jane didn't eat. She was thinking.

The next day she turned her camera toward places and people that she had, since her arrival, carefully avoided. She filmed at the rough edges and rotten spots of Blue Lake – grimy, dented single-wide trailers slumped amid wrecked machines, beaten down houses little better than shacks on grassless patches of dirt, flimsy wooden four-plexes that shivered in the wind, rooms with vacant windows over Main Street stores. She filmed too, from a distance, the inhabitants, women waddling or gaunt, bruised or toothless or slack-dugged; ssilent or shrieking children, unkempt and hungry looking; and men ugly inside and out. She complained that she couldn't interview Mina Pasco, who was in Reno with a hydrocephalic child recuperating from a recent operation.

I had an inkling of what she might be about. "You need to be careful, Jane."

"I know Mina," she said. "I – we're friends."

"Maybe," I said, "But Mina is what she is and will do what she must."

"She already apologized for that day in the street, Miz Waner." Jane smiled her smile. "And she'll want to help me. Everyone wants to be in a movie."

So despite my warning, Jane would proceed, to calamitous ends. But she could do little at the time, with Mina Pasco absent and her own few remaining days in Blue Lake taken over by concerns of a different sort.

The fire started shortly after midnight. If Troy Hardaway hadn't been watching in the dark, Jane surely would have perished.

Troy was parked in a driveway several houses down, wallowing in the muck of his obsession. Pete Haas was out there in the night, Troy was convinced, soon to assault Jane's psyche and person. Troy would watch and wait, would be there for her, would earn her gratitude and regain her love and esteem by saving her.

Save her he did, but not to the effect that he had fantasized.

When he noticed a faint glow in the window of the small bedroom she used as an office, Troy thought first that Jane had awakened and turned on a lamp. Then the light altered, shivered and danced, took on color, and with a shock he recognized the flare and shadow of flames.

A few seconds later, his pickup skidded to a stop at Jane's driveway, and Troy, racing across the lawn, hurled himself at the front door, sheering it from a hinge. Inside, he made his way through the thickening smoke to Jane's bedroom, where he found her on her hands and knees, terrified, disoriented, gasping for breaths of acrid air that her lungs rejected in harsh retchings. Quickly draping her nakedness with bedclothes, he raised her up and half-carried, half-led her back through the smoke and out into the night.

Seeing Jane safely to his pickup, Troy then foolishly went back into the heat and smoke of the house, returning soon with an armload of film canisters. He made one more trip into and out of fire before flames barricaded the doorway.

By now others had gathered to watch the old frame structure burn. Just as the roof collapsed, the Fire Department pumper arrived. Soon the crew had hoses trained on the blaze, but to no real point.

I slept through some of the excitement. Then Cletus awoke to the smell of smoke and, after determining its source, awakened me. Shocked, I was frantic after Jane's welfare until Cletus pointed her out in the cab of the Troy's pickup. Then we watched the final fulmination: a lovely, flower-like unfolding of flames, a dramatic shower of bright fiery brands, and a slow subsiding into smolder and char and ember and ruin.

I took Cletus' hand. I had been happy in that house.

George Burleigh drove Jane and Troy to the emergency room, where she donned scrubs and a sweater someone found for her. An intern listened to her lungs. At the same time a nurse tended to Troy's hands, blistered on the metal film canisters, slathering them in unguents and swaddling them in gauze. Jane ignored the suggestion that she sleep the rest of the night in a hospital bed, under observation. Instead, she told George, she wanted to come to me.

Cletus and I greeted them, he settling Troy and George at the table with coffee. I showed Jane to my bathroom, and while she showered, I got out pajamas and a good robe and warm slippers and I changed the sheets on my bed. Jane was in the shower for a long while. When she finally sat at the table with us, her damp hair pressed to her skull, her face bloodless, her hands wrapped around a coffee cup from which she didn't drink, she looked down at the smoking, steaming mess at the bottom of the hill, her eyes glittery: "It wasn't me, Miz Waner. I didn't – "

"Haas," Troy said, holding up his swathed hands as if they somehow proved his claim. "Has to be."

Hatless, reeking of smoke and singed hair, his boots muddy, his jacket smudged with soot, his hands bandaged, Troy was at once swollen to swagger at his rescue of Jane and deflated by her response. She avoided his eyes.

"The fire was set?" I was dubious.

"Haas. He was there," Troy insisted.

"Maybe so," George said, his tone carefully neutral, "but he wasn't actually seen. Why don't we wait to hear what the Fire Marshal says before we make accusations?"

"Haas," Troy said again, as if to make it so.

George rose. "I need to take your statement at the office, Troy. Might as well do it now. Then I'll drive you back out to the ranch, so you can get some sleep."

Troy clearly did not wish to leave. "I'll come in tomorrow."

"You're not driving with those hands," George said.

"They're not that bad."

"Bad enough." George moved to the door and waited. "Last thing we need now is to have to pull you out of a ditch."

Troy looked at each of us. Whatever he was looking for he didn't find. He got slowly to his feet.

George, his hand on the doorknob, paused. "Sorry about your house, Miz Waner."

"I couldn't call the fire department first," Troy said earnestly. "I had to get Jane."

"I'm glad you did," I said. "You saved her life."

Troy looked at her. She stared into her cup.

"And the film," he said, encouraging her approval.

Jane looked up, out the window. "That was... brave of you."

Troy stood before the door, silently pleading for a word to justify his hope, a smile to avow a renewed affection.

He would have been better off if he'd turned and stepped out into the darkness.

"You didn't have to, though. The negatives are in L.A."

"Oh." The single syllable hung in the room, empty, naught.

"But thank you for trying."

"Sure. Yeah," Troy said, dazed. "Anyhow... I'll be back in the morning."

"No, you don't need to," Jane said softly. "I'm fine."

"I'll check, just in case," he insisted rather desperately.

And then Jane looked at him. She took him in. And she said to him what she had said to his sister out on the highway at the edge of town the day she drove her car into the ditch.

She said, "Leave me alone."

The next day, Blue Lake had Troy Hardaway a hero. Saving Jane's life, he had earned, as local parlance had it, "an atta boy in capital letters." However, from the first Blue Lake discounted his claim that the fire had been the work of Pete Haas, who was known to have been otherwise engaged: after an evening of bowling at Lucky Strike Lanes, he had gone home and spent the night with Mary Jane Copleston, the bartender at the alley, which she confirmed. And in any case, lurking, prowling, and setting fires – this wasn't his style, Blue Lake agreed. Pete Haas didn't peep, he leered and sneered and assailed. Norman Casteel, now – he was a sneaky sort, all right, and he always talked a lot of nonsense about Jane, enough once to convince Mina Pasco that she had a rival for her man's affections. But Norman had driven his ailing aunt to Reno, where while she doctored he rooted about in downtown refuse. So Blue Lake praised Troy's courage and Jane's luck, even as some wondered, too, what Troy had been doing outside Jane's house at that time of night, as others wondered how Jane would view her erstwhile lover now, and a few speculated about who, if anyone, might gain from all this. Blue Lake began to considered whether, maybe, it just might possibly be the case that the fire had actually been set by, well, Troy.

Until, a few days later, the Fire Marshal reported that the cause of the blaze was a frayed computer power cord, an accident caused by not paying attention.

Of course, Blue Lake said: Calamity Jane.

Jane gave no indication that she heard what Blue Lake said. For some time she huddled in a stupor of self. All that she had brought to or bought in Blue Lake was destroyed, but only after my repeated nagging did she prepare a list for the insurance adjustor. The first day, while she slept, I found in local shops a few articles of clothing I thought she might like, but she preferred and continued to wear the hospital scrubs. The toiletries and hygienic items that I brought her she made no attempt to augment. She didn't run or ride, rarely leaving my patio or kitchen table or bed. She was polite to Ione, and to Ruby and Irene, when they stopped in, but unengaged. She retreated to the bedroom when Troy appeared; after the third day, he didn't return. She showered frequently.

She was depressed, of course, as was I, a bit. The spring air sometimes caught, in its stirring, the faint scent of scorch and char, drawing my gaze to blackened plumbing and unconsumed bits of cabinetry that leaned in the ash and ruin like obscure sculpture – my old home was gone, as was my now ever-youthful husband with whom I had shared it, as soon would be my aging lover. The new leaves and buds on the lilac bush seemed a mockery. I tried to write about these but, no Anne Bradstreet, could not.

So we were a somber pair, Jane and I. During the day, while I fussed about the house, Jane sat on the patio with Cletus, as if under his tutoring studying solitude. Evenings, she talked to me about her life, in a sober, odd summing up. She might have been repeating stories she'd overheard about a distant relative, for all the detachment with which she spoke of fruitless aspirations and empty achievements, of crippling love affairs and marred work. Some of this I had heard before, of course, but now her matter-of-fact accounts – scenes, mostly, and observations, and anecdotes – constituted a dispensation, a setting aside, revealing her as a woman with a past but no history. She made her family seem merely people she once knew, and not well. She had friends, but none close, had had lovers but none she herself could actually love. She had lived in various places but remained unsettled. Always going, she got to nowhere. In all innocence she ruined opportunities, her own and those of others. She took in the world and reshaped it to satisfy her own dimly understood urges but could not, so doing, make herself happy. She seemed to me in all this a pure product of America.

What had driven Jane was ambition. What had mattered to her finally was her work. What sustained her was a constantly regenerated, constantly replenished hope.

What all this might mean I couldn't have said. Cletus, however, could, and did. "Desquamate."

"She's shedding a skin?"

"Sloughing everything off."

"Everything being what, exactly?"

"Whatever she doesn't want to deal with."

"She was nearly killed," I said. "Doesn't that justify a reassessment?"

"She'll slither out all slick and shiny," Cletus said. "Watch."

I was dubious, until the morning I returned from running errands to find Jane's car gone and Cletus on the patio with a note of three words: "Thank you. Goodbye."

"She didn't sign it," I said.

"Doesn't know who she is yet."

News of the fire took two days to arrive in Southern California. Carlyle Walden had immediately called to offer me conventional consolations, although it was clear that his primary concern was Jane. They spoke briefly, long enough for him to offer as a haven a bedroom at the Malibu ranch. She declined, but when she left – I want to say fled – I assumed that she'd gone to L.A. So when Carlyle flew up to Nevada, we were as surprised that he hadn't seen or heard from Jane as he was that she wasn't here.

After Carlyle loaded the ranch van with Cletus' few belongings – a couple of changes of clothes, a clutch of books – the two men sat with me on my patio and drank iced tea. Surveying the now bare, blackened earth and budding lilac at the bottom of the hill, Carlyle again tendered sympathy. But where, he then wondered, could Jane be? Why hadn't she gotten in touch with him?

"Our collaboration was developing into a genuine symbiosis. Our minds are so different, she is so marvelously visual, I…"

He trailed off, perhaps sensing that to continue would require him actually to say something. Something like "I'm in love with her – how could she abandon me?"

"Time to go," Cletus said.

We embraced.

I watched the van down the hill and out of sight.

A week later Eleanor arrived, and we tended graves. I enjoyed her company, as always, but soon she too was gone, and I was alone as I hadn't been for some time.

On the Fourth of July, Cletus called, the celebration of Independence Day being an old joke between us. After satisfying my enquiries after his health, he told me that Jane had arrived in Malibu a few days earlier. Where she'd been the past month, and with whom, if anyone, and to what purpose, she hadn't said. She said only that she wished to make a film about wild horses and Brock Walden.

I DIDN'T KNOW that I would be writing so much about myself — about old emotions, intuitions, and uncertainties. I sense these relevant. I hope I'm not merely maundering.

Of a hot and windy day much like the one, fifteen months earlier, on which Jane Harmon gawked at a billboard image of Brock Walden and ended up in the ditch, she arrived back at Blue Lake. I was dozing that afternoon when I heard a car pull into the driveway, and, a moment later, a metal chair leg scrape against flagstone. Rising, I peeped out onto the patio, where Jane sat at the shaded table and looked out over treetops to the playa, dry once more, and beyond to distant hills blurred with dust. A rush of pleasure, surprising in its force, swept over me. I hadn't known if I would see her again. Now her return, accomplished, seemed inevitable: a homecoming.

Quickly preparing a tray with iced sun tea and apple wedges and macaroons, I stepped out to greet her. Her smile spoke delight in, it seemed, her own presence: "Miz Waner Ma'am, I'm back."

"And welcome."

I sat and served. Jane chatted. Carlyle and B. W. were flying in. She would meet them at the Rocking W, where B. W. wanted to stay for a couple of months, at least until deer season. She needed to film some more in one or two Gull Valley locations, and around town, and with Mina Pasco, so she'd be busy, but she would try to stop in often. Carlyle would be helping her. He was competent with the camera, and he was going to write the narration for her film, which would both celebrate the Real, the Wild West and mark its passing.

Jane hesitated. "I — maybe you heard from Cletus that we've formed a production company, Carlyle and I."

I had heard that. I'd heard too that Carlyle had augmented the insurance check so that Jane could purchase new, top of the line equipment. He'd given her access to the material he'd collected for the biography of his father and helped her to film interviews with some of B. W.'s old partners in work and riot and bed.

"And that we..."

Jane and Carlyle had become lovers. "Yes."

"I'm not sure how that happened."

"Carlyle has been courting you for quite a while," I said. When she didn't respond, I asked: "Are you happy?"

After a moment, she said: "He's better for me, Miz Waner."

"Are you good for him?"

The question startled her. "I – he says he loves me."

I let the evasion pass. "And do you love him?"

"Yes. Of course. How else could I...?" Her gaze met mine and slid away. "I didn't plan this, Miz Waner. It just...happened."

I offered her a macaroon. "I hope it won't be too awkward, you and Carlyle staying at the Rocking W, with Troy around so much."

"Troy? Why should it be awkward?"

She seemed serious.

When I didn't reply, she went on: "He's been seeing to Virgie, and I need to, not pay him, exactly, but...reimburse him somehow. I'd like to do something nice for him."

"That might not be too easy."

She smiled her bright, reassuring smile. "If Brock Walden and I can become friends, I don't see why Troy and I can't too."

Before she left that day, Jane had more to say about Brock Walden, who over the weeks she'd spent in Malibu apparently had charmed her. "He can be vulgar and crude, but he's really a...decent man, inside. Don't you think so?"

"I don't know Brock Walden well enough to have an opinion," I said, although I nevertheless had one.

"He's...complex. But he's been really helpful, getting materials for us, making introductions. And he tells wonderful stories. He told me about his life, about his mother and father, the real story, and about growing up on the streets, being on his own out in America. It's...inspiring, really, a real rags-to-riches American story. A lot of what he did wasn't right, but I can see why he...I mean, people don't know, don't understand. Nobody really knows him."

That, I thought, was probably true.

"And even now, sick and in a wheelchair, he has a kind of...charge about him. I can understand why women..."

I remembered the tingling on my skin as, many years before, Brock Walden reined his horse into fancy steps in the Rocking W ranch yard.

"He likes me." Jane smiled a different smile. "And he admires my work."

"As well he should," I said, struck by the notion that Jane had reconstructed her fantasy. She was speaking of Brock Walden now as she might of a lover.

"He's the last Western hero. Not the kind in a white hat, there's a dark streak in him, not evil, really, just... animal. But where would we be without men like him?"

I wasn't sure what that meant, but I wasn't inclined to pursue it. "And he'll be the subject of your film?"

"And the ranch. And wild horses. His life will be story enough, I think. It will work."

"So," I said, "your film will also be a memorial to Brock Walden."

"Yes. I mean – I hadn't actually thought about it that way, but yes."

A memorial, and, I thought, Brock Walden's final hoot of disdain. He would laugh his way to the grave.

"There they are now," Jane said.

A faint groan of engine trailed a dark speck in the sky that arced in a looping turn out over the desert hills. As the sound thickened, slowly the mote took shape, becoming an aircraft that, with a sort of sigh, dropped toward the playa and its own shadow, which it confused in a roiling of dust, and then rose to skim over town and trees before climbing sharply and circling back out over the hills, growing smaller, quieter.

"He seems to be going the wrong direction," I said.

"No, look," Jane said.

The plane had turned again, climbed higher, and now, heading once more toward Blue Lake, seemed to hang motionless in the vast blueness. Then the pitch of the engine changed as the nose of the plane dipped. In a steep dive, the plane grew large, red and white, the engine growl louder. I could not believe what seemed to be happening, even though soon I could see the shudder of wing struts, the lettering on the engine cowl, the faces in the cockpit. Suddenly unable to breathe, to move, I clutched the iron arms of my chair as Brock Walden aimed his airplane at me. Glasses rattled on the metal patio table. The umbrella shook. Brock Walden grinned. Then the roar came to crescendo as the plane swooped upwards and away from the rock face behind us.

The sound of the plane was long gone before Jane found her voice. "Carlyle says it's a kind of test – not of courage, of reflexes. Eventually he'll be too slow."

"And kill everyone in the plane, and some of us on the ground as well?"

"Cletus and Carlyle are the only ones who fly with him any more," she said. "As for us, well… he has that way of not caring. Even if he cares."

I had no idea what that meant either. "It's a wonder he hasn't already killed somebody."

Jane didn't answer. She sat looking out to the playa, where the dust the plane had raised was drifting. Then she said: "Carlyle isn't B. W.'s only child, is he?"

"I don't know. There have been rumors about paternity settlements and payoffs."

"Rumors," she repeated. "I – that… Haas, some say that he's B. W.'s son."

"They say a lot of things, Jane. Most of it nonsense."

"It is pretty unlikely, isn't it," she nodded. "I mean, he's never made any claim, Carlyle says, never approached him or B. W. They don't look anything alike. Still…"

"He's a drug dealer and a brawler and bully. He'll end up dead or in prison, and probably soon."

"Yes, yes. Of course."

Something in her tone, in the way she positioned her body on the edge of the chair, alarmed me.

"Stay away from him, Jane."

"Yes," she said, "he's a hateful man."

"He's a dangerous man. Every molecule in your body, every stirring in your psyche has warned you against him."

"Yes," she said again. Then, despite the heat of the late afternoon, she shivered. "He's like one of those ugly, scarred stallions out at Mud Springs, isn't he?"

"He's nothing like them. They're brutes. He's human and malign."

"Yes," she said, "I know, Miz Waner. I know."

But of course that didn't stop her.

Only after Jane left that afternoon did I realize that she'd made no mention of the fire. The conflagration might never have occurred, my old home and life never have been. So too, I suspected, her affair with Troy Hardaway.

Blue Lake has no account of the meeting of the ex-lovers. The evening of her arrival, Carlyle drove Jane and a horse trailer to the Hardaway place, where they loaded up Virgie. Troy was there. What transpired at this meeting none of the three involved ever said. Since then Virgie has been stalled at the Rocking W.

Over the next week, Troy did his work, twice he had supper with his sister, and at night he puttered about the house that had sheltered generations of his family or he drove about in the dark as his sister once had. At the Rocking W, when Jane and Carlyle were not listening to Brock Walden sing the myth of himself, they rode, she on Virgie and he on Hop, or they filmed, or they talked of their project, and they fed each other dreams before retiring to a ranch house bedroom for the night. They could hear Brock Walden in the next bedroom, his shiftings and soft groans, his cries in dream and distress.

Then one afternoon Troy Hardaway inexplicably stopped in the middle of a fence repair, drove into town to Brunson's, and bought a quart of Jim Beam, which he sipped from on the way back to his house. Hooking up a horse trailer, he loaded Tango, slipped his .30-.30 into the rack behind the seat, and started off toward Mount Adams. Late that night George Burleigh got a call from a BLM ranger patrolling county roads after cattle rustlers. He'd come upon Troy, reeking of bourbon, sitting slumped on the slope of the ditch in which his pickup stood slanted, the wheels on one side held two feet off the ground by a trailer hitch violently twisted but still fixed.

The trailer itself lay on its torn and crumpled side. Tango's leg was broken, his brain shattered by a .30-.30 bullet.

Troy was uninjured. He was still drunk when George arrived, but, George said, not enough. He mentioned a deer.

Over the next few days, Blue Lake picked at the story. So a deer had leaped into his headlights and Troy, trying to avoid it, had ended up in the ditch. That happened. He'd been drinking. That wasn't unusual on desert roads in darkness. But leaving a job unfinished? That wasn't Troy Hardaway. And where was he going? Roundup would start soon, but Walden Ranch had no grazing allotments on Mount Adams, so there was nothing for him to be checking. And why had he brought no saddle or blanket or tack? And why the rifle – Troy hunted but was not known to poach. And what had he been thinking, after he shot Tango, as he sat in the dark and drank? To these questions Troy offered no answers. He never spoke of the incident, not even to his sister.

"Can't get anything out of him, Miz Waner," Ione angrily told me later that week. "He just looks at me like I'm not even there."

There was nothing I could say.

Troy, she said, had, by hand, dug his horse a deep grave in the north pasture.

"Between him and B. W., the place's like a mental ward." She scowled angrily. "I don't know why the old goat's even here. He can't ride, he can hardly negotiate his chair around the ranch yard. He flies a little, when Carlyle can go with him, but mostly he just sits on the porch and gawks."

"Taking stock?" I paused. "Putting his life in perspective?"

"Wouldn't be like him," she said. "Though I guess Cletus is putting some of his affairs in order for him."

Cletus had told me on the phone, somewhat vaguely, that he had stayed in Southern California to "make arrangements." I took this to mean that he was engaged in a final cleaning up after Brock Walden.

"Maybe he just doesn't want to die in Los Angeles." I thought of our meeting in the hallway of the Community Center, of his odd moment of self-reflection. "But who knows what he really wants?"

Ione didn't have time to contemplate the question, for it was the end of summer, time to ready all for roundup. Neither did Jane give the matter much thought, occupied as she was in putting to use another relationship.

Making her earlier films, Jane had gained considerable experience working with abused women, so that when Mina Pasco came to her door that day to warn her off Norman Casteel, she quickly turned the situation to her advantage. Could she and Mina meet, at the Wagon Wheel Café perhaps, and discuss the possibility of Mina appearing in her film? Mina, after very little persuasion ("Everybody wants to be in a movie") agreed. The next day, over coffee, Jane talked of her film about the Real Wild West, Mina of her life. Raised with four other children of absent fathers, pregnant and abandoned at sixteen, she was at thirty the mother of three, subsisting on food stamps and ADC and infrequent baby sitting or house cleaning jobs, with her children and her mother and two of her sisters and their children living in a ramshackle two-story frame house across the street from Cottonwood Creek Park. (Filmed, the house is grimy white clapboard with two dormered windows in which tattered curtains whip out on the wind.) Men drifted in and out of Mina's account, Norman Casteel being the latest. He could get nasty when he'd been drinking or was upset, and he was always fussing about and competing with Pete Haas, but he was a good man, they might get married soon.

About that unpleasantness with Jane's soiled panties: Mina hadn't known what the men had planned; Norman had wanted her with him, so she had to go along, didn't she? Jane had accepted the apology.

When Jane came to me, I could tell her only that Mina had been, as my student, a young woman for whom I'd had some hope, intelligent and pleasant if self-consciously alert to affront ("nice but touchy," a classmate had labeled her), one who could do better in life than immediate circumstances might suggest. But as with so many, dreams did her in, romantic visions of love leading to the limited future of a high school dropout in rural Nevada. She had managed better than some women in her situation: neither ravaged to skin and bone by methamphetamines nor swollen by starches and sugars, she kept herself up and her children clean and appropriately dressed. She volunteered her services to her mother and sisters and, sometimes, the community. She smiled, Blue Lake came to know, even after a beating.

"We connected right away," Jane said. "My early films were all about victims."

"I thought you were trying to move beyond that subject."

"But it's there, Out Here, isn't it," Jane said. "It's part of this larger story. It's like the wild horses."

I saw no likeness at all, but I didn't say so.

Now, returned, Jane reestablished contact with Mina Pasco. She filmed in and around her house, and with Carlyle she interviewed Mina and her mother and sisters and friends, let them speak of children and men and America and the desert. They didn't mention drugs and alcohol and battery and rape, but Jane's camera found the effects of these in their faces and eyes. They seemed, these women, a constant, generations breeding generations.

Not so the men lurking in the background – shadowy figures, transients, always the same if not the same man. One, Norman Casteel, his facility for fantasy exercised by Jane's presence, crept closer, exchanging a word with Carlyle, then with Jane, who eventually suggested to Mina that Norman's mountain man outfit – beard and bulk, elk tooth and turquoise hat band, bobcat skin waistcoat – would show to advantage on the screen. Norman agreed to an interview, to be filmed down near the fairgrounds, at the corrals of the nags he rented the few times he actually guided hunters into the Turquoise Mountains. As much for the benefit of his Aunt Shirley and Mina and a glut of local wastrels as for the camera, Norman, scratching and sweating in the desert heat, struck manly poses as he proclaimed the virtues of the Real Wild West, vanished to all but men like himself, and he boasted of his skills with animals, with Out There incompetents, with women. He strutted through a showing of hunting and trapping gear. He pronounced America effete, its spirit lost, he himself a throwback to a hardier era. He proposed, with a snigger, to restore the country's manliness by putting himself out to stud.

His twenty-second appearance in Jane's film would reveal him a buffoon, constitute a savage burlesquing of all he pretended to be. Thus, Jane would avenge her humiliation on Blue Lake's Main Street.

The only on-looker who seemed to have understood what Jane was actually up to was Pete Haas. And discerning her plan, he began, it turned out, to formulate his own.

That day Carlyle noticed Haas speaking softly to Mina, his words raising color in her throat, injury and anger in her eyes. After that, her smiles to Jane were stiffer, forced sometimes, and her enthusiasm for the film project artificial. At the same time, she began to confide to Jane that Pete Haas was misunderstood, a rebel who drew the wrath of conventional authority, a man peaceable until provoked, and one more of Jane's many distant admirers. Mina crossed her heart and hoped to die that Pete Haas was the son of Brock Walden.

Jane believed, really, none of this. She caught the change in Mina, suspected collusion, sensed that she was being set up for... something. Yet Haas now was often about the house across from the park, moving quietly, speaking softly, and Jane, wary, studied him, once or twice passing a civil word.

I was bewildered. I had to acknowledge then that I didn't understand Jane at all. I especially didn't understand her fascination or her fear.

Jane, I realized at last, was afraid of men – certainly of men like Norman Casteel and Pete Haas, perhaps ultimately of all men. But why I didn't know.

Why, taking Ione Hardaway for a man advancing across the highway toward her, had Jane retreated into the hard shell of herself? Was it Ione's angry aggressive lean? Was it her pistol? Or was it something other, some old image appearing before her, some old terror clutching at her heart?

Why her near hysteria when first accosted by Pete Haas and his pickup and his question? Some in Blue Lake would think him merely to have been having a little fun, "messing with her," as young people say today.

How much of what she feared, how much of what she heard and sensed and felt, was real, of the present, and how much memory or imagination?

Why had all her films taken as a subject abused, battered, injured, betrayed, and oppressed women?

Why had she been unable to love any of her lovers?

I could almost believe that Jane herself had been abused. Almost. But Jane, in all she said about her past, never hinted that she was a victim of violence. If she'd ever been assaulted, violated, she would have told me, I believe, Jane being Jane. Nevertheless, she seemed to bear old, unhealed wounds. Were these simply ideas to her, ideological givens, or the sympathetic stigmata of sisterhood? Had she taken in and made her own the fears and sufferings of other women? I don't know.

All of which is to say that I don't know what made Jane Harmon do what she did. If pressed I would admit that, ultimately, I don't care. Motive matters only to the actor. To the woman who is acted upon, knowing the complexities that drive the hand slashing across the face does not soften the slap.

If I could make little of Jane's fear, I could make less of her fascination with Pete Haas. It certainly had some connection to the possibility of his being of the blood of Brock Walden. Beyond that – but perhaps I am naïve. Perhaps Jane is merely one more woman sexually drawn to danger. Perhaps there is in her psychosexual makeup an impulse to destruction, which she inevitably avoids by bringing it down on others.

I don't know. Although there was one small story...

At thirteen, Jane was a gymnast betrayed by her body. She didn't mind, terribly. For all her coordination and strength, she hadn't been really good – she was too tall, her muscles were too long to produce the explosive bursts of energy required by tumbling and the vault. Now her flesh was reshaping itself, transforming her into a different kind of creature, and gymnastics was becoming one more childhood treasure to slip into a scented drawer in her memory. She would miss the rhythmic exercises, though, with a hoop or ball, but especially with a ribbon.

Jane loved herself dancing barefoot on the mat. She loved arranging her limbs into arcs and pointed tips, twisting her torso into attractive forms as she streamed the ribbon sinuously, continuously through the air. She loved making something beautiful of herself, knowing herself both dancer and dance. She felt herself, like the ribbon, flowing and afloat, somehow freed and purified.

Until the day that, dancing alone at the end of practice, the ribbon waving in graceful loops and flutters, she came slowly, oddly to feel imperiled.

As always, from the gymnasium door there lengthened a line of men waiting for their daughters. She knew some of these men, fathers of friends, and others she had seen before; all were in some sense familiar to her, had always offered a kind of comfort. Now, this day, disturbed, she finally looked, and she saw the eyes – not the faces, only the eyes – of three or four men, she could not have said who they were, watching her move over the mat, watching her arranging her changing body, looking at her as she had not been looked at before. And she was suddenly afraid. The ribbon settled to the floor as she stopped dancing.

Jane had tried to smile, telling me that little story, tried and failed.

JANE SOMETIMES SAID that she had come Out Here looking for the Wild West. Other times she said she wanted to find the Real West. Or she used the terms, always capitalized by her inflection, together, one intensifying the other.

Blue Lake does the same. I'm not sure why. Using language this way, what are we trying to say about ourselves?

Near the end of August, the BLM began a major gather in the desert and foothills of Gull Valley, hoping to round up and remove from the range thirty-five hundred wild horses. And one evening

Carlyle Walden met with Blue Lake at the Community Center to discuss his plans for Walden Ranch.

Carlyle's letter to the newspaper, short on specifics as it was, had satisfied no one.

Blue Lake didn't really know what, exactly, he had in mind, how serious a disruption he intended, or how significant a change he envisioned. He had solicited opinions and suggestions, but, with no plan to discuss or debate or dismiss, Blue Lake could suggest only that he do nothing. Now, when in town at the drug or hardware or ranch supply store, or going to and from AA meetings, he was interrogated. His responses – thoughtful, considered, intricate – only increased the frustration of those seeking simple reassurances, until at last, although no one could say quite how it came about, a convocation was scheduled: Carlyle Walden would address all questions about his planned memorial to his father.

Of course, the meeting disappointed everyone. Some present, those of a certain age, had hoped to see and hear from Ol' B. W. himself, from whom, they liked to believe, straight talk always issued. But Carlyle came to town only with Jane, explaining that his ailing father no longer involved himself in business matters. Beyond that, on this question B. W. had no opinion. Those who knew Brock Walden would understand when Carlyle told them that the old man didn't care what happened to the ranch.

Some did in fact understand, but many did not. This crowd was younger than the men and women who had danced and mourned in this same room over a few hours not that long before. While some of my generation attended, most were economically active, many of them my former students: hay growers and shopkeepers and teachers and clerks and builders, the odd buckaroo and trucker, a handful of professionals and local officials. A few barroom habitués were also present, perhaps in search of fun, although Pete Haas and Norman Casteel sprawled over their chairs as if presuming to have a legitimate stake in the concerns at hand. Troy Hardaway was absent, which seemed fortunate.

Carlyle, after joking about a splinted, bandaged index finger (he didn't tell us that Jane had slammed a car door on it) had just begun a formal greeting when Ione Hardaway came in. Her work clothes pale with dust, hat sweat-stained, boots caked with mud and manure, she scanned the room as if for something on which to reckon. When Jane approached her, filming, Ione glowered and seemed about to speak but then did not.

An old rancher, one of Bill Hardaway's pallbearers, sang out: "Don't worry, Carlyle. She ain't packin' her little gun."

Ione's grudging smile authorized our laughter. She looked around the room again, and for a moment I thought she might turn and leave, let all be what it would. But this was one more situation to tough out. She moved to the back of the room, where, in a rich funk of dirt and sweat and cow and horse, she took a seat beside me. Removing her gloves, she returned my quiet greeting with a touch of her fingers on my arm as if in consolation – for what I didn't know.

Carlyle began again, and quickly the crowd stirred to shift and mutter. If Carlyle Walden stood a little straighter and gripped life a little more firmly, as it seemed to those of us who had long known him, he still could dither Blue Lake to despair. In his carefully composed, constantly qualified listing of possible projects at Walden Ranch there was no fissure that a rhetorical pry bar might fit into. Everything was tightly, rationally sealed; all was accounted for, and nothing was settled. The questions, when they came, were the old questions, the speculations and arguments those that had floated about for months.

Beside me, Ione sat silently. Only then, studying the sag of her shoulders, the tightness around her mouth, did I perceive how much the previous months, all the to-do with the ranch, with Carlyle and Jane and Troy, had taken out of her.

Perhaps she felt my concern. Without speaking, she closed her eyes, felt for my hand and held it. For a moment I found myself moved nearly to tears.

The meeting droned on, speeches were made, motives questioned, insinuations issued, and accusations leveled. Chair legs scraped against the floor, voices raised, faces flushed with anger or anxiety, and Carlyle came to say: "I understand your apprehension. Uncertainty can rot the spirit. But surely you see that we have to resist the impulse to a hasty decision."

"Rot the spirit, huh?" The impudent drawl came from Pete Haas. "Don't look like all this's done your spirit any harm."

Carlyle frowned, as if not quite able to take the point.

"Must make you feel like a big man, keep the whole town hanging." Haas swung his hard smile around the room, stopping it finally before the lens of Jane Harmon's camera. "Blue Lake's turn in the barrel, huh?"

"I'm sorry, I don't quite – "

"Giving it back to everybody who give it to you when you was a kid, is that it?"

Murmurs confirmed the favor the idea found in the room.

"This has nothing to do with – "

"You're enjoying this, ain't you, brother?"

Before Carlyle could consider an answer, Norman Casteel, as if challenged by Haas' boldness, brayed: "Why change? Leave things the way they are."

The room grumbled accord. Other speakers seconded the notion. Change was threat – this was the unspoken argument. Security lay in sameness and cycles. Call it tradition, as Blue Lake did that evening, call it our Out Here heritage, call it desert tough-it-out stubbornness – the way we live now in an inhospitable, beautiful land, however much it limits us, however severely it twists us, works. We get along, make do, get by. Change brings uncertainty, and problems, and, in the desert, most often failure. Better to leave things alone.

"What do we celebrate each Wild West Days if not change?"

Carlyle's question startled the room into silence.

"Opening the West altered the land irremediably," he said. "White men came to Nevada, and nothing in it remained the same. Settling Gull Valley transformed it."

"Yeah. Made it a place we could live in," croaked a young hay hauler. "And now you want to ruin it all."

"Most of it's long ruined," Carlyle rejoined calmly. "My father built Walden Ranch out of what was left of other men's failures."

"Ain't the same thing," someone said, but the claim had no energy, argued against the unease that subdued the group.

Then Ione Hardaway, releasing my hand, rose. "So you'll commemorate B. W.'s achievement by destroying it."

Carlyle was silenced as much by her tone – somber, richly layered with feeling – as by her words.

"Walden Ranch is beautiful," she said. "The way B. W. put it together, all the places fitting in around the Rocking W. It's beautiful. And it works."

"As it will continue to do, even – "

"No," Ione said, and in that single syllable I heard, for the first time, her sadness.

Carlyle, I think, also heard, and felt at last her sense of impending loss. "Ione – "

"You take out a piece, it all falls apart. Walden Ranch, and everything on it, every one on it, stops working. So you sacrifice what is for what was."

"As for who will be working on the ranch, Ione," Carlyle began again, "you and I can discuss this privately – "

"This isn't about me, Carlyle," she said quietly. In the room now nothing stirred but Jane Harmon, as she altered the angle of her lens.

Carlyle and Ione looked at each other. In this public occasion, the moment had for them become intensely private. Finally, he spoke. "What is it about, then?"

"That's it. That's what it's about, right there. You don't get it." Ione's smile was rueful, ironic. "B. W. gets it. He knows how we ranch Out Here, and why. You don't get it, Carlyle – and that's what this is all about."

She stepped into the aisle and was nearly to the door when she stopped, and turned, and addressed not Carlyle but Blue Lake: "It doesn't matter what any of us say, you know. He won't quit."

As Ione stepped out the door, Jane Harmon took the empty chair beside me. "Isn't she... magnificent, Miz Waner?"

So the meeting resolved nothing. It did give Blue Lake something new to talk about, however. Was Carlyle Walden deliberately frustrating the community, causing anxiety among those who, years before, had abused his innocence? Was this memorial business, the transforming of the Rocking W into some kind of tourist trap and the dismantling of Walden Ranch, was this all Carlyle Walden's revenge?

The meeting also gave Jane Harmon something to worry: "Miz Waner Ma'am, why did Pete Haas call Carlyle 'brother'?"

But both Blue Lake and Jane Harmon had other things to talk about. The BLM roundup was raising dust all over Gull Valley as helicopters herded mustangs toward traps, where men funneled the horses into corrals and chutes and loaded them onto trucks that hauled them to temporary holding facilities. Raising more dust were the SUVs of media teams, television crews and print journalists from local and national outlets, and observers from animal rights groups. As the BLM tallied horses, and the mustang advocates catalogued abuses, Blue Lake counted cash and credit card receipts. As federal agents publicly debated those arguing against the need, efficiency, and humaneness of the roundup, Blue Lake privately castigated both sides as Out There meddlers.

Jane found her allegiance divided. She knew Barry Shantz, the local BLM chief, to be a sincere official doing his best for the land and the animals on it. She had heard from locals of the deterioration of the range, and of the rate of population increase among a species with no natural predators, and of the irony of wild, free animals – symbols of independence – having to be kept alive in drought by trucked-in water, during blizzards by air-dropped hay. She'd also heard stories of how ranchers had once controlled and profited from the herds, improving the bloodlines with their own stallions, shipping excess or inferior animals to the slaughterhouse. But now she was learning from the media and activists of the number of animals dying in gathers, the number of mares aborting; she saw their exhaustion and fear, and the stress brought by the breakup of the band structure that ordered their existence. She was informed that desertification of the range was caused not by wild horses but by cattle, which had overgrazed the land for a century or more. Wild horses, she heard again, were symbols of American freedom, but threatened and in need of protection.

Jane took it all in and got it all on film. In the air with Carlyle and, when he was feeling up to it, B. W., she got wonderful panoramic shots of men and machines and animals crawling though the sage and rock, scurrying over the torn and buckled terrain, and scuffing earth into dust that drifted in heat shimmers or dissipated in the wind. She and Carlyle rode Virgie and Hop to a knoll from which she filmed swaying helicopters herding frantic horses; they drove to the BLM pens and filmed as the animals shied and shuddered. She interviewed phlegmatic federal agents, who intoned statistics and schedules, and she listened to impassioned activists. She spoke with and filmed Gull Valley hay ranchers and Blue Lake businessmen. Over the first phase of the gather, at the far end of the valley, she got enough material, she told me one day, for a documentary on the subject.

"It's... well, I don't know what the word is for it, Miz Waner, but everything is turning out perfectly, all by accident. I was struggling to find one film, and now I've got two of them."

"Serendipitous might be the word you want," I said.

We were on my patio once more, shaded in the late-morning heat, sipping iced tea. Before she arrived, I had been trying again to write about my burned house and the still-living lilac bush. I was happy to have her company.

"When the BLM moves closer to the ranch next month, I'll be able to get a different set of images." She smiled brightly. "I'll be glad when Cletus is here to show me what I've really got."

That would be soon. Brock Walden had been having breathing difficulties, and the next day Carlyle was flying him to L.A. to see a pulmonary specialist. The plan was to bring Cletus with them when they returned.

"I wasn't clear," Jane said. "Cletus, he will be staying with you again?"

"He'll be at the ranch. There's nothing to keep him occupied here."

Jane frowned. "I'm not sure I understand, about Cletus and B. W. I know that B. W. got him sober and everything, and gave him a job, but…"

"As different as they are, they're a lot alike," I said. "They respect each other. And their relation has something to do with their war experiences too, I think." That was not a satisfactory answer, but I didn't have a better one. "Cletus always jokes that B. W. threatened to beat him to death if he didn't stop trying to kill himself."

Jane immediately believed that she understood. "It's all about fighting, isn't it? It would be, with men like them."

The night that Cletus and I sat over coffee in a Hollywood diner filled with street people and denizens of the night, he had told me something else: "Remember Lonnie? I'm just like him."

I had never seen any similarity in the hard-bodied, kind-eyed ex-cowboy and the maimed and malodorous unfortunate I'd met years before in the Rocking W ranch yard. As with so much else about himself, Cletus hadn't elaborated. I was content not to understand.

I was also content with the notion that if Cletus Rose could stay with him for nearly sixty years, Brock Walden must be a man of, if not exactly virtue, at least some value.

"So he'll be out at the ranch, watching over B. W., while you're here, writing…" Jane nodded at my pen and notebook, temporarily set aside, "your little essay things."

"And you will be making two films."

"We're really alike too, aren't we, Miz Waner, both of us working all the time. You really are my mother, in a way. Creatively." Then came one of her skips. "Carlyle says you read a story he wrote, years ago, about an Indian girl and a newspaper reporter from back east."

My reply came cautiously: "A youthful effort."

"Oh, he knows it isn't any good," she said. "He showed it to me so I could see why he failed as a novelist. It's pretty cheesy. But there are things in it, Miz Waner…"

"I suppose you mean the picnic scene," I said.

"I – that was real, wasn't it? In a way."

Some months after his long summer in Blue Lake, Carlyle Walden had sent me a manuscript. The accompanying letter, in his formal and circumspect style, begged to hope that I would read the fiction upon which he had labored since leaving Nevada. It was not, he modestly allowed, up to the standards of Max Brand or Louis L'Amour, but perhaps neither was it devoid of all worth. He would deeply appreciate any comments, criticisms, or suggestions that I might be kind and interested enough to offer.

I read the story. Two hundred or so carefully typed pages of fussy prose narrated the adventures of a young reporter in Comstock era Nevada as he sought silver, fought off claim jumpers and road agents, helped to drive beef to hungry miners, and wrote up his exploits for an admiring readership in the East, among whom he was securing a glorious future. Through all this he also managed to win the heart of a Shoshone maiden, who nevertheless insisted that he return east to fulfill his authorial destiny while she remained in the desert to work for the good of her people.

Carlyle's characters were cutouts speaking a patois heard nowhere in the West and stumbling stiffly through scenes from B-movies, his story bearing the stamp of adolescent male fantasy. The one exception to all this was a picnic scene, in which the young couple consummate their love. Here, suddenly, was a real world in which a real young man and young woman, speaking the words of real people, came together. The encounter was charged with real emotion: the young man's stunned, innocent uncertainty at his lover's unanticipated offering of herself; his hesitancy before her eagerness; his wonder at her body and his own body's response to the touch of her beautiful hands; his burgeoning sense of his feeling for her, and for himself, as he slowly settled into pleasure and what he thought was ultimate wholeness.

"He was writing about her. Ione. About them."

I had nothing to say. Not that Jane would have heard me anyway.

"I've never felt that way with anybody," Jane said. "Have you?"

Again she didn't notice that I didn't answer her question.

"Carlyle and Ione – why didn't they ever…"

"They were teenagers," I said, "and his story was fiction."

"That doesn't mean it wasn't true." This time, when I didn't respond, she went on. "And there's something else happening there.

Something the young man doesn't understand. Or the author. Isn't there?"

"If so, it's none of our business, Jane."

"He really loved her, Miz Waner. He still loves her, in a way. I mean, he's not in love with her any more, but he still – " She broke off, for a moment lost in herself. "It's all right, though, I don't mind, I admire him for it. Sometimes I wish…"

But what she sometimes wished she did not say.

"Miz Waner Ma'am – you know where Troy is?"

Ione, this time, was not angry. She was disheartened.

She drove up not long after Jane departed, as I was preparing lunch. Surprised to see her at mid-day, puzzled by her question, I insisted that she share my tuna and tomato. While I set her a place at the kitchen table, she washed up. Refreshed, she sat, hands in her lap like a schoolgirl, as I served.

"Jane said she was going to stop and see you. I thought you might have noticed Troy lurking around, tailing her. That's what he does, anymore, when she's not with Carlyle."

"I didn't see him," I said. "I – he follows her? To what end?"

"Same old thing. Thinks Haas is after her, and he'll rush to her rescue again. He's… gone over the edge, Miz Waner."

I had never seen her so dejected.

With her fork, Ione scraped gently at her ball of tuna salad, as if to uncover in it some delicate truth. "It's my fault."

I bit into a tomato wedge.

"I spoiled him. Didn't toughen him up. I let him get away with things, let him think he was God's gift to – "

"Oh, hush," I said. "I don't want to hear this nonsense."

The old Ione was suddenly present again, flushed, glaring. I thought she might rise and leave. Instead, her scowl slowly shifting into a small, repentant grin, she said: "I guess that's why I'm here, Miz Waner. To hear you say that."

I smiled. "Take the rest of that tuna, will you please?"

"The thing is," she said, "sometimes he does his work, and other times he just leaves it and drives off after her. Everybody in Gull

Valley is watching to see if I'll fire him – if it was anybody else, he'd be long gone. They've been willing to cut him some slack because of Tango, but now they're waiting to see if I've got the sand to do what needs doing, or if after all I'm just a sloppy, sentimental woman."

"Jane won't be here much longer," I ventured. "No one will begrudge you a couple more weeks, in these circumstances."

"You think?" she said. "Tough it out till she's gone, then see what happens?"

I nodded. "And whatever happens, accept it. Troy will do whatever he will do. He's the one with the problem, and he's the only one who can solve it."

"That's what B. W. said to me, remember?" She tried a smile. "Maybe I should of shot Jane instead of the projector last Thanksgiving."

"I've told you – "

"I know. It's not Jane's fault, she's not responsible for what Troy does. I know. But shooting her would have been ever so satisfying."

I had to smile.

"I can forgive her Carlyle, the refuge idea, the ranch. But Troy – she thinks it's all like a movie, Rio Bravo or one of those, she told me." Ione shook her head. "Maybe she isn't responsible, Miz Waner, but she should have known better."

I saw nothing to be gained by dispute. On this issue, Ione was fixed.

After our meal, Ione helped me wash up before we returned to the table with more tea. "I'll finish this and be on my way," she said, but she did neither. Instead, after a moment, she asked: "Did she come to ask you about an old story Carlyle wrote? One that has something to do with me?"

"It's about a young man and young Shoshone woman with beautiful hands. There is a picnic scene in it, in a shady cove along what seems to be Molly Creek."

A quarter century after the fact, Ione colored in embarrassment. "That yahoo – from what Jane said, I thought that might be it. What does it say about... them?"

"That she's an admirable young woman. That he's a love-struck young man. Just what Blue Lake, watching you and Carlyle, noted at the time."

"Yeah, well." Ione had regained her composure. "It was a pretty day, the shade was delicious, the creek whispering sweet nothings ever so seductively." She couldn't maintain the ironic pose. "It was a mistake, Miz Waner. A lulu. And I paid for it."

"So did Carlyle, didn't he."

"I pay for that, too, every time I see him," she said. "Jane — why is she poking around in that piece of business?"

"Her interest seems natural enough. They're in love. She wants to know all she can about him."

"That doesn't mean I want her knowing all there is to know about me," she said with something of her customary ire. "She wants to dig into ranch doings, that's fine, but my private life's none of her affair."

"A teenage summer romance," I said. "That's hardly something for her to get excited about. Or you."

"May be, Miz Waner," Ione said grimly, "But everything she touches either falls down or blows up. I'll feel a whole lot better when she's gone."

We walked out to her pickup together. Ione tugged at her hat. "Terrible time for the BLM to be gathering. This heat won't do scared horses any good."

"Maybe the weather will break before they start up again."

"Nevada in August, not much chance." She looked out at the playa. "I have to let him go, Miz Waner."

"Troy? If I see — "

"I don't mean today. I mean…" But she didn't say what she meant. She got into her pickup and backed out and without a wave rolled down the hill.

THAT SATURDAY Carlyle flew Brock Walden and Cletus back to the Rocking W. At mid-afternoon, Cletus called to ask me to dinner.

B. W. hankered for a bloody steak and the ring of slot machines, he said. Jane and Carlyle would be along, as would Ione, who had somewhat unexpectedly accepted Carlyle's invitation.

I met them, a bit late, in the Silver Sage dining room, where they sat in the center of the room at tables rearranged to accommodate a wheelchair, but I didn't immediately greet anyone. I was too disturbed by Cletus' appearance, all teeth and eyes in a face from which the flesh seemed eaten away under the skin.

As he rose to seat me, he said quietly: "I don't feel as bad as I look."

"You look ghastly," I said, shaken. "What have you been doing down in Malibu?"

He smiled. "Dying, Winnefred, a little each day. Like everybody."

Tears sprang to my eyes. "Cletus – "

He touched my shoulder. "Bad joke. I'm fine."

But he wasn't fine, and we both knew it. Brock Walden, however, seemed much as he had at Bill Hardaway's funeral. His color high, he joked with Con Geary, the casino manager, one hand hoisting high a dark drink while the other gestured expansively, as if to draw into an embrace everyone in the crowded room. All present appeared pleased to be in his company, even Pete Haas, in a booth with Mina Pasco, across from Norman Casteel and his aunt Shirley.

I managed a smile for Carlyle, whose finger had shed its splint, and Jane, who for once had no camera. That evening she might have been posing for a portrait herself, her hair perfectly arranged, eyes and mouth touched by make up, a lovely silk blouse and a lacey fichu showing her to her best advantage. Her body brushed against Carlyle's in comfortable intimacy. Cletus, catching me considering her, smiled. "All slick and shiny and new."

Across from me, watching too, was Ione, at the crowded table in the crowded room somehow alone.

We ordered and ate. Brock Walden, whose appetite for rare beef had brought us here, enjoyed more his bourbon, continually refreshed, and the attention of those in the room who approached him: an elderly couple remembering when, a son of old you-know-who, the fan who recently rewatched *Under the Mountain*. He had come to town not to eat but to see and be seen, with charm and humor to connect with people. Jane, catching the spirit of his performance, now and then pertly, prettily asked questions, to which he offered quips and hackneyed phrases that mildly mocked his film career. Cletus, called on to confirm fanciful claims, made an unflappable straight man. Carlyle watched his father drink and joke, and he attended to Jane, and he seemed happy. I said little. Ione said nothing.

As we were being served coffee, music tugged my glance toward the entryway to the lounge, at the edge of which a haggard Troy Hardaway stood watching us. Meeting my eyes, he vanished.

Ione had not seen her brother. I smiled at her: "It's nice that you can get a night out. I know how busy you are."

I thought she would tell me about her day, about work. Instead she said: "The idea was to show I'm human like everybody else."

"Who would doubt it?"

"Everybody but you, Miz Waner." Her small smile faded when she looked over at the old actor. "Doesn't seem to be working."

The meal had ended, but Brock Walden, his head drooping with weariness, was nevertheless unwilling to leave. When he ordered brandy, which he obviously didn't need, Cletus made clear that this would be the culmination of the evening.

The dining room was half empty when Mina Pasco and Shirley Casteel stopped at our table on their return from the ladies room. Shirley turned positively girlish as Brock Walden, rousing himself, grinned, addressed her as "Darlin' Shirl'" and joked about an encounter in the Country Clerk's office thirty years before. Mina offered me a nod that meant nothing if I did not recognize her. When I smiled and said her name, she nodded more emphatically, but then turned to speak softly to Jane, who, when Shirley paused for breath, surprised Mina into pleasure by introducing her to Brock Walden. The old man's absurd flirting brought to the cheeks of both women a color to match his alcohol flush.

They skittered off, finally, to rejoin the men and make as if to depart.

"Mina's switched boyfriends," Jane said. We watched as the young woman, taking up her purse and shawl, managed to keep a hand on Pete Haas: shoulder, arm, hip.

"She was trying to get Norman to marry her," Jane said. "You don't suppose she believes that... he, Haas, will?"

"People can get themselves to believe almost anything," Ione said.

As if they knew we spoke of them, Haas and Mina glanced at us while they conferred quietly. Then, gesturing for the others to wait, he came over to our table.

I'd seen him about town, and at the recent meeting at the Community Center, but always across a street, a room. Jane, straining to describe him, had once referred me to Robert Mitchum in *The Night of the Hunter*: quite unlike the actor physically — bony and ponytailed and tattooed — Haas, she said, nevertheless projected the same pure masculine psychopathic menace. That hadn't helped me then and didn't now. Slouched before us, calm and smiling in jeans and a T-shirt from Darla's, he bore nothing minatory in his manner or carriage, no malice in his expression.

"Walden," he said easily, impertinently, "I'm Pete Haas."

The only threat in the room, I realized with a shock, issued from Brock Walden. Old and bloated, ill and intoxicated, he nevertheless pulsed with cold, hard hostility.

"So?"

"I thought before you croaked I'd let you know I was around."

"Why'd I care?" The old man's voice had gone soft, promising violence.

"A girl named Angela." Haas' smile became a lewd grin. "In Palm Desert, thirty five years ago. You were making a movie there."

"Angelas all over," B. W. said.

From the casino floor came the ring of a slot machine win. Haas held up a hand, as if listening to a favorite song, before he said: "I'm thirty-four."

Brock Walden's smile deformed his face. "Bastards everywhere I been, those that weren't scraped out and flushed."

"Me too," Haas said, still grinning.

"What do you want?"

"Nothing from you, old man," Haas said, his voice too now soft and seductive and chilling. "Just wanted to let you know your genes'll be alive and kicking when you ain't anymore. Don't look like number one son here's got the cojones to get 'em where they might do some good. I'll keep the bloodline going."

"Get the fuck out of here," Brock Walden said, nearly whispering.

Haas smiled and turned to Jane. "See you got both of them along tonight."

"I – what?" Jane, as if startled out of a dream, gaped.

Haas nodded toward the lounge entrance, where Troy Hardaway once again stood, watching,

"You might want to take a look at my birth certificate. For your movie. Let Mina know if you're interested." His smile broadened, took in all at the table. "Been a pleasure. Ladies."

From the lounge came country music imperfectly played. Coins rattled into slot machine trays in the casino. No one at the table spoke until the two men and two women had left the room.

"Is he…" Jane now sat eagerly on the edge of her chair. "Is he right?"

Brock Walden snorted an obscenity.

"We hear things, and we check," Cletus said. "His mother's name is Angela, nee Lesser. His father's Oscar Haas, a part-time bartender and full-time burglar. Those are the names on his birth certificate."

"But why would he want me look at it, then? I don't – "

"It's bull shit." Brock Walden had gone fractious. "You so stupid you can't see that?"

Jane flinched, but to her credit she did not slink. "So how many illegitimate children did you… father?"

"Who knows? Who cares?" He was suddenly quite drunk, exhausted and mean. "Maybe you're one of them, girlie. Maybe that wasn't imaginary, that idea you had. Maybe your mother was one more hot little – "

"Shut up!" Ione was up, angry. "You're an ugly, pathetic old man, boozing."

"And you, miss," he said: "What makes you think that buckaroo over there is your brother?"

The silence at our table changed as Ione looked at Troy, who still stood in the doorway. Finally, pale, she managed to speak: "What did you say?"

"No secret." His leer was slyly stupid. "Everybody knew old Bill Hardaway wasn't very careful about his womenfolk. Dumb bastard didn't – "

"That'll do," Cletus said, rising. "You've had enough, B. W., and we've had enough of you."

"Goddamn you, Clete!" Brock Walden's flush deepened until his face seemed raw meat. "Who you talking to!"

Silence hollowed a depression in the sounds from the lounge and casino. Into it Cletus evenly spaced his words. "We're finished here."

And then we all watched Brock Walden, his emotions ebbing, slowly become again a dying old man who'd had too much to drink. He looked at us as if trying to recall who we were.

"He says things to get people's goat, Ione, you know that." Cletus moved behind Brock Walden's wheelchair. He spoke over the old man's head, as a parent might over a child's. "It's just meanness."

"But why? Why is he this way?" This was Jane. Even as she spoke, some thoughtlessness sent her fork cartwheeling onto the floor. She paid no attention.

"Because he's angry," Carlyle said unexpectedly, "and he's alone."

Cletus nodded. "And when he says he doesn't care that he's dying, he's lying."

"Must be dead already, the way everybody's talking about me like I'm not here." Brock Walden said with his old drollery. Then something like sadness softened his tone as he looked at Ione. He seemed to struggle just to hold up his head. "Sorry, miss."

"Saying so is easy." She was no longer angry, but beyond that I couldn't read her mood. "Let's see you do something about it."

"Too late. I'm too old. You're too..." He trailed off, his gaze going distant.

I realized that I didn't know what they were talking about.

And then, suddenly, I did know.

Or, more precisely, I became aware of what I had always known.

Ione said a hasty good night to us all and entered the lounge, going after, no doubt, her brother. It took some time to settle the bill, gather our things, and determine who would drive Brock Walden back to the ranch, but we finally left without seeing either of the Hardaways again.

Cletus had planned to return to the ranch, but I insisted that he stay in town with me. We watched Carlyle drive the van off into the desert night. Cletus put a hand on my shoulder. "I'm not up for much more socializing tonight."

"I have something I want to say to you."

"Fine," he said, "but first let's just stand here for a while, shall we?"

The night sky was a deep black emptiness bristling with stars. From the hillside around the water tank came the soft chirr of cicadas, and the autumn air smelled of dry decay and overheated engines. Here and there on the street a shadow moved or took on substance. Cletus and I, old man and old woman, stood on the sidewalk in front of the small shabby casino in the small shabby desert town, casting our own single, substantial shadow.

I waited until we were at tea at my kitchen table: "I won't ask you to betray a confidence, only that you tell me if I'm wrong."

"You could just leave things be, Winnefred."

But like Jane, that's just what I couldn't do. "Carlyle Walden did not impregnate Ione Hardaway. Brock Walden did. "

His kind eyes took up an old sorrow.

"He was over fifty, she was fifteen, not that he cared. When she got pregnant, he worked out a scheme. There was no way she could cover up an abortion, Blue Lake being what it was, so she would seduce Carlyle and let him, and everyone else, think that the child she was carrying was his. To this day Carlyle doesn't know that he didn't father the fetus she aborted."

Cletus turned and stared out into the dark August night.

I went on: "She was underage, but the authorities would look the other way when it was teenagers, when the fathers had agreed on how to handle it, when one of the fathers was Brock Walden."

Cletus said nothing.

"But had the truth been known, and Bill Hardaway made a fuss, Brock Walden would face a statutory rape charge. His career would have been over."

Cletus still said nothing.

"Bill Hardaway didn't know the truth either, I imagine."

"I'm tired, Winnefred," he said. "I'm glad you made me stay in town tonight."

"Drink your tea." After a moment I smiled. "Do you remember the day we met, out at the Rocking W?"

"Every minute."

"Do you remember what you were reading?"

"I... what was it they said was the second thing to go when you got old?"

I smiled. "I know what the first was. I won't make up the guest bed for you, since my virtue is in no jeopardy."

"Don't be too sure about that, Winnefred."

I awoke some hours later, suddenly alert. But beside me Cletus breathed easily, evenly. His rich male smell was soured slightly with age and, now, a faint medicinal rot.

As I lay beside him, I thought of Faulkner, and of Yoknapatawpha County, its humidity and hanging moss so different from the arid Nevada sageland, its old secrets and human intensities so like those in Gull Valley and Blue Lake.

I thought of Ione Hardaway's anger and pain. Had she, years ago, feeling Brock Walden's eyes following her, his hands on her, ever imagined that her life would be a long emptiness?

I thought too of Troy Hardaway, lurking in the doorway of the room where his affair with Jane Harmon had begun. Had he, over the edge, any sense of an ending?

DAYS PASSED. High on Mount Adams, aspen and alder leaves began to turn. On the flanks and foothills of the Turquoise Range, buckaroos trailed cattle off allotments. In Gull Valley, activists and news people looked on as government employees in helicopters and pickups found and collected mustang bands around Mud Springs and other seeps near Walden Ranch. And at the Rocking W, Brock Walden sat on the ranch house porch, shaded from the September sun, and watched his meadows and his corrals fill with his cattle, which, under Ione Hardaway's direction, seasonal hired help sorted and doctored and shipped. Cletus, when he wasn't in town with me, or out puttering around the corrals, sat on the porch watching Brock Walden and reading. Carlyle, sometimes alone, more often with Jane, rode out to look anew – through Jane's eyes, as it were – at a land he'd known from boyhood; or, in what had once been his father's office, he studied the responses he'd received to his letters of inquiry, looked at still photos Jane had taken, reread old studio public relations material, and began to write. Jane, in no need of more material, filmed little now, spending more time in the house, planning cuts and junctures, designing motifs, experimenting with bits of music, and constructing a narrative. She rode, and she ran. Restless, eager to begin the actual composing of her film, she talked of a return to Los Angeles, but for some reason she didn't leave.

Over the same days and weeks, Troy Hardaway began to climb back into himself. George Burleigh had a talk with him, which seemed to help, and his sister kept him as far away from the Rocking W as she could – he had manned the Walden Ranch stall at the Nevada State Fair, which allowed for a purgative weekend debauch, and he spent a week in a line shack in the Cress Creek range enjoying the adulation of two high school boys who wished for nothing more than to be just like him. He worked cattle and rode fence and fixed water systems, and he no longer walked away from a job. If he followed Jane now, no one ever saw him.

So life went on, and other small scandals squealed for Blue Lake's attention, other human messes offered amusement, and I took heart. From early childhood, the succession of the seasons had always encouraged me, the slant of autumn sunlight not intimating an inevitable decline and darkness but awakening a sense process, of cycle and continuation: constancy. And nearly fifty years in a schoolroom argued that September was a time for fresh starts. As at the beginning of each new term, I had hope that perhaps all would turn out well.

Having Cletus at hand helped. At the ranch he had little to do, for Carlyle had hired Betty Johnson's sister Sally, an RN, to look after Brock Walden's nursing. Two or three times a week, Cletus came in from the ranch, grumpily insisting that his efforts to help out with the cattle just got him in the way of those doing the work. He found things to fix around my house, and we walked, and sometimes dined out, and we talked. His presence was comforting, although when he spoke of death, which he did too often, he distressed me, which he just as often failed to notice. But I made allowances and remained positive: he had a bit more color, a bit more energy, and had regained some strength. When he did look at me, his gaze lingered.

Cletus spoke more of himself and his life over those few weeks than he had in all the years of our intimacy. Telling his stories, he seemed to be brushing off the suit he would be buried in. Most of what he had to say he had said before; nevertheless, I attended to his tales, for he was reaffirming for me, and himself, who he was.

His boss and friend featured in many of the stories, of course. When Cletus retold to me, one evening, how Brock Walden had saved his life, this telling was not quite like those earlier, in which truth had twisted elusively through the cowpoke funning. This time there was no spit-and-whittle joshing. And more than one man's life was measured.

A second son born on an Arizona ranch big enough for only one, Cletus had the feel for the work that his brother lacked, the skills, the strength of muscle and character, the love of the land. It sometimes seemed to him, he said, that the first thing he knew was that there was no place for him on the place where he belonged. It sometimes seemed to him that the first thing he felt was anger. In high school he learned that alcohol abetted escape, even if into a blackness he returned from sore and dirty, remembering little, to confront the accusing or disappointed faces of those who cared for him. Once graduated, he could only, like an excess son of a medieval baron, become a warrior, and he sailed a world away to be twice wounded by Asian men he had been trying to kill. After alcohol and anger got him a bad conduct discharge, he found himself back in Arizona, trying to take out his self-disgust on Brock Walden.

"He beat hell out of me. I drank out of a tube for six weeks. When I left the hospital, he hauled me and a fifth of Jim Beam into the desert, and told me to get out. Said I could have the bottle and the desert, or I could get back in the car."

I allowed him the drama of his pause.

For the first time, Cletus smiled. "Took me a while, let me tell you."

"But you got back in the car."

"Then he heaved the bottle into a creosote bush. I wanted to cry. Then he told me to get over myself. My innocence. My anger."

"At not being able to stay on your father's ranch?"

"At being passed by by history. Like it never happened to anybody else."

I hadn't heard this from him before. "If I understand you, Cletus, that's what Jane told Ione. That ranching Out Here was an exercise in nostalgia."

"That's not quite right. But it's not wrong either. As if Ione didn't know it. She's always known it."

I considered what he had said. "And at fifteen she found herself bargaining for a place on the place where she belonged, as you put it."

Cletus shrugged.

"And now the old goat is reneging."

"He said it the other night. It's too late. Carlyle's in control of things. B. W.'s like the rest of us now, waiting to see what Ione will do."

Because Ione, being Ione, would do something, certainly.

"Working with her when she was a kid – she learned so quick. Show her an inch and she saw a yard," Cletus said.

"She could be like that in the classroom too," I said. "When she chose."

"I always knew I'd never marry. Never have a family."

"Only me," I smiled.

He didn't smile. "She's the child of my heart, Winnefred."

I looked into his kind eyes, and my vision smeared.

So we all waited. Worked and waited. But nothing happened, even as things were in fact going on.

In Foodmart one afternoon, I left Cletus in conference at the meat counter and was inspecting strawberries when around the corner came a loaded cart and Mina Pasco.

I offered a greeting. "How are you, Mina?"

"Your movie friend, Jane – she hasn't been to visit us for a while." Her tone was barely civil.

Surprised by her rudeness, I nevertheless smiled. "She's out at the Rocking W, mostly, filming the round up. I see little of her these days."

"Little's more than I do. I guess now she's got what she wanted, pictures and interviews and that, we ain't – aren't – important enough to keep up a friendship with."

Her complaint held both malice and injury.

"Couldn't of been much of a friendship to start with, I guess. Maybe none at all."

Mina stared at me, as if daring contradiction. When none came, she abandoned all subtlety. "Your friend Jane, she uses people like me and Pete. We're just stuff to go in her movies. Otherwise we're nothing to her. Not even that."

Mention of her new man suggested the source of her attitude. "I'm sorry, Mina. I can't speak for Jane, but – "

"Sure you can. You're just like her, just as phony."

I knew to remain silent.

"All your English teacher talk, the book you wrote, your stuck up airs – you think people don't know your mother was grass-eating crazy and your old man scratched dirt out in Amargosa Valley? You think we don't know you're all fake, you're really just like the rest of us?"

Cletus, coming down the aisle with a package wrapped in butcher paper, saw us and instinctively slowed.

"Everybody laughs at you. *Miz Waner Ma'am.*" Her color had deep-ened, her tone hoarsened as she worked herself into hissing outrage. "Strutting around like you're something special. Brock Walden's secret lover – all the while you're sleeping with the hired hand."

I thought she had finished. "I'm sorry you feel this way, Mina — "

"You and Jane Harmon, you need a man just like every other woman Out Here. Except she must think she's such hot stuff she can have them all."

Cletus was standing just behind her. As Mina caught my glance and turned, he tipped his hat. "Afternoon, ma'am."

Mina turned back to me, her features gathered bitterly. "Calamity Jane, is right. The bitch wrecked one relationship for me. She won't wreck another."

She pushed off down the aisle.

I didn't refer to the incident until we were home. "Jane should know that Mina is not her friend."

"Yours neither, Winnefred."

"Phoniness. I've heard the charge before. I don't let it bother me."

"So I see." Cletus too had a talent for irony.

I ignored him. "I am what I am. I love words and sentences, but I live among people suspicious of language used for anything other than expressing simple sense. I believe in being civil even when it's easier to be unpleasant. I believe what I told Ione once, that we might be animals but we don't have to be brutes. So yes, I've created a persona. I play a role. Miz Waner Ma'am. I've played her so long I've become her. So be it."

Cletus knew this already. Now he quietly proposed: "You and B. W."

I was not prepared to accept that. "He was brutish enough the other night."

"Walter Waldo Broekenworth," Cletus continued, "that's who tangled with Haas and abused Jane and Ione. Brock Walden is the man the folks joked with and fussed over. You can't tell them B. W. isn't real, even though he made himself up. That's why they love him."

"Out Here being real seems to atone for all evils."

"Could be real is just a role well played. Like yours."

Cletus sounded weary, ready for his nap. And I suddenly wished to be alone. I altered my tone. "And what role do you play, Mr. Rose?"

"Ah," he said, "everyone knows I'm the Constant Lover."

With that the conversation took a different turn, and soon he was asleep, and I was at my kitchen table, drinking tea and mulling over what we had said.

Only much later, preparing for bed, did I return to the grocery store incident.

"I'll have to pass on Mina's sentiments the next time I see Jane," I said, not knowing that I wouldn't see her in time.

Events both Out There and Out Here then made demands. Brock Walden had skirmished with the IRS for years, and now his accountant phoned for someone to come to Los Angeles to confer with her and federal agents and to sign a stack of forms. His father being in no condition to travel – he would die at the Rocking W, everyone now accepted; he had returned to the ranch expressly to do so – Carlyle determined to fly down and see to things. It happened too that the old flatbed power wagon from which ranch hands had for decades fed wintering Rocking W cattle had broken down beyond, finally, repair. Ione located a replacement on a ranch in foreclosure in Orange County, and she proposed that Carlyle fly Troy to John Wayne Airport before going on to L.A. Troy could hire transport to the truck and drive it back. So off the two men went, uneasy in each other's company, Cletus said, but not hostile.

"Carlyle's a forgiving soul, and Troy's scabbing over his hurt. I don't guess they'll get into it at ten thousand feet."

Then, the evening of the day after Carlyle and Troy left, George Burleigh came to see me. Sitting with coffee at the patio table in the twilight, as the day declined and the air took on a chill, George asked after Jane Harmon.

I'd last seen Jane several days earlier when she and Carlyle stopped on their way to the drugstore for liniment. Carlyle had been kicked by a horse. Jane hadn't done anything to startle Hop, she insisted, had only been adjusting her camera settings when suddenly the mare drove a rear hoof into Carlyle's thigh. It wasn't Jane's fault, Carlyle at once insisted, acknowledging his own culpability: he knew not to walk so close behind a horse. Fortunately, he had twisted to avoid the full force of the blow, but he was nastily bruised and would be sore for a while. The two of them were rather mawkishly solicitous of each other's sensibility, even as they made shy small jokes about massaging muscles.

"I happened onto her car this afternoon," George said. "On The Rise, about where she went in the ditch that first day. I thought she might've had trouble and walked or got a ride, until I noticed her out in the sage. Sitting there. Being a photographer, she could have been just looking at things, but I thought I'd check. I…"

George was not a hesitant man. His pause now signified.

"Twenty yards away, I could smell the booze."

I was confused. "Jane doesn't drink."

George knew that. But there was more than the reek of alcohol to suggest that she might be intoxicated. She neither noticed his approach nor responded to his inquiry. Her gaze was empty and unfocused.

"Her blouse was crinkled up, drying but still damp over her chest. That's where the stink of booze came from." George frowned. "But something was wrong. She wasn't in pain, wasn't injured, and I finally got that she wasn't drunk – she was in shock."

George frowned again, as if at his own inability to understand.

"She saw me and came to, but she wasn't really right. She was calm, with a quiet little smile… I'm not sure how to describe it."

"She didn't offer an explanation?"

"Acted like there was nothing to explain. She was just thinking, she said. She'd been talking to a man in a bar and accidentally spilled a drink."

"You didn't believe that?"

"She might have been in a bar. But it was a lot more than a drink soaking her shirt. And I know the difference between day-dreaming and shock, Miz Waner." George twisted his thick shoulders, as if to relieve tension. "She'd come out of her daze, like I said, but she still wasn't normal. I couldn't get anything more out of her. I couldn't get to her, either. Everything I said just sort of slid off."

I too was perplexed.

"When she got up to go, I didn't like the idea of her driving, but there wasn't much I could do. Later I called the Rocking W, and she'd made it back okay, but…"

"And you don't know what was causing her odd behavior?"

"I know a little," George said. "I was hoping you might know the rest."

After watching her drive off toward Gull Valley, George had returned to Blue Lake to ask questions. Jane, he learned, had come into town near noon, meeting Mina Pasco at the Wagon Wheel. After a short while, the two women had crossed the street to the Adaven. Both had entered, Mina remaining for only a few seconds. Jane did not step back out for nearly an hour.

Blue Lake knew all this. Blue Lake didn't know for certain who else had been in the Adaven, although Norman Casteel and Pete Haas were thought to have been among them. Blue Lake also didn't know, then or later – Blue Lake does not know to this day – exactly what took place over the hour that Jane was in the bar.

"I called out to the ranch again, to see if she had anything she wanted to tell me, but she wasn't there. I thought maybe she'd come in to see you."

"I wish she had," I said. "You're sure she hadn't been assaulted?"

"I've seen rape victims act like that, but there were no physical signs. Except for the damp blouse she was all neat and tidy. And calm – like if anything had happened, it didn't matter. But something did happen, Miz Waner."

I didn't doubt it. "What will you do now?"

"Try to find her, unofficially. At this point, nothing I know makes any of this my business, but I'd like to be sure she's safe. I'd like to give her a chance to tell me what went on in there, if she wants to." He shifted in his chair. "And I think I'll have a talk with Mina Pasco."

"She enticed Jane into town, into that bar?"

"I don't think Jane stopped in the Adaven for a Perrier," he said, rising. He hadn't touched his coffee.

George left me feeling guilty, of course. Had I made it a point to let Jane know of Mina's bitterness, maybe whatever had happened wouldn't have. But more than that I was worried. Where was Jane?

George called an hour later to ease my concern. Jane had returned to the Rocking W from Mud Springs, where she'd been watching the small mustang band the BLM had left on that part of the range. Thanking George for his concern, she insisted that she had no complaint to make. She had stopped in the Adaven to speak with Norman Casteel, whose drink she had clumsily spilled, and with whom she had then had an interesting conversation. Nothing more.

George didn't believe her. Neither did Blue Lake. By the next day, word had it that in the Adaven Jane Harmon had been raped by Pete Haas, or forced to fellate Haas and Norman Casteel, or abused by the obscene taunts and touching of greasy drunks, or terrified and toyed with, made an object of the crude jests and vile epithets through which boorish men express their fear and hatred of women. It was just a little barroom high-jinx. Blue Lake inclined to this last, citing Shirley Casteel's overhearing her nephew talk of having a little fun with Calamity Jane. Mina Pasco told George Burleigh that, you bet, she'd lured Jane into town and the bar with the promise that Pete Haas waited with the certificate proving he was Brock Walden's son, which Jane was gullible enough to believe; the men just wanted to scare her a little, to show her that her artsy-fartsy, hoity-toity manner meant nothing Out Here, that Out Here, where real Americans lived, she was no better than anybody else. Pete Haas hadn't been in the Adaven, no, no – that would have been a violation of his parole: he was with Mina's sister, Patty Coombs, he said, discussing her move out of the white house so that he could move in, which Patty subsequently swore to. Blue Lake, knowing that no one involved was telling the truth, nevertheless came to consensus: no serious harm seemed to have been done, Jane certainly should have known better than to go into the Adaven in the first place, and whatever grievance she suffered in the bar she probably had coming to her. (This last incensed me; Cletus suffered my rage.)

Carlyle flew back to the ranch that evening, and the next day he and Cletus drove into town for a meeting and then lunch with me. We ate on the patio, enjoying beef stew and the day, clear and bright and cool. Leaves were turning on the cottonwoods along the creeks, and the rabbit brush was yellow with pods, and we spoke of endings:

the year's calves had all been shipped – the animals in good shape and of good weight; the BLM gather was also over, although there was talk that too many horses remained on the range. We spoke too of beginnings. Scouting hunters were stirring up dust in Gull Valley.

"Will anyone at the Rocking W be hunting this year?" I asked.

"B. W.'s done with it," Cletus said. "But I'll go out with Ralph Johnson and see if I can't harvest something for the folks at the Community Center."

My displeasure no doubt altered my expression. Cletus was in no shape to be riding or hiking about the hills. But I remained silent, and he only smiled. He would do what he would do.

"I won't hunt again either," Carlyle said. "I never really enjoyed it. I was merely showing my father that I was capable of killing. I don't have to do that anymore."

Neither Cletus nor I commented. The conversation shifted. Carlyle spoke of the flight to California, which had been quick and quiet, Troy's silence one that Carlyle, hearing in it no complaint, chose not to disturb. The tax business had gone quickly too, and reasonably well. But what Carlyle especially wanted to talk about was flying back to the ranch, when, for the first time, he looked at the land he flew over.

"Really looked," he said.

And what he saw, really looking, was nothing, or next to it. The few small towns between Los Angeles and Blue Lake seemed from the air almost abandoned. Isolated mines and ranches interrupted the emptiness to no clear purpose, roads over bare earth or through scruffy brush led nowhere, and life was reduced to slither and skitter. Nothing. No one.

"There are beautiful places Out Here, where there's water, but they're so few, so small, and the waste lands so expansive." Carlyle spoke almost sadly, as if of loss. "The desert wasn't settled. People just passed through on their way somewhere else. If they stopped where they found something of value, they took it and left."

I smiled. "Yet here we sit, Carlyle."

"We few," he said, smiling too. "But I saw what Jane meant. We have no business Out Here. Except for mining, we're not engaged in any enterprise that couldn't be done better, and more economically, somewhere else. I understand what she means when she says that we should all leave. Let it be, big and empty."

"Okay, let's go," Cletus said. "You first."

Carlyle smiled again. "Ione says I don't understand desert ranching, the rationale for it. She's probably right. But I wonder if she understands the sheer perversity, the blind stubbornness of running livestock in a country so desolate that people come to it only because they have nowhere else to go."

"She understands," Cletus said quietly.

"Do you really believe that, Carlyle?" I asked. "Do you really believe that I couldn't go elsewhere if I chose?"

He thought for so long that I began to despair of an answer. Then he said, with his old sincere seriousness: "I believe, Mrs. Waner, that if you were to live somewhere else, you would cease to be you."

Cletus laughed.

"I was thinking, too, of your essay about women going mad in the desert. When I read it years ago, I took your point, but I didn't really feel it. But in the plane, seeing the land whole, as it were, I could nearly experience their loneliness. That kind of emotion, the overpowering sorrow and dread, could easily unbalance a sensibility that – "

"It wasn't loneliness." Cletus interrupted rarely. His doing so now commanded attention. "They weren't alone. They were with their men and their children."

"Well, yes," Carlyle said. "But then what drove them over the edge?"

"Winnefred has another essay about women on their way West having to toss away their furniture, their possessions."

"It was a defacement of sorts," I said. "A loss of identity. Then, settled in the desert, surrounded by all the nothing, they – some of them – lost themselves, lost their humanness. The keening of a mad woman is the wail of an animal."

I hadn't expressed myself well. And I didn't know if I still would make such an argument. Maybe I just wanted to enquire: Do desert places, isolating one from another, preclude intimacy? Does the gritty desert wind scour away the thin veneer of civilization? Has each of us Out Here nothing but her sense of herself as defense against the elements and the Other?

"There's a line in one of B. W.'s films," Carlyle said somberly: "You don't have to be crazy to live out here, but it helps."

Cletus laughed again, and rose. "Time to stow this furniture for the winter."

That afternoon, trying to work, I couldn't keep from thinking about Carlyle, his growing confidence, his apparent reevaluation of his father, and his relation to Jane Harmon. During lunch, I had waited for him to bring up the incident of the previous day, but he hadn't, although he spoke of Jane repeatedly, easily, with pleasure, as one in love does. I could only conclude that she hadn't told him that she had spent an hour in the haunt of base, mean-eyed men. Cletus appeared to be equally ignorant. But Blue Lake knew. And Blue Lake talked.

ACCIDENTS AND inevitabilities – to these the story that I am trying to tell myself seems always finally to reduce. What happened must have happened, even if the result of lapses and missteps and the thoughtlessness that Ione Hardaway called "gawking." Individuals acted, accidents occurred, and Brock Walden died. If his death were the actual subject of my story, however, I wouldn't trouble to tell it. Leave that to his son and biographer or, better, to those who chronicle the doings of celebrities and such. But the other story, made of the stories of Jane Harmon and Troy Hardaway and Carlyle Walden, of Ione Hardaway and the Rocking W, of Cletus Rose and Winnefred Westrom Waner, and of Brock Walden and his relation to and effect on us all – a story, finally, of men and women seeking lives and love in the desert and one another – that's the story I would put on paper, fit together so as to make it mean. But what if it means only that accidents happen and what will be will be?

For my tenth birthday, my father bought at auction a radio, a large, backless old mahogany case of vacuum tubes, which, I discovered, gave off a pale yellow light. For an hour or so each night, supposed to be asleep, I would place my book in the illuminated space and, craning my neck uncomfortably, read. I would also listen, for sometimes, through an atmospheric aberration, the signal from a Los Angeles station brought into my tiny room, in our tiny house in the Amargosa Valley, dance music, the tunes to which a generation that fought World War II had loved and dreamed: blends of reed and brass, bland or perky or smoky voices, sentimental notions of love and longing advanced in now simple, now sophisticated forms. All these years later, reading over what I have written, I hear, faintly, the rhythms and phrases of that music, and I wonder where else I might find its traces. I wonder if those delicate harmonies and elaborate improvisations offered a young girl in the desert models of human attachment. I wonder if those maudlin couplets may have directed and confined her young heart's affections. I wonder if those patterns of sound and sentiment gave form to the world that she was becoming part of even as it was becoming part of her.

Sounds arranged in time, words arranged to rhyme...

The truck Troy was driving back from California developed transmission trouble outside Bishop. Parts could not be had locally, and those first shipped from Los Angeles were for a newer model, so for six days Troy, restless and sober, watched television in his hotel lobby or walked the streets, while in Nevada Ione fumed and Brock Walden sat on his porch and Jane and Carlyle rode or worked and Cletus Rose and Ralph Johnson took up the hunt. The evening of his return to Walden Ranch, Troy came into town.

Early the next morning, Carlyle called me. During the night Cletus had suffered what Sally Keogh called an event: awakening to sweats and dizziness and chest pain, he had fumbled on his bedside table for his angina pills, knocking them to the floor; as he leaned to retrieve the vial, he had fallen out of bed, alerting Sally. Returned to bed, medicated, Cletus gradually became comfortable again and slipped once more into sleep.

Nevertheless, Carlyle was concerned. "I volunteered to take him to town to have Dale Carson examine him, Mrs. Waner, but he refuses."

I concealed my anxiety: "That shouldn't surprise you, Carlyle."

"Sally believes the event was probably precipitated by helping drag out the buck Ralph shot yesterday. Cletus agreed not to hunt today, but he insists that he will soon. I hoped you might convince him to reconsider."

So that I might attempt to dissuade Cletus from hunting, Carlyle invited me to lunch at the Rocking W, a ruse that would deceive no one. Not that it mattered. And not that I believed I could keep Cletus from doing what he had determined to do. But I would try.

The day was bright and October cool, the wind ragged gusts and swirls that hurled grit as if to scour to blankness the billboard picture of Brock Walden welcoming all to Blue Lake, where the West gets Wild. I was a mile into Gull Valley when I noticed, far ahead, a disheveling of dust and a pickup, which hurtled toward me at a speed that made it seem larger, dangerously, until it, and a grim-faced Troy Hardaway, were past me with a roar and a buffeting blast of wind and gone down the highway.

Shaken, uncertain, I proceeded cautiously toward the ranch.

I met no other vehicles. The wind shivered the sage and stirred the dust but nothing else in the valley seemed to move. Then, some miles down the road, I came upon a horse: out in a patch of scrub sage stood a solitary mustang, shaggy and thin and old, unmoving, head drooped earthward as if in despair. An old mare missed by the BLM? A stallion driven off by a younger, stronger rival? I couldn't tell.

Near the Rocking W I saw another horse, gray, and a rider I recognized, after a moment, as Carlyle Walden. He raised a hand in greeting, reined in, and the horse reared up impressively before leaping forward to gallop through the sage and disappear into a fold in the earth.

Nearing the ranch, for a moment I saw again the Rocking W of a half-century before, the June day I met Brock Walden and Cletus Rose. For all its litter and junked equipment and weathered sheds and ramshackle corrals, the ranch had been a vigorous, vital enterprise. Now, neat and scrubbed of history, it seemed in the chill October sun less a place than a thing, a device of some sort. A few cows grazed in a far pasture. The horse corrals were empty, and the vehicles lined up before the house looked unused. The two men on the porch watching my arrival were old and ill.

Jane Harmon too had watched me drive in and park. She stepped away from the barn door, much as Ione Hardaway had a year earlier. It might have been the quiescence of the scene that leant her life, made her a glow of fresh color in the autumnal drab. She attributed her radiance to exercise.

"I've been currying Virgie, Miz Waner. I love having her under my hands. It's like..." No simile suggested itself. She didn't seem to care.

One of the hands she had held up was adorned by a ring, a lovely oval sapphire in a simple setting. I nodded, admiring: "It's beautiful. Does it signify?"

"Oh, not really. It's not an – it's a friendship ring. Carlyle got it in Los Angeles."

I smiled, even as I sought in her signs of recent trauma. But she carried herself with the same natural elegance, spoke with her customary enthusiasm. Richly redolent of horse and sweat and a lilac scent that hung in her hair, she beamed.

She walked with me to the house, after her camera. She had already filmed in the barn, she said, done the birds, pigeons and swallows, so beautiful, and the sunlight that slid through cracks and chinks in the wall and roof, but just now she had noticed the lines and shapes of the old tack and equipment hanging stiffly from pegs and nails, the leather strapping and little machines and tools. Material.

Then in one of her skips, she said: "Carlyle apologizes for not lunching with you. He rode out to check on a well pump."

"I didn't know he was interested in such matters."

"It's an excuse to get up on Hop. He's so proud of the way he can handle her."

"I saw him," I said. "He seemed to be enjoying himself."

"He's what he couldn't be at sixteen, when everybody laughed at him," she said, in her voice that familiar air of discovery. "A rider. A buckaroo."

And more, I thought.

Ione's pickup was across the yard by her trailer. "You and Ione will be joining us, then?"

"We'll let you talk to Cletus alone," Jane said. "Ione's doing paperwork. That's why Carlyle is checking the pump, so she could finish up. She wanted to send Troy, but he... isn't here."

The small uncertain silence that preceded her last words gave them an odd resonance.

"I met Troy near the Gull Valley turnoff," I said. "He was driving at a reckless speed."

Jane twitched, as if under a faint electrical charge. "Well, he's a big boy now. He can take care of himself."

The remark seemed not quite appropriate, but I let it pass.

Our approach to the house was observed by two old men, one a reprobate who had earned fame and fortune pretending to be a cowboy, the other a real cowboy, displaced, disinherited, the possessor of virtues known to no one but, I fancied, myself.

Cletus got to his feet. He looked neither worse nor better. His smile was amused.

Brock Walden wheeled his chair to the ramp. Even on the smooth, level porch the task took something out of him, so that I could almost believe that he, not Cletus, had suffered in the night. He sat for a moment, gray and panting. Then he said: "The schoolmarm."

He too spoke with an air of discovery. I realized, with a pang of sadness, that he had forgotten my name.

"Good morning," I said.

"The schoolmarm," he repeated, now as if making an accusation. Jane and I stepped up onto the porch.

"Girlie, wheel me over to the barn, so's I can see Clete's kill."

Jane gave his thick shoulder an absent, almost maternal pat. Their relation had altered once more, apparently. "Let me get my camera first."

Cletus carefully rolled Brock Walden away from the ramp, smiling at me. "Looks like it's just the two of us for lunch. Imagine that."

"We do need to talk," I said. "Last night, were you trying to slip away without saying goodbye?"

"Nothing wrong with me that a good burp couldn't fix."

The tenor of our upcoming negotiations established, we went in to lunch. Betty Johnson had prepared spinach salads and a spiced consommé and sectioned BLTs, of which Cletus, I was pleased to note, partook heartily. I quickly set to my task, offering the obvious arguments. Cletus, as I expected, conceded little to mortality. He would adjust his diet and routine, he would restrict his activities, he would modify his habits, but he would not stop for death: he would continue to be what he was, and death would have to stop for him, sooner or later.

"I prefer later, if you please," I said.

"No, you're ready to bury me, Winnefred." He didn't allow me to object. "I'll ride a slow-footed nag, but I'll ride. I'll fill my deer tag, even if I have to find myself a rock and just sit all day and wait for a buck to mosey into my sights. I'll dance with my best girl," he smiled, "but only to the slow songs."

"Did I just hear Brock Walden say you'd already killed your deer?"

"He's... confused." I heard then in his pause, saw in his kind eyes his great fear. "Let me fall off a horse and break my neck or work myself into a heart attack, Winnefred. I'm not man enough to take to a chair like that."

My adjurations ended. We finished our lunch, talking of reading and writing: he had taken up again, after nearly fifty years, the stories of Melville; I had been trying to compose a poem about dust.

A sudden crash from the office indicated Jane's whereabouts. Cletus smiled: "You suppose B. W. will get to the barn sometime today?"

"She must have found something to occupy her interest."

"Sure did a while ago." Jane and Troy had been in the barn, angry, he said, but suddenly silent as he passed. Neither spoke until he was again out of earshot. A few minutes later, Troy stormed out of the barn and leaped into his pickup and raced off toward town.

I told Cletus what I had seen of Troy. After a thoughtful silence, he said, "In the barn, he was badgering her. You suppose it was about that business in the Adaven?"

So the story had reached the Rocking W. And Troy would have heard about it in Blue Lake, no doubt.

Before I could reply, Betty Johnson came in with her sister. A member of the last class I'd taught at Blue Lake High School, Sally Keogh had been in Las Vegas for some time and would catch up, so names rose and drifted off as if on the wind. As we women chatted, Cletus began to sag and yawn. In a pause he injected: "Nap time."

Betty and Sally slipped out. I proposed to beg a cup of coffee from Ione while Cletus rested, then to join him on the porch and share the view and the afternoon. He concurred, pleasing me by his obvious pleasure in the thought that I would, for a while, remain with him.

He wandered off to his bedroom. I went into the kitchen to thank Betty for the lunch. Then I made my way out onto the porch. Brock Walden sat where Cletus had left him, his chin resting on his chest. I thought he was asleep until, as I was passing, he said: "He could have jumped."

He raised his head and was wholly present, looking at me.

"Had plenty of time to get out." Something in his dark eyes, darkly ringed, and his raspy drawl made me feel exposed, vulnerable. "Stubborn. Thought he could out-wrestle gravity."

I didn't understand.

"Never would have guessed a man could survive that kind of banging down a mountainside."

Two thoughts rose suddenly, simultaneously into my mind. I was an old woman, dried up, used up. He was talking about Henry.

"What are you telling me?"

"Came at him out of the sun, to spook him. Brown his britches. Didn't know about the black ice. He ended up hanging on the edge. He could have jumped."

He was telling me that he was not responsible for the death of my husband. I heard it otherwise.

"In your plane, you dove at him, Henry. You... he lost control. You killed him."

"If you want it that way." He shrugged. "Said I was sorry."

I felt then no new sorrow, no anger, only a deep weariness of spirit. "Are you saying it was an accident, just a stupid prank that — or was it me, and the dance and…"

Brock Walden looked at me as if my confused question did not merit a response.

"I – does Cletus know all this?"

His laugh came from low in his throat, like a death rattle: "Had to fly over that damn canyon four or five times before he finally saw the wreckage. He probably figured. Never asked."

"You knew," I said slowly. "You knew where he was. And you left him there."

"Had to be dead, after that fall," he said. "Mangled the cab like a beer can."

I found that I was sitting on the edge of the porch. "Why are you telling me this? Why now, after all these years?"

His grin held a kind of hatred. "You been innocent too long, Win."

I couldn't bear to look at his face. Instead, I looked out onto the ranch yard, where the wind scoured earth into dust.

I sat for some time, resting. I thought about death, not the accomplished death of Henry Waner, not the imminent death of Cletus Rose and Brock Walden, but of my own unavoidable end: to die seemed to me, at that moment, not merely inevitable, not only necessary, but good.

Brock Walden said nothing else. When I could look at him again, I saw that once more he didn't know me. I didn't know him either, this real fake, this reprehensible hero. What did he mean, innocent?

I struggled to my feet and made my way across the ranch yard to Ione's mobile home. Exhausted, I could hardly lift a hand. Dust puffed up under my knuckles as I knocked on her door.

Ione's coffee, biscuits, and gooseberry jam brought me back, eventually, to myself, so that I could more or less calmly relate to her what had transpired on the porch.

"Could be he's just having you on, Miz Waner," she consoled. "Remember what Cletus said, how he likes to do that. He did it with me, too. As if he could be Troy's father! Troy and dad, peas in a pod."

"I have no reason to doubt him," I said.

"Would of been an accident, if he only meant to scare Henry. I don't know what the law would be, if the statute of limitations hasn't run out – manslaughter? Negligent homicide? We can ask George – "

"I don't care about the law," I said. "I don't know what justice would be in this case, and certainly I don't want revenge. He's an addled old man sitting over there on the porch barely breathing. I just want…"

But I couldn't finish the sentence. I didn't know what I wanted. Henry Waner was long dead, Brock Walden was dying, and I was old. What did any of it matter? Maybe I already had what I wanted, which was simply to know.

For some time we sat silently. Then she shifted and spoke: "This probably isn't the right time for it, Miz Waner, but I've wanted to talk to you for a while now."

I was glad to be able to get away from myself. "Yes, all right."

She refreshed my coffee. Her hands, bare, suited small domestic tasks just as, gloved, they did ranch chores with machines and animals. Dressed in her usual denim and leather and plaid, hat and gloves at hand, she had been about to set off to doctor a hobbling cow when I arrived at her door.

"As soon as B. W. goes, I'll be going too."

For the second time that afternoon, I was confused. "Going?"

"Leaving the Rocking W. Quitting Walden Ranch."

Blue Lake had been waiting, certain that Ione would disabuse Jane Harmon and Carlyle Walden of their Out There notions, end the memorial nonsense, remove the refuge threat, and ensure that nothing would change. How anticipate this?

She had been making enquiries, she said, sending letters to a Salt Lake City CEO whose company owned cattle operations in Deeth, and to the manager of a ranch in Independence Valley, and to two brothers who ran cows along the Idaho-Nevada line. She had many contacts among livestock grazers in Nevada, in Idaho and Utah and Montana. She would have no difficulty finding a position for herself. And for Troy.

I wasn't completely recovered from my surprise. "I – what prompted this decision? Is it Carlyle and Jane?"

For a moment she didn't answer. She seemed tired but at ease, relieved of a long-borne burden. The lines left on her face by worry and weather had softened, as if under a caress.

"It would be hard, working for Carlyle," she said then. "The last couple of months he's been here – if it was only that, though, I could handle it. But there won't be a Walden Ranch much longer."

"Because of the memorial, you mean."

She scowled. "The other day, Carlyle started talking about grass-fed beef. You know what that is, Miz Waner? You raise cattle not to ship but to butcher. You go from the livestock business into the meat business. Took me half the morning to get him to see the problem with that for an outfit like ours."

That idea was not the problem, however. The problem was that there would always be ideas, suggestions, proposals and projects never thought out or through, and they would come not from Carlyle Walden but, as had the memorial idea, and the refuge idea, and the grass-fed beef idea, from Jane Harmon. Some Ione might manage to deflect or circumvent, but others no doubt she would not. Jane would always have ideas. "One way or another, she'll ruin the place."

Yes, Jane was a woman of enthusiasms. But if she was spontaneous and often unthinking, she was not mean-spirited or malicious or spiteful. I said so.

"Yet look what happened to your house, Miz Waner."

I moved past that. "Once her film is done, we may never see Jane again. She may have no interest in returning to Blue Lake. And who knows? She and Carlyle may not last – she seems to go through men at an alarming rate."

"She'll be back," Ione said shortly. "She's already told us this place will be her refuge. And now, with Hop, Carlyle's got something to come back to himself."

"But the two of them – "

"She'll stick with Carlyle, if she can, Miz Waner. He admires her, and he'll take care of her. He'll put up with her notions. He'll always be there for her, the way he…"

We both knew what she had been about to say. Her flush was faint.

"He'll stick to her, and she knows it. He'll make her as happy as any man could, and he'll be happy with her, if she doesn't kill him." She shook her head in mock wonder. "Every time I see him he's got another bruise or bandage."

Despite the circumstances, I smiled. Calamity Jane. Poor Carlyle.

"This is very unlike you, Ione – walking away from a difficulty. Especially as you would be leaving your home."

She sighed, on the edge of anger. "I should tough it out, you mean. You're like Carlyle – you think I'm so tough. Well, there's a difference between tough and stupid. I know when what I'm getting isn't worth what I'm giving. As for this being home…" She looked around her, at the china and chintz, the wonderful photographs. "I haven't had a home since I was nine."

Since the death of her mother, she meant. An orphan myself, I remembered how I had felt without a place in the world. Sometimes I still felt so. Nevertheless, her solution seemed extreme.

"You love the Rocking W. You've given your life to it."

"All the more reason not to stay and watch it go to ruin," she said, angrily. "They don't get it, Carlyle and Jane. They don't know how fragile it all is. We almost went under this winter, for crying out loud. Nobody knows how close to the edge we work."

I knew. All my life I had heard ranch folk talk, thanking God or their ancestors or their lucky stars that they could live the life they did, even with all its labor and fretting, and in the same breath lamenting that they might be the last generation to ranch the desert.

"One crack-pot idea – refuge or memorial or whatever – and a bad hay crop and it'll all be over. And there's nothing I'd be able to do to stop it. They come out here with their ideas and their ignorance and they destroy – "

Her anger seemed to choke her, to distort her features.

I watched her. She spoke of Carlyle Walden and Jane Harmon, but her ire had no simple object. She was raging against the times. Hers was the kind of wrath that deforms.

Seeing this, I thought that maybe she was right. Maybe she should go, find a place that mattered less to her. Before her anger turned her ugly.

"I'm sorry," I said at last. "I wish there were something I could do."

"I suppose," she said, with an ironic quivering at the corner of her mouth, "you could write a poem about it."

I smiled, slowly. "You've discovered my little secret."

"Well, Miz Waner, when you're always scribbling in one of those notebooks, and your lines don't go all the way across the page, you could be making the world's longest grocery list, but it isn't likely."

"Blue Lake had enough to talk about without my verse."

I had written essays to establish that that I was of this place, a creature of the desert; I had written poems to confirm for myself what I had always, in a small, private place in my heart, felt: I was a stranger in a strange land.

I paused, silent, until Ione looked at me; then I said: "Other people have secrets of far more consequence."

She busied herself with the coffee pot. I thought she would let my invitation pass, but after she had refilled my cup and her own, she said: "I suppose you mean my perpetrating a fraud on Carlyle."

"You and his father together," I said.

She looked at me over the rim of her cup. Her equanimity signaled acceptance. "You figured it out. I thought that damn Indian maiden story could give the game away. I thought it would be Jane who saw it, though."

"And you feared that she'd tell him?"

"I hoped she wouldn't," she said. "He loved me, in his goofy way, and I used that, and him, and I hurt him doing it. The truth would hurt him more. Why cause him pain? But she'd have to tell him, wouldn't she – what good's a story if you don't tell it?"

"Maybe," I said. "In any case, he's a grown man. He could deal with the truth."

But as soon as I spoke, I had doubts. Carlyle could come to terms with his betrayal by Ione, but for all his maturation, he might have real difficulty with his father's duplicity.

"I'm sorry, Miz Waner," Ione said then, strangely. "I hate to disappoint you."

"You've never done that," I said. "But if I had a horsewhip, I'd use it on that vicious old man over on the porch, dying or no. Taking advantage of a fifteen – "

"B. W. is right, Miz Waner." Ione's smile was odd, ironic and despairing. "You are innocent."

I felt a constriction in my chest. "I'm not following you."

"You ever know me to do anything I didn't want to do?"

I attended to respiration. When my breathing was again smooth and even, I suggested, carefully, "A fifteen-year-old may be brought to believe that she…"

I couldn't finish this sentence.

I started another. "You initiated the plot, when you became pregnant. You involved Carlyle."

"I initiated everything, Miz Waner."

Of course she had. Feeling Brock Walden's eyes on her, she had presented herself to him.

The full force of her boldness, the intensity of her fifteen-year-old will struck me, so that I didn't know whether to be appalled by or proud of her. Her mother had died. Her father had lost their home. She had a brother to raise. She had taken steps to secure her future. She had done what she could do.

"That doesn't exonerate Brock Walden," I said. "A grown man."

"He is what he is. If anyone's to blame – if there has to be blame – it's me."

"And you are what you are," I said, "which even Jane Harmon admits is remarkable."

Ione folded her hands in her lap and looked down at them. Then she looked at me. "There were times, Miz Waner, when you getting my jokes was the only thing that kept me from falling into a hole in myself."

"My dear…" Now I saw her through a shimmer of tears.

We said no more.

I didn't know that we would never again speak intimately.

"Right now I have to find my rambling brother," Ione said then. "Jane's here and he isn't – I take that as a sign of progress."

"He was racing out of Gull Valley as I was coming in," I said. "Apparently he and she had a dispute of some kind."

"Headed for town?"

"I assumed so – "

"Damn! What's she done now!" Angry and alarmed, Ione sprang to her feet, clapped on her hat and took up her gloves and, before I quite knew what was happening, was out the door.

For a moment I sat quietly, feeling too old for this toss and tumble of emotions. I thought to straighten up for Ione, or to refresh myself with soap and water and a comb, or simply to finish my coffee, to let Jane and Ione do to one another what they would. Instead I rose and went to the door and through it.

Brock Walden was in the middle of the ranch yard, a small front wheel of his chair turned and caught in a rut. Arms and shoulders heaving, he struggled, issuing imprecations into the gusty wind, his efforts to shove free threatening to topple him.

Jane Harmon stood some distance off, where she had been filming him. Now she swayed under a gust of wind and the assault of Ione Hardaway.

I hurried over to the two women. Ione, like Brock Walden, was in a rage: "…what happened at the Adaven? Is that what he's upset about?"

Jane seemed not so much imperiled as frustrated. "Even though it's none of his business, which I kept telling him."

"What else did you tell him? What happened to you in there, anyway?"

Jane flushed, growing angry herself. "That's none of your business either."

Ione leaned, raised a gloved hand as if to deliver a blow. "What did you tell him!"

"Leave me alone!" Jane's face contorted, her features misaligned.

I stepped closer, placing a hand on her arm. "Jane, please, tell us."

"He wouldn't leave me alone, Miz Waner," she said. "He kept at me and at me. He put his hands on me, just like..."

"Did you tell him what they did to you, those men in the bar?"

"He made me. He's just like them."

To forestall Ione's angry objection, I quickly interjected: "Pete Haas was there?"

"Of course. Of course."

Ione was suddenly still, her voice low and hard. "You sent him after Haas?"

"I didn't send him after anybody. Why can't you see that? He did it. It's him." She turned to me, angry and pleading. "It's them, Miz Waner, you know that. It doesn't have anything to do with me."

Ione wheeled, and in a few strides was at her pickup, jerking open the door.

I called out over the wind: "Phone George. Maybe he can stop it."

After a moment's hesitation, Ione turned and hurried into her mobile home. Did she have the pistol in her hand then? I don't know.

A screen of dust blew across the ranch yard. Once it passed, I could see that Brock Walden had ceased to struggle. Leaning in his chair, his head bowed, he gave no indication of being alive.

Jane had collected herself. "I won't be made responsible for whatever happens, Miz Waner. They can kill each other for all I care."

I couldn't believe that she was serious. "Jane, you can't – "

"Oh, look," she said, raising her camera.

Carlyle had ridden into the ranch yard. Seeing us watch, he took a tight rein, nudging and kneeing the mare into a pretty dance step. Hop was a beautiful, powerful animal, and Carlyle, demonstrating his control of her, allowed himself a satisfied smile. I remembered his father putting on a similar exhibition for Eleanor Broadhurst and me fifty years before.

Jane filmed as horse and rider approached, until Carlyle brought the mare to a halt a few feet from the old man in the wheelchair. Dismounting, the son handed his father the reins. "Why don't we get some footage of you and Jane and Hop?"

Brock Walden looked at his son. "Good looking animal, mister. Yours?"

Carlyle's smile faded as he gazed down at his father, but when Jane and I approached, he held out his hand for the camera. "Get up in the saddle, Jane. The juxtaposition, machine and animal, you and B. W., will tell."

"It works better without me," Jane said. "Him, horse, chair – the fate of the cowboy."

"We can do both." Carlyle raised the camera, let the lens linger on his father and then on the horse standing quietly, her head bowed as if in submission. Finally he turned the camera toward Jane, who had stepped forward and reached for the reins.

Jane, later, would use the film to establish her innocence. She would rely as well on my testimony, for like the camera I saw nothing that might explain what happened. Perhaps it was a glint of sunlight on Jane's sapphire friendship ring. Perhaps it was the wind tugging at her sleeve or tousling her hair. Perhaps it was Carlyle creeping closer with the whirring camera, or Brock Walden twitching his reins-holding hands, or the animal sensing a threat in the arrangement of human forms around her. But when Hop jerked her head and reared, Brock Walden, unthinking, resisting, pulled sharply, his grip fast on the reins, and the horse, rearing again, pulled the chair over, and the old man was on the ground and under the frightened mare's iron-shod hooves.

Even now, so long after it occurred, that last accident remains vividly present to me. I can watch once more as Brock Walden performs his final scene before a camera. I can see again the sun flashing on the spinning spokes of the toppled aluminum wheelchair, see the dust rising from the ranch yard, and hear the old man's obscene ejaculation and the mare's scream. I can follow the flailing of the hard dark hooves under which Brock Walden's mottled, pouched, no longer handsome face becomes a smear of bone and flesh and blood as his once powerful body, now bloated by excess and age, jerks and trembles and sighs into a final stillness.

That is what happened. Or is it what Jane made of what happened?

Carlyle of course had operated the camera, but Jane's editing worked a kind of magic, creating a sequence of highly stylized images. She made the brute violence and sudden gore of Brock Walden's death beautiful and moving and meaningful, the climax of *The Last Roundup,* the end of an idea and an era.

Blue Lake, hearing about it, would ask why B. W. hadn't just let go of the reins? Was he old and out of it? But that would hardly do for a hero, and a hero Blue Lake would, and will, have him. No, Brock Walden had been fighting down the horse, as buckaroos do. He had been hanging on, toughing it out. He had never given in to man or woman, machine or animal before, not Ol' B. W., and he wouldn't start with a frightened mare.

Carlyle, shocked, aggrieved, oddly guilty, would say in a rush of emotion that, viewed within the frame of the lens, the pounding of hooves onto flesh and bone had seemed somehow staged; he felt himself not filming a real action but watching a movie. Later, trying to explain more precisely how it was that he would film his own father's death, he discovered that words for once failed him.

Jane insisted that she had done nothing, that what happened wasn't her fault.

And I would try to account for Jane's cries as the shoes of the horse flashed and grew bloody. Brock Walden was being stomped to death, yet she seemed concerned only with her film, pleading with Carlyle: "Shoot! Shoot!" Not until much later would Cletus explain that she was urging not Carlyle but Ione, who stood watching, her pistol in her hand: shoot the horse.

And Ione, whom Blue Lake had been expecting to do something, had done nothing.

If she had killed the horse, or even fired a shot, the report of which would surely have put Hop to flight, could she have saved Brock Walden's life? That was doubtful. My sense of it, at least, was that he died the moment a hoof struck the thin, brittle old bone of his skull.

Did Ione ever show any regret for not having tried to save him? Not in my presence.

But these considerations came much later. At the time, I remember, I noticed Hop, shivering, hooves shuffling in an uncertain and solitary dance, twenty yards away, and Cletus, who had seen the accident from the porch, slowly approaching, speaking quietly, calming her. Then Sally Keogh raced from the house, to no point, we who stood over the body knew, and to no point knelt and felt at the bloody flesh, between the broken bones, for a pulse. Cletus gave the mare over to Ralph Johnson and then came to me. Jane, as she had the day she met Brock Walden, buried her face in Carlyle Walden's shoulder. Carlyle looked at the body of his father uncomprehendingly, as if he were stepping from a darkened theatre into the brightness of a sun-bleached and alien day.

Ione had not moved. Still holding her unfired pistol, she seemed to me then a most solitary figure, profoundly alone. I remembered what she had told me about her drives through the desert darkness, feeling herself the sole still point in a perpetual swirling.

When the sheriff's cruiser drove into the yard, Ione finally roused herself. As George Burleigh climbed out of the car, she moved to meet him. I watched them, the big deputy in his carefully pressed uniform, the wide-shouldered woman in her workaday buckaroo outfit, even as I wondered how he had managed to get to the ranch so quickly. When George removed his hat, I saw from his expression that something was wrong.

They spoke. Then the wind carried to us Ione's cry, the wail of a woman crazed.

Ione whirled and ran toward her pickup. Then suddenly she stopped, seeming frantic and lost, as if she had forgotten what she was about. She turned once more, saw us standing over the gruesome body of Brock Walden, and her face changed. With long sure strides, her hat tugged down, leaning against the wind, pistol still in her hand, Ione advanced on us.

On Jane Harmon.

Jane, with a whimper, shrank into Carlyle's embrace.

Cletus slipped his arm from my shoulders and stepped forward, hands up as if to ward or warn her off: "Ione."

Ione ignored him, intent only on Jane and the kill.

And then George Burleigh was there, somehow, between Ione and Jane. Incensed, Ione lashed out, as if to swat him aside, striking him on the cheekbone with the barrel of her pistol just before he circled her with his arms. As Cletus had to the horse, George spoke softly to her.

Ione thrashed against, writhed in his restraining arms, silent, as if in an exercise of will, or madness, or sexual ecstasy. George soothed, consoled, comforted. He laid his bleeding cheek against hers.

For what seemed a lifetime the two stood in the wind, George absorbing her rage. Then he no longer restrained her. He held her. Ione, now hatless, leaned back into his loosening embrace and looked at him. Removing a glove, she gently touched his bleeding cheek.

I had a sudden sorrowful sense of what might have been. For the first and only time I hated Brock Walden.

Cletus left me then and went to them. After a few moments, Ione and George parted. Giving Cletus her pistol, Ione allowed George to lead her to and seat her in his vehicle. He raised a cloud of dust as he urged the car out of the ranch yard.

Cletus returned and told us.

The louts had been waiting for Troy in the Adaven, he said. Pete Haas used his boots on him.

I **HAVEN'T TOLD** the story I set out to tell. Fitting life into language warps what was lived. Beginnings and endings frame and falsify. A story, like a poem, like a play or film, does not mean but is.

I would have told a story woven of stories, but I have narrated merely moments. I would have plumbed emotions but only offered impressions. I would have construed events but only felt once more their force. I would have shaped time and circumstance into meaningful form but have only, I fear, fashioned a pretty tale. Trying to account for the way we live and die Out Here, I have composed, as did Jane Harmon in her film, an elegy.

As I began this effort, I asked if Jane Harmon had been right about our having no compelling reason to live in the desert. I have not come to a reasonable answer. That is, yes, of course, Jane was right, as Ione and Cletus always knew, as Carlyle came to understand. But this does not matter. We live Out Here because we choose to. We will stay in the desert as long as we can.

Jane accused us of nostalgia. Here too she was right. Out Here, Out There – even a half-century ago the terms might have signified. Now they are only figures, at best. Now the world is compressed, and Out There is but a wish away. Our children speak the language of the ghetto, boys stuff into their back pockets iPods instead of snoose cans, girls wear the same shirts as the Bangladeshi. How can you keep them Out Here on the ranch, after they've seen youtube?

I had wished, writing this, to understand. Instead, I have borne witness.

And so to finish.

Eleanor Broadhurst and I continue to exchange visits, tending our graves in Nevada in May, our memories in Los Angeles in December. She grows frailer and smaller; she will be a second sibyl, she says, will live forever like a cricket in a cage.

Cletus Rose died in Malibu six months after Brock Walden. The arrangements that he had been making, alone in Southern California, had been not for Brock Walden but for himself. All that he owned he had given away. His aged brother claimed the body and returned with it to Arizona.

Pete Haas was tried and convicted on several charges stemming from the assault on Troy Hardaway. Norman Casteel, after a drive into the desert with George Burleigh, testified for the state. Mina Pasco did not attend the trial.

Troy survived the attack, physically. His bones have healed, but his brain is irreversibly damaged. He spends his time in an aluminum wheelchair, much like that in which Brock Walden rode out his last days, in a long-term care facility in Las Vegas. He can neither feed nor clean himself, and he doesn't speak. Doctors say that he might live for many years. Or not.

Blue Lake knows that Carlyle Walden bought out Ione Hardaway's ten percent interest in Walden Ranch. Carlyle is thought a pathetic businessman, paying an exorbitant price for what was, after all, a tiny piece of an operation that returns little. Meanwhile, his biography of his father has been published to mixed reviews, some complaining of the author's ambivalence toward his subject. His plans for Walden Ranch and the Rocking W remain unsettled. For now, Ralph and Betty Johnson manage things, he seeing to cattle and feed, she to finances. Both are confident that they can hang on, unless they're hit by storms or drought or disease or…

Blue Lake also believes that Carlyle knows where Ione Hardaway is. If he does, he hasn't said. Most think that she's in Las Vegas, or Clark County generally, near her brother. She has been sighted dealing Twenty-one in a downtown casino, reported working on a ranch outside Pahrump, and said to be caring for horses at a racetrack. I wait for a letter or card or call, which I am certain will come.

Ione has been proved prescient. Over the period during which I have been writing this account, Jane returned twice to the Rocking W. There she rode with Carlyle, she cared for her horse, and she relaxed. At the moment, she is in Los Angeles, where her short film on mustangs in Nevada is about to appear on PBS. At the same time she is making final arrangements for a film, financed by a mid-level studio, based on an original script that Carlyle admitted to me was a much revised version of his story about himself and Ione Hardaway.

Jane stopped in to visit when she was at the ranch. We had tea and talked about her art and her career and her affections. She spoke of the The Last Roundup as if it were the work of someone else, admiring, analyzing techniques and effects. She worried that she might never again find a subject so rich in possibilities for aesthetic expression. She has not yet brought herself to accept Carlyle's marriage proposal, although she doesn't know why.

The Last Roundup has now been shown again on television. I watched it with Ruby and Irene, sharing with them a sad pleasure at the sight of those who are gone, enjoying Jane's rendering of our Out Here landscape and ethos, and coming to a deeper appreciation of her artistry: all in the film connects. However, I saw too that the very coherence of image and event, words and music – the wholeness, as it were, of Jane's vision – intensifies that which gives the film its power, which is an absence.

Those Out There can only sense that something is missing. They feel it in the images of the empty playa and sage plain, the abandoned homes and fallen-down corrals, the dark holes in the earth, the blank blue of the Nevada sky.

Some of us Out Here, slipping from the film's emotional grip, have discovered what isn't there. We are all in Jane's film, all of us who appear in my pages, all but Ione Hardaway.

Jane, when I asked, said vaguely that she had at first thought she might make a separate film about Ione, to that end having cut out and saved the footage in which she was featured. "There's a story there, Miz Waner."

"But now? Are you are going to tell it?"

She looked at me. For the first time, she seemed actually to see me. Now, somehow, we were not speaking of stories or films or art.

"No," she said. After a moment, she said it again: "No."

And I think I know why.

Composing a film about Ione Hardaway would force Jane to raise the question that everyone seems to have forgotten.

I would prefer to forget the question again, but I cannot.

What did Brock Walden mean, that night in the Silver Sage, with his remark about Troy and Ione and their parents? Was it, as Cletus had said, merely an attempt to rile her? Was it just a perverse prodding by a drunken old man? Surely he could not have meant that he was Troy Hardaway's father – the young man had Bill Hardaway's features and frame, his mannerism, his ways: he was his father's son, they were peas in a pod, as Ione had observed.

Or was it something other and unspeakable?

Jane, I believe, came to that question, took it in, and, finally, refused to ask it. In that refusal, in deliberately choosing not to pursue the story to its end, which is to say to its beginning, she has, so far as I am concerned, redeemed herself.

Bernard Schopen was born and raised in Deadwood, South Dakota. He attended the University of Washington and the University of Nevada, Reno where upon receiving his Ph.D. in English he taught for many years. He is the author of three Jack Ross novels, as well as a study of the novels of Ross Macdonald.

Colophon

Designed by Corinna Wilborn, Paula Robison and Baobab Press.
Title and header font is Sackers Gothic, based on designs
of ancient Roman inscription, and designed by Monotype
Design Studio in 1994. The author name is set in Adobe's
Rosewood, released in 1994 as a digital version of Clarendon
Ornamented, a wood type first seen in the late nineteenth
century, inspired by typefaces of the American Wild West.
The body face is Joanna, designed by Eric Gill in the 1930's,
who described it as "a book face free from all fancy business".
Printed by McNaughton and Gunn, Inc., Michigan.